# Praise for Ally Blue's
## *Love, Like Ghosts*

"This story is told with Ally Blue's usual deft hand, detailing the relationship between these two young men as they ~ very gradually, with fits and starts, with mistakes and really hot sex ~ fall in love."

~ *Rainbow Reviews*

"Yet another winner from a great author!"

~ *Fallen Angel Reviews*

"The detail and setting of North Carolina comes alive vividly and crisply with hues and landscapes that draw the reader's eye."

~ *Reviews by Jessewave*

# Love, Like Ghosts

*Ally Blue*

A Samhain Publishing, Ltd. publication.

Samhain Publishing, Ltd.
577 Mulberry Street, Suite 1520
Macon, GA 31201
www.samhainpublishing.com

Love, Like Ghosts
Copyright © 2010 by Ally Blue
Print ISBN: 978-1-60504-791-1
Digital ISBN: 978-1-60504-676-1

Editing by Sasha Knight
Cover by Kanaxa

First Samhain Publishing, Ltd. electronic publication: October 2009
First Samhain Publishing, Ltd. print publication: August 2010

# Dedication

To my lovely daughter, Veronica, who put up with her mother's constant questions about everything from the best shortcuts across the UNC campus to what those big round things all over the ground are (horse chestnuts, by the way). She did her level best to help and any mistakes are totally my own fault. Sweetheart, you are the best, thank you!

*"True love is like ghosts, which everybody talks about and few have seen."*

—François de la Rochefoucauld

# Chapter One

Adrian Broussard expected to encounter the ghost of Lyndon Groome at some point. He just never expected it to happen his first afternoon at the castle. In broad daylight.

The apparition floated just above the dark gray stone floor, spectral brains leaking from its shattered skull. A blotch of nearly transparent blood wavered in and out of existence on the floor beneath its bare feet.

Adrian found those particular details terribly intriguing. According to the stories he'd heard since arriving on the UNC campus three years ago, Lyndon Groome had vanished without a trace on Halloween night, nineteen-oh-five. Since then, Lyndon's sad, blood-soaked ghost had been occasionally spotted here in the tower room on Halloween night. Some stories claimed he ran away with an older, married woman. Another rumor had it that Lyndon, distraught over the loss of a lover, had run from the castle in the dead of night and been murdered by persons unknown. There were other stories, of course, but those two were the most persistent, probably because Lyndon had never turned up anywhere and no body had ever been found.

It fascinated Adrian to come across a ghost story in which so many visible details appeared to fit with at least one of the more popular tales, even if the spirit itself happened to show up a bit early.

From his spot in the doorway of the small octagonal room, Adrian darted a swift look down the narrow stone staircase spiraling into the distance behind him. Laughter, conversation and the echo of hammers drifted from the group of fellow college students working three stories below, but as far as he could tell no one had followed him. Which was a good thing, since he was pretty sure he wasn't supposed to be up here.

Adrian returned his attention to Lyndon Groome, who floated nearly invisible in the sunlight streaming through the window. The specter's pale eyes stared straight into his. The colorless lips moved, shaping a word Adrian couldn't quite hear.

Moving with careful precision, Adrian paced forward one slow step at a time, his hand stretched toward the diaphanous figure. He opened his mind just enough to let a trickle of his psychokinesis past the absolute control he'd gained over the past decade. His power attracted paranormal entities like a magnet, which was one reason he kept such a tight lid on it. Maybe a little taste would lure poor, sad Lyndon close enough for Adrian to communicate with him. He'd been able to interact in a limited way with spirits in the past by touching them, so he saw no reason why it wouldn't work this time. With a bit of luck, maybe he would be the one to finally learn Lyndon's fate.

As if in response to Adrian's thoughts, the apparition wafted closer. Adrian stopped moving and waited, his gaze holding Lyndon's. *Come on, Lyndon. Don't be afraid.*

Lyndon's shade drifted nearer. A chill raised the hairs on Adrian's arms. "That's it," he whispered. "Come here."

"Who're you talking to?"

At the sound of the unexpected voice from the doorway, Lyndon vanished, taking the puddle of brains and blood with him. Adrian shut his eyes for a moment to calm the brief flash of irritation before it could get away from him. Between the set-up and the actual work of running the planned Halloween haunted house here at Groome Castle, he had three whole weeks of work ahead of him. Surely he would have another chance to attempt communication with the entity.

Opening his eyes, Adrian turned to face the newcomer. It was a boy he'd never seen before. A very good-looking boy, with a dancer's body poured into snug jeans and a long-sleeved Carolina T-shirt. Adrian swallowed. "Um. Hi. I'm Adrian Broussard."

The big gray eyes lit up with a definite spark of interest, and the pretty lips curved into a flirtatious smile. "Greg Woodhall." Crossing to where Adrian stood, Greg held out a hand. "Very nice to meet you, Adrian."

"You too." Not knowing any way out of it, Adrian took Greg's hand and shook. As soon as he politely could, Adrian retrieved his hand and stuck both in the front pockets of his jeans. "Are you part of the haunted house?"

"Yep. I'm playing the ghost of Lyndon Groome." Greg brushed past Adrian. "I figured I'd come up here and get a feel for the place, you know? Since this is where the ghost is supposed to be."

"That makes sense." Adrian watched Greg wander across the room to peer out one of the four tall, narrow windows set in the stone walls. God, those jeans were tight. Adrian looked away.

"What about you?" Turning, Greg leaned on the windowsill, crossed his arms and flashed a wide grin. "Are you in theater? Because I gotta tell you, that would make me very happy."

That made Adrian laugh in spite of himself. No one had ever mistaken him for a theater kid before. "No, I'm majoring in physics."

13

Greg's mouth formed an "O" that made Adrian think of things he hadn't thought of in a long time. "Physics. Wow. What brings a smart boy like you to our theater department's humble haunted house?"

"Work study." Adrian shrugged. "The castle's an interesting place, though. There's a lot of history here."

"That's true." Unfolding his arms, Greg tucked a curl of golden brown hair behind his ear and pinned Adrian with a curious look. "Who were you talking to earlier? When I came in?"

"Lyndon Groome."

Greg gaped. Adrian stifled a smile. He did love to shock people with the truth.

"Um. Okay." Greg pushed away from the window, eyeing Adrian with rather more caution than before. "Seriously?"

"Yes."

"You're telling me you really think you were just talking to the ghost of Lyndon Groome?"

"I don't *think* so. I *know* I was."

"Seriously?"

"Again, yes." Adrian grinned. "You're repeating yourself, Greg."

That got him a sly smile that made his pulse pick up. "Well, Adrian, it's not every day a guy hears a handsome physics major say things like *I just had a nice chat with a ghost*, you know?"

A blush heated Adrian's face before he could stop it. He forced it back, annoyed with himself. He hadn't let simple physical attraction get to him like this since high school. Of course, he hadn't actually felt this attracted to a guy since...well, ever, really. Not even his one and only lover,

14

Christian, back in freshman year, had given him the same quick thrill through his blood that this stranger did.

Before the silence could stretch on long enough to become awkward, footsteps pounded up the stairs and a young woman in paint-splattered jeans and a UNC sweatshirt burst into the room. "Adrian, there you are. We need you downstairs. We can't figure out how to get the frame straight for the false wall."

Adrian breathed quietly through the brief surge of impatience. No matter how many times he'd tried to explain it, the group of freshmen he'd been working with all morning just couldn't seem to understand that being a physics major did not make him a carpenter. If anything, the theater upperclassmen would know more about it than he did, since they had years of experience in building sets. But the younger students hadn't listened to him so far, and the older ones seemed happy enough to let him deal with it.

*Be calm, Adrian. This is only a little thing. You've helped build a few things at home. Surely you can help these kids puzzle out how to put together a simple frame.*

"All right, Chelsea, I'm on my way." Adrian glanced at Greg, who was watching him with a grin that made Adrian not want to turn his back on it. "You coming?"

Greg sauntered forward, the predatory grin widening. "I will if you want me to," he murmured, brushing Adrian's shoulder as he passed.

Greg and Chelsea were already out the door before Adrian got it. Groaning, he clapped a hand to his forehead. His brother Sean would tease him without mercy for not having picked up on what was, in retrospect, obvious innuendo. Thankfully, Sean was a few hundred miles away right now, playing his fourth game as a freshman for the Auburn Tigers. He would never have to know of Adrian's humiliating cluelessness.

Of course, it was exactly the sort of thing that would make Sean laugh, and that just happened to be one of Adrian's favorite sounds in the whole world. Maybe it wasn't a cool thing for a guy to admit about his little brother, but Adrian didn't much care about being cool. Staring death in the face at the ripe old age of eleven tended to strip away all such unimportant things and leave behind only what mattered. Like hearing your brother laugh.

Making a mental note to videocall Sean that night, Adrian followed Chelsea and Greg downstairs.

By the time Adrian got back to his apartment that evening, he had two video messages waiting for him—one from his mother and her husband, Lee, and one from a wildly excited Sean, both bearing news of the Tigers' landslide victory over the Bulldogs.

Adrian smiled to himself as he viewed his brother's video on his laptop. Maybe he ought to wait until the next day to call Sean back. Judging by the noisy crowd of kids clustered around Sean, the celebratory party promised to be a long one.

After a moment's thought, Adrian decided to work on his paper for his Quantum Mechanics class. It wasn't due for nearly two weeks, but he saw no sense in putting it off. Besides, it wasn't like he had anything else to keep him busy. The few people here who he could call friends would be down on Franklin Street by now, celebrating UNC's afternoon win over Virginia Tech. Adrian had tried joining in the parties at first, but he'd never felt comfortable with the rowdy crowds, the drinking or the sex so thick in the air his skin burned with it. These days, he spent game nights the same way he spent most other nights—alone in his apartment, studying.

Which was another good reason to wait until tomorrow to

call Sean, Adrian reflected as he settled into the overstuffed chair with his laptop and clicked open his "QM" file. He knew Sean meant well, but he didn't much feel like listening to another lecture about *getting out of that damned apartment* or *meeting a nice guy* or any of the other things Sean tended to worry about. Adrian wasn't in college to meet men. He was here to get his doctorate. And after that? To take the theory and practical application of multidimensional physics as far as it would go, and beyond. To finally understand the science behind the mysterious and deadly gateways which still opened from time to time between the human world and a distinctly unhuman one.

At age eleven, he'd hungered for revenge on the creatures from the other dimension which had come within seconds of killing his entire family, and had haunted his nightmares for years afterward. A decade later, his goals had changed. Instead of a child's nebulous dream of vengeance, he now had a solid plan. Learn. Understand. Destroy.

Not that he would ever tell his family that. His father especially. Though he had a feeling his dad's now-husband, Sam, suspected him of more than a simple interest in physics.

Realizing his mind had wandered off course, Adrian shook himself. He hated it when that happened. Usually he had better control.

"Focus," he reminded himself in a stern voice. "You have another full day at Groome Castle tomorrow. You need to get as much done on your paper tonight as you can."

Nodding to himself, Adrian clicked into the university library. He needed to hunt down the latest research on the practical applications of quantum entanglement.

He was deep in the midst of his work when the videochat alert on his Mac trilled.

17

For a second, he considered ignoring it. He was well and truly on a roll with this paper, and he hated to stop now.

Of course, quantum mechanics came as naturally to him as English Lit did to some other people. He could pick up where he left off without any trouble.

The alert sounded again. He glanced at the chat icon on the dock. Sean's name flashed neon green over the top of it. Smiling, Adrian clicked over and accepted the chat invitation.

Sean's beaming face popped up onscreen in front of the old Tokyo Police Club poster hanging in his dorm room. "Adrian! Why didn't you call me back?"

"I thought you'd be out partying." Adrian stretched, working some of the stiffness out of his spine. "Congratulations on beating the Bulldogs, by the way."

"Thanks." Sean bounced in place, hazel eyes shining. "Man, it was *awesome*. I wish you could've been here."

"Yeah, me too. Mom called me earlier, she said she and Lee went to the game."

"They did. Dad and Sam came too. And so did Dean and Sommer, and Danny and her husband. Hell, Andre even brought Lucy and Bella with him."

The thought of Andre's elegant wife and their rambunctious toddler at the football game brought a grin to Adrian's face. "That's awesome."

"It totally was." Sean chortled in obvious delight. "The whole Bay City Paranormal gang was here, except David and Cecile, and they called from the office. It was cool."

Adrian laughed. "Dad and Sam are leading a Haunted Auburn tour this weekend, aren't they?"

"Yep. You know Dad, never waste a trip on one thing when you can do something else at the same time."

"Sean, come on, you know he'd never consider any of your college games a waste of time."

"I know that. I was just joking." Sean tilted his head sideways. "What the hell are you doing, anyway?"

"A paper."

Sean's mouth fell open. "On Saturday night? Are you nuts?"

"I *like* quantum mechanics." Adrian tried not to sound defensive, but it didn't work. It never worked with Sean. They knew each other too well.

"Quantum mechanics. You're spending Saturday night alone with a bunch of quarks and shit."

"Entangled particles, actually."

"Hell, I don't even know what that means." Sighing, Sean shook his head. "Speaking of tangling your particles, when's the last time you got laid?"

Even though he had no intention of answering that question, Adrian couldn't help thinking back to the last time he and Christian had sex. God, had it really been a year and a half? "Um..."

Evidently Sean could read minds. He groaned. "Jesus, Adrian."

"Give me a break. It's hard for me to meet guys here."

"Are you kidding? There's almost thirty thousand students there! It's the size of a town, for Christ's sake. And I know damn well there's a lot of gay dudes there. So how does a smart, good-looking guy like you have trouble getting a date?"

Adrian smiled. "I appreciate your faith in me, but you know I have a harder time talking to people than you do."

"It doesn't take that much. Just smile and say hi, is all."

"Easy for you to say. Everyone likes you."

The second he said it, Adrian wished he could take it back. A lifetime of jealousy lay behind those three words, and they both knew it.

The easy smile vanished from Sean's face. He leaned forward on his elbows, staring at Adrian with an intense determination that had become all too familiar over the years. "I know they do. But everybody would like you too, if you gave them the chance. You're a great guy, Adrian. You just have to open up enough to let other people see that."

*Yeah, because everyone loves a guy who can move things with his mind.*

Adrian shoved the bitter thought to the back of his brain and pretended keen interest in his keyboard so he wouldn't have to meet Sean's painfully sincere gaze. He hated being discussed, analyzed and advised, even by his beloved brother. Fortunately, he knew just how to make Sean stop.

Straightening his shoulders, Adrian forced himself to look into Sean's eyes. "Actually, I kind of met someone today."

Sean lit up like a spotlight. "Well why the hell didn't you say so in the first place? What's his name? How'd you meet him?"

"His name's Greg Woodhall. We met today at Groome Castle. He's a theater major. He's playing the ghost of Lyndon Groome at that haunted house I told you about." Adrian felt an uncharacteristically goofy smile spread over his face. "He was coming on to me like you wouldn't believe."

"Wow. Sounds promising." Sean leaned closer, grinning. "Is he cute?"

Adrian couldn't help mirroring his brother's smile. Sean's eagerness on his behalf was infectious. "Yeah, he's cute."

"You gonna ask him out?"

A sudden tension drew Adrian's shoulders upward. If he could only bring himself to lie, Sean would go away happy, and Adrian would be left in peace. But he couldn't do it. Lying just wasn't in his nature. "I doubt it."

Sean wrinkled his nose. "Why not?"

"It wouldn't work, that's all."

"Again I say, why not?"

*Yes, Adrian. Why not?*

He tuned out the inner voice which prodded him now and then to expand his scope of experience. It rarely worked out for the best. Sometimes, yes. Like when he'd finally gone to bed with Christian and discovered sex for the first time. But the tempting whispers had hurt him more often than not, and he'd sworn to himself that he wouldn't listen anymore.

"We're too different," Adrian answered, though he wasn't sure if he was talking to Sean or himself. "We wouldn't have anything to talk about."

Sean made a rude noise. "Bad excuse."

Sighing, Adrian rested his head in his hands. "Sean, come on—"

"No, dammit."

Adrian looked up, surprised at the heat in Sean's voice. The spark in Sean's eyes matched the expression on his face. It made Adrian feel unaccountably ashamed. "Sean—"

"Look, you're always like this. Always so damn careful." Sean jabbed a finger at the computer screen. "Let me tell you something. If you don't loosen up a little bit, you're gonna careful yourself into dying alone."

Anger swelled in Adrian's gut. Years of hard-won control kicked in before the unwelcome emotion could even raise his heart rate. He arched a cool eyebrow. "I'm only twenty-one,

Sean. It's a little early to be condemning me to a lifetime of loneliness, isn't it?"

Sean shook his head. "Just ask the guy out, Adrian. What's the worst that could happen?"

The memory of Adrian's last date, just over five months ago, flashed into his mind. The boy had called him a frigid, self-loathing emo fag before stalking out and leaving him alone at a club in Raleigh with no ride back to school and not enough cash for a thirty-mile cab fare. He hadn't even known about Adrian's abilities. That particular rejection was based purely on Adrian's sparkling personality.

Adrian elected not to mention the incident, since Sean would only point out that he'd managed to get a ride to the bus station and catch a late bus back, and anyway such a thing wasn't likely to happen again. "Okay, I'll think about it." Adrian heaved an exaggerated sigh. "You're worse than Mom."

Sean snickered. Their mother pestered Adrian for details of his nonexistent love life every time she talked to him. It irritated him on one level, because he wasn't looking for a relationship and wished everyone would just leave him alone and let him concentrate on his studies. Deep inside, however, a part of him loved that his mother accepted his sexuality so completely.

When he'd first come out to his family in ninth grade, it hadn't been that way. His announcement had torn open wounds everyone had believed healed. His mom had blamed his dad and Sam for Adrian's "problem", and Adrian had blamed himself for the renewed rift between his parents. The psychokinesis he'd worked so hard to gain control over had begun to leak through again. He'd lost sleep to endless nightmares and watched his family fall apart right before his eyes.

He still remembered the moment of crystal clarity which

changed everything. At three in the morning one rainy Sunday in April, he'd woken his mother and told her that he was himself, that no one made him who and what he was, and that she could either accept him as he was or not, but he would no longer listen to her or anyone else—including himself—assign blame where there was none. He'd turned away from her stunned expression, gone back to his room and fallen into an exhausted and dreamless sleep. The next day, his mother had called his father and Sam to talk. There had been no more blame, no more nightmares, and now Adrian's mother nagged him about his love life just like everyone else's mom did. It was nice to have a bit of normality in his life.

He flexed his well-honed psychokinetic muscle to pull a Carolina mug across the room into his hand, just to remind himself how far from normal he really was.

"Hey. Okay there, bro?"

Shaking himself, Adrian nodded. "Fine. Just thinking."

"Thinking about asking out Mr. Cute Theater Major?"

Adrian laughed at the hopeful gleam in Sean's eyes. "Good grief, you're relentless."

"That's what Coach Rodriguez says too." Behind Sean, someone called something Adrian couldn't hear through the dorm room door. Sean turned and yelled for whoever it was to wait just a minute, then faced Adrian with an apologetic expression. "Some of the guys want me to go to another party with them."

"So go on. You *should* be out having fun tonight, not sitting in your room videochatting with your stick-in-the-mud older brother." Adrian grinned to show he was only kidding about the stick-in-the-mud part, even if he really wasn't.

Sean narrowed his eyes, but didn't argue. "Okay. Well, next time I talk to you I'd better hear about your date with Theater

Guy."

"Greg. We'll see." Adrian waved at his brother. "Night, Sean. Have fun."

"Night." Sean stood and leaned down into the field of view with his usual sunny smile. "Love you, bro."

"Love you too."

Sean's image stilled on a fuzzy capture of him in motion, turning off the chat function as he straightened up. Adrian studied the blurred outline of Sean's face, thinking about the things he'd said. As usually happened when Adrian thought about it, Sean's words made sense. Would it really be so terrible to ask Greg out? Sure, it would hurt if Greg rejected him up front or said hateful things to him later. But he'd survived before. He could survive again, and come out the other side stronger for the experience.

It all sounded suspiciously like something the voice in Adrian's head—his demon, he called it in his darker moods— would whisper to him. Maybe it was Sean's evil twin.

Chuckling, Adrian switched off the videochat and clicked back to his paper. He could decide what to do about Greg later. Right now, he had work to do.

# Chapter Two

When Adrian arrived at Groome Castle the next morning, only one car sat in the circular gravel drive outside. Which didn't necessarily mean anything. Many of the students working on the haunted house, including himself, preferred to walk. Freshmen weren't allowed cars on campus in any case, and at least a third of the haunted house staff were freshmen. Still, the place seemed much more quiet than it had the day before.

Frowning, Adrian tromped through the piles of crisp brown leaves and up to the wide front steps of the house. Maybe he'd misunderstood the time they were supposed to start work today. He'd thought Marisa, the project manager—or the director, as she preferred to be called—had said ten a.m., but he could be wrong. The high arched ceiling and stone walls of the castle's tremendous downstairs hall magnified any sound above a normal conversational tone into an echoing boom. Having thirty-something people in the room all trying to talk over each other at once created enough noise to drown out even the loudest single voice, and Marisa had been on the other side of the room from him when she'd told them when to be back the next day.

He found the heavy wooden double doors unlocked. They creaked as they swung open. "Hello?" he called, walking into the foyer. "Anyone here?"

"In the main hall," a very familiar voice answered. "C'mon in."

"Be right there." Adrian shut the door and leaned his forehead against it until his hammering heart slowed down. Didn't it just figure that the one person already here was the one person he didn't want to be alone with?

*You don't know he's the only one here. There might be a whole room full of people in there. Being very, very quiet.*

"Bullshit," Adrian muttered, pushing away from the door. He and Greg were here alone, no doubt about it. He'd just have to deal with it somehow.

Gathering his courage, Adrian turned and strode across the foyer toward the arched entry into the main hall before he could change his mind. His sneakers barely made a sound on the oak plank floor. It wasn't a real advantage, when Greg knew he was there, but it felt like one anyway. Especially when his silent entrance into the huge room earned him the sight of Greg's pale skin between the top of his low-slung jeans and the ragged hem of his black Cats T-shirt as he stretched on tiptoe in a vain attempt to reach a sagging cloth on the wall.

Adrian swallowed. God, it really *had* been too long since he'd gotten laid if the mere glimpse of a strip of smooth bare back could make his mouth go bone dry and his armpits prickle with sweat.

He cleared his throat. "Hi."

Greg twisted enough to grin over his shoulder. "Adrian. Am I ever glad to see you. Can you help me out here?"

"Um. Sure." Adrian edged closer, trying to act as if his heart wasn't attempting to pummel its way through the center of his sternum. "What do you need me to do?"

"See if you can get this cloth back over the hook there." Stepping back, Greg pointed toward one of the adhesive-backed plastic hooks attached to the stone wall. A loop of dark gray gauze had come loose and sagged just below the white peg. "I can't reach the stupid thing."

"Oh. Yeah, okay."

Adrian walked forward, thinking surely Greg would move out of the way. He didn't.

God.

Trying to ignore Greg's nearness, Adrian planted one palm on the wall to brace himself, grasped the cloth in his other hand and reached upward to replace it on the hook. He only had a couple of inches over Greg, but it was enough. Barely. By standing on his toes and straightening his fingers, he managed to get the thin material looped over its hook.

"Okay, that's got it." Adrian dropped his arms. "Who hung this, anyway? I know for a fact we didn't have a ladder down here yesterday."

"Linda Torino. You know her, right? Redhead, killer body, 'bout nine and a half feet tall?"

Adrian laughed. "Yeah, she used to date my roommate in sophomore year. Nice girl. Though she got very tired of being asked to hang things up where other people couldn't reach."

"Speaking of which, thanks for helping me out here. I just couldn't get it up." Greg moved closer, a playful smile curving his lips. "The cloth on the hook, that is. For you? I could get other things up just fine."

Half the blood in Adrian's body rushed into his face. The other half siphoned southward to his crotch. His head whirled. He put a hand on the wall to keep himself upright, trying to act casual. Maybe Greg wouldn't notice.

Of course he couldn't be so lucky. Grin widening, Greg sidled so close Adrian could feel the heat of his body. "Hm.

Something tells me you could, um...get up more than a piece of gauze for me too. Am I right?"

*Oh God.* Adrian shut his eyes. Only mortification and vertigo kept an erection at bay, and the faint, spicy scent of Greg's skin threatened to erode those two fragile barriers any second now. "Uhhh..."

Greg let out a low chuckle that sent gooseflesh racing up Adrian's arms. "Oh, man. You do. You want me."

An arm slid around Adrian's waist. He yelped, eyes flying open again. "What?"

"It's okay." Greg pressed close and nuzzled Adrian's throat. "I want you too, in case that wasn't totally obvious."

"Greg, no." Adrian's voice sounded weak, breathless and unconvincing, even to himself. He laid both palms on Greg's shoulders, though his hands shook too hard to push Greg away. "Stop."

"Do you really want me to?" Warm, soft lips followed the line of Adrian's jaw, making him shiver. "Please don't make me stop. We could leave, right now. We could go to my dorm." The tip of Greg's tongue traced the shell of Adrian's ear, sending electric jolts up his spine. "I want you to fuck me, Adrian."

Sheer panic at the bald declaration galvanized Adrian into action. He grasped Greg's arms and shoved hard enough to send Greg stumbling backward. Greg stared, mouth open and eyes wide. "What the hell, man?"

Adrian hunched his shoulders, face flaming. "I'm sorry, I just...I don't..." Frustrated, Adrian ran a hand through his hair and tried to marshal his thoughts. "I can't pretend I'm not attracted to you. But I don't do casual sex. So if that's all you're after, you can forget it."

Greg's expression turned hard. He drew a breath, as if to speak, but the sound of several people entering the house at once interrupted him. He cut a swift glance toward the din of footsteps and conversation from the foyer, then pinned Adrian with a cold look. "Fine."

Before Adrian could say anything else—though what exactly he would have said, he had no idea—Greg strode across the hall to greet the cluster of six students who'd just come into the room. Adrian pretended to inspect the nearby framework he and his team had built the day before, while watching Greg from beneath his lashes. If he hadn't seen those gray eyes bright with lust only moments before, he wouldn't believe it had ever happened. He wondered if all actors hid their true faces that well.

*As well as you hide yours? Hypocrite.*

Adrian scowled. Keeping his psychokinesis to himself was different. No one would consider it lying, or being two-faced. What reasonable person would reveal such a thing to someone they barely knew? And who would believe it anyway?

*You never told Christian.*

He was saved from having to deal with that particular truth when two girls he had worked with the day before broke from the group and walked toward him. He drew a couple of slow, deep breaths. By the time the girls reached him, he had his roiling emotions under control.

He managed a smile that didn't even feel forced. "Hello, Erin. Chelsea."

"Hey, Adrian." Erin stuck her hands in the back pockets of her jeans and flashed a flirtatious grin. "What're we doing today?"

Deliberately turning his back on Greg and the knot of boys and girls gathered around him, Adrian rubbed his chin in an effort to channel his thoughts where they needed to go. "More building. We got a lot done yesterday on the false walls, but there's a lot more to go."

Chelsea wrinkled her nose. "Building frames isn't very exciting."

Adrian laughed in spite of the tight, sick feeling in his gut. "No, it isn't. But you know they're necessary if we're going to turn this giant room into smaller areas that people can walk through and still leave spaces in between for the cast and crew to operate."

"Yeah, I know." With an exaggerated sigh, Chelsea gathered her shoulder-length black curls in one hand and secured them into a ponytail with a red band she took from her pocket. "All right, let's do this thing."

"I'll get the tool kit," Erin offered. "We should be all set to go when the rest of our team gets here."

Adrian nodded. "Good thinking."

Erin's pallid cheeks flushed pink. Beaming, she brushed past him and practically floated to the alcove across the room where they'd stored their tools. Adrian turned away and busied himself with inspecting the heavy black cloth they'd stapled to the frames the previous day. He'd never had a straight girl crush on him before. It was a very strange feeling. He had no idea how to handle it.

"You realize why she's fixated on you, right?"

Startled, Adrian blinked at Chelsea. "What?"

She rolled her eyes. "Don't be dense, you know what I'm talking about."

He shot a glance at Erin, who knelt at the alcove entrance digging through the pile of various implements. "Yes." He looked at Chelsea again, curious. "So why is she fixated on me, then?"

"Because you're safe. You're gay, and she knows it. She can moon over you all she wants, but there's no way you'll ever return her interest so she won't have to put any effort into a relationship."

Adrian frowned. "How do you know that?"

"What? That you're gay, or what her motivation is?"

"Both, really."

"Word gets around. You used to date one of my suitemate's older brother's roommate's best friend, Christian. As far as Erin's motivation?" Chelsea flashed a wide, evil grin. "She and I have known each other since middle school. And I'm a psych major."

Something unpleasantly familiar squirmed in the pit of Adrian's stomach. "What if I wasn't gay? What if I was to show interest in her?"

"She'd push you away with both hands. Find some reason why you weren't compatible, pick fights. Anything to keep from having to work at a relationship." She gave him a narrow look. "Why?"

"No reason. Just idle speculation." The tiny falsehood came out sounding stilted, but there was no help for it. As much as he valued truth in all things, there was absolutely no way Adrian was telling Chelsea the real reason for his question.

God, he could hear Christian now, accusing him of inventing reasons to end it between them. Adrian had scorned Christian's claims at the time, but now the parallels between Erin's behavior and his own seemed clear, and he had to wonder if Christian had been right after all. *Had* he been the one to destroy their relationship? And if so, had his subconscious prodded him into doing it in order to avoid telling Christian about his psychokinesis?

Adrian shook his head. He'd never believed himself capable of such things—especially without even being aware of it—but there it was. He couldn't ignore the possibility.

At that moment, Greg crossed Adrian's line of sight, arm in arm with a ridiculously handsome boy whose name Adrian couldn't remember. The two had their heads close together, talking and laughing. Greg didn't so much as glance in Adrian's direction. Adrian tried not to watch them, but he couldn't help following Greg with his eyes for a second before snapping his focus back to Chelsea.

He forced his face into a blandly pleasant mask. "Well. Okay, so. Erin's on her way back with the tool kit. I think we have enough boards cut to start on a new frame before the rest of the team arrives. We'll begin with that. Hopefully once everyone else gets here, we can finish the frames by lunchtime and start working on some of the effects after lunch. Sound good?"

"Sounds great."

Erin walked up with the toolbox, and the three of them settled down to work. Every now and then, Chelsea would cast a thoughtful look in Greg's direction, followed by a more calculating one at Adrian. He cringed to think of what that might mean. The last thing he wanted was a well-meaning freshman psych major interfering between him and Greg. Even if he really did unintentionally sabotage his own chances at a healthy relationship—and he had to admit the available evidence pointed in that direction—such a chance did not exist with Greg. Physical attraction didn't provide a solid enough foundation for a relationship.

Halfway through the morning, while leaning a newly built frame against the wall, Adrian felt the back of his neck prickle. Following a gut instinct, he turned his head. Greg's gaze locked onto his from the other side of the room.

For a few heart-stopping seconds, everything went still. Adrian's vision tunneled. The blood whooshed in his ears. Then

Greg blinked and turned away, and the world started moving again.

Adrian stood without moving and breathed, in and out, in and out, until his pulse slowed and his racing mind quieted. He hadn't really seen the intense longing and regret he thought he'd seen in Greg's eyes. It was just his imagination. He couldn't allow himself to think of such things.

Shaking off the lingering memory of Greg's lips on his skin, Adrian hefted his hammer and went back to work.

~ \* ~

By the time the group stopped for lunch around one, Adrian remembered why he normally avoided being around large groups of people. Especially a bunch of theater kids who all knew each other and did not know—or, apparently, *want* to know—him. He hadn't felt this out of place since the last time Christian dragged him to one of those ridiculous Mystic Society of the Scythe parties, where the level of world-weary pretentiousness was always thick enough to suck all the air from the room.

Not that these kids were at all pretentious. They weren't. But like gazelles sensing a hyena in their midst, they tended to shy away from him in nervous clumps. Even his own team— with the notable exceptions of Chelsea and Erin—interacted with him as little as possible. He wondered why that hadn't happened the day before. Or if it had, and he just hadn't noticed.

A few not-so-subtle hints got the two girls to join the other kids for lunch and leave Adrian in blessed solitude. As he sat against the wall munching sausage pizza and watching Greg laugh with his friends on the other side of the room, Adrian thought he knew why he felt so particularly invisible today. For a couple of glorious, horrifying moments, he'd been wanted. Not in the general way of all the men and women who admired Adrian's dark good looks from a distance, or the futile and ultimately sexless way Erin stared at him. No, Greg had *desired* him, on a very personal level. Then in the time it took for him to say no, that desire evaporated and Adrian became the same thing to Greg that he already was to everyone else—the weird science geek who never talked to anyone.

For some unfathomable reason, losing Greg's regard left Adrian feeling bereft, lonely and awkward in this tightly knit crowd. For such a long time now, he'd successfully avoided situations that made him feel this way. Now here he was, once again the odd man out. He hated it.

A sudden wave of anger rolled through his brain like a tide. The wooden frames he and his team had just finished building rattled against the floor. A few of the other students glanced over with puzzled frowns on their faces.

*Shit.* Abandoning his last half-eaten slice of pizza, Adrian scrambled to his feet and crossed to the archway leading toward the back part of the house as fast as he could without drawing further attention to himself. The last thing he wanted was anyone following him upstairs this time. He needed to be alone for a while, to gain control of himself before he brought the whole damn place down around their ears.

The second he was out of the main hall, Adrian took off at a dead run toward the entrance to the tower, located at the southern corner of the castle. He took the stairs two at a time, arriving at the top breathless with a combination of exertion and fear.

Crossing the room, he threw open the window, leaned his elbows on the rough stone sill and drew the sharp October air deep into his lungs. He hadn't experienced anything less than perfect control of his psychokinesis ever since he broke up with Christian. The fact that his control could slip even a little simply because he felt uncomfortable worried him.

"It can't happen again," he declared to the red, gold and orange leaves rustling outside. He couldn't start letting his emotions get away with him. It was dangerous, not only for himself but for everyone around him.

An icy draft brushed the back of Adrian's neck. Although there were three other windows in the thick stone wall, all of them were shut, and anyway the outside air wasn't nearly this cold.

Keeping his movements slow and even, Adrian pushed himself upright and turned to face the apparition he knew would be there. Sure enough, Lyndon Groome's ghost stood only inches away, regarding Adrian with eyes far too intelligent for those of a mere residual haunt. Spectral gore dripped down his translucent neck to stain a shirt and brown leather vest old-fashioned enough to have been part of a costume even at the turn of the twentieth century. Adrian hadn't noticed that before, but he wondered about it now. Had Lyndon died during a Halloween party or something?

Lyndon's face took on a mournful expression that made Adrian's heart go out to him. Holding one hand palm up in front of him, Adrian let the shields restraining his psychokinesis drop enough to sense Lyndon's spirit.

Growing up with a father who owned a paranormal investigations company, Adrian had seen his share of residual hauntings. He'd even faced down terrifying otherdimensional creatures bent on death and destruction, though not by choice. But he'd never encountered a real apparition before Lyndon. He'd certainly never made a deliberate attempt to open himself up to one. For some reason, he'd expected the experience to be unpleasant, like a blast of freezing water to the chest.

It was nothing of the sort. Instead, a pulse of warm, welcoming energy flowed through his veins to burst like fireworks in his skull.

His knees buckled. He sat down hard on the cold floor, legs sprawled out in front of him. Planting his hands behind him to brace himself against the dizziness making his head spin, Adrian tilted his head back and squinted up at the spirit hovering above him. Lyndon hadn't moved, except to track Adrian's undignified fall with that sorrowful gaze.

"I wish I could talk to you." Adrian had no idea what made him say that. It was the truth, though, so he had no wish to take it back.

Lyndon's bloodless lips curved into a melancholy smile. The heat of his energy thumped through Adrian's mind, and his heart clenched. Something told him that if Lyndon Groome were alive, the two of them would be fast friends. Maybe even more than that.

Adrian let out a soft laugh. Only he could encounter a blood-covered phantom and want to be its lover. *There's a safe object of desire for you.*

The idea was sad, ludicrous and frighteningly close to the mark. Groaning, Adrian bent his knees up and dropped his forehead onto them. Was he really that pathetic? Had he truly fallen so far that he preferred the company of a ghost to that of a living, breathing human being?

He didn't know quite what to make of the fact that his honest answer was yes.

# Chapter Three

"You want to do *what*?"

"Would you keep it down?" Adrian cast a nervous look around the crowded hallway. A couple of passing girls laughed at Ryan's outburst, but no one else seemed to have noticed. Grasping his classmate's arm, Adrian steered him out the nearest set of double doors and down the steps into the afternoon sunshine. "I said, I'd like to go to your fraternity's party tomorrow night. If the invitation's still good, that is."

Ryan stopped at the bottom of the stairs and gaped at him. Adrian waited, clinging stubbornly to his somewhat ragged calm. Ryan was arguably the best friend Adrian had here. They shared a major and thus most of the same classes, and often talked between classes or at lunch. Still, they mingled very little socially. Approaching Ryan with this request had taken every ounce of courage Adrian possessed. But he had to try. Yesterday's realization that he'd rather spend his time with dead people than live ones had shaken him. He'd promised himself that he'd make an effort to get out more. Meet people. Maybe even start dating again, even though the thought made his stomach churn. A frat party seemed like a logical place to start.

At least Ryan's fraternity was an academic one. Maybe their parties would be more subdued than most.

"Yeah, of course the invitation's still good." Ryan gave him a sheepish grin. "Sorry. You know all the physics majors have a standing invitation. It's just that you've never gone before. You kind of threw me for a loop there."

"I know." Relieved, Adrian smiled. "Thanks, Ryan. I really appreciate this."

"No problem." Ryan clapped him on the back. "Hell, it'll be good to see you set foot outside that apartment for something other than class for a change."

Adrian started down the sidewalk, trying to get away from the sudden tension between his shoulder blades. "I get out."

"For what, groceries?" Ryan strode along beside him. The dried leaves crunched under his sneakers. "What you need, my friend, is to find some hot piece of tail and have yourself one glorious night of wild sex."

Heat flooded Adrian's face. He stared at the enormous oaks dotting the quad so he wouldn't have to look Ryan in the eye. "Good grief. You sound like my brother."

"Yeah? Well, clearly your brother is a wise man." Ryan kicked a horse chestnut out of the way. It skittered off through the grass. "A couple of the guys in my house bat for your team. Want me to set you up with one of 'em?"

"No, thank you." The words came out before Adrian even thought about it. He decided not to take them back. Yes, he needed to get out more, and this party was definitely a start. However, he knew himself well enough to know that a blind date with a frat boy was likely to push him further into his shell, not draw him out of it. Maybe a few weeks from now, he'd be ready for something like that. But not yet.

Ryan shook his head. "Too bad. Scotty's had his eye on you, and I'm told by people who ought to know that he gives a damn fine blow job."

The latter declaration was uttered just as the two of them approached the Pit, crowded as always with students and teachers eating lunch. Adrian groaned and hid his face in his hands as everyone within hearing distance laughed. "God, Ryan. Don't you think you could've said it a little louder? I think there are a few people who didn't quite catch that."

"Adrian, trust me, nobody but you cares." Ryan patted his shoulder. "I have to be at the computer lab in fifteen minutes for work study, so I'm just gonna grab a sandwich at Alpine Bagel and run. I'll see you at the house tomorrow night, yeah?"

Adrian licked his lips and forced himself to speak. "I'll be there."

"Good. I'll tell Scotty." Grinning, Ryan turned and made his way through the crowd before Adrian could say a word.

"Great. Wonderful. Thanks." Adrian shuffled over to the nearby steps and sat with his shoulders hunched, staring at the ground. He wished he could teleport straight to the tower room at Groome Castle. Lyndon's silent company would be welcome right now.

Somewhere behind him, Adrian heard a male voice express the opinion that Scotty did indeed give an amazing blow job. A second man laughed. A woman told them both to shut up. Adrian tuned out all three of them and breathed quietly until the knot in his gut eased and the burn of humiliation cooled from his cheeks.

Slipping the strap of his laptop bag onto his shoulder, Adrian pushed to his feet. He had just enough time to eat before his last class of the day. After that, he had a couple of hours free before he was supposed to be at Groome Castle. The theater group had made plans to meet there at one, but Adrian was exempt from that since he was on work study and so could only work a certain number of hours at the haunted house.

Guilt tugged at Adrian's insides as he strode across the Pit to the dining hall. A great deal of work remained to be done in order to get the Castle ready for its haunted house debut on Friday night. There was no rule saying Adrian couldn't volunteer his time toward that goal if he wanted. The truth was, being around Greg after yesterday's debacle had made Adrian feel at once horribly conspicuous and utterly insignificant, and he dreaded feeling that way again.

*On the other hand, there's always the tower. You could go early. Sneak upstairs, quiet your mind for a while. Maybe visit with Lyndon.*

That, even more than the fear of Greg's mocking gray eyes, convinced Adrian to wait. After all, that was the whole reason he'd gone to Ryan in the first place—to drag himself back into the world of the living. He'd become far too set in his solitary ways. He had to fix that, and hiding in the Groome Castle tower with a ghost wouldn't fix anything. Maybe a frat party would help and maybe it wouldn't, but it couldn't hurt.

At least, Adrian hoped not.

*Of course it won't. Just stay away from Scotty and his magical blow jobs.*

Adrian snorted. A normal guy would seek out a person who'd expressed an interest in giving him oral sex, not avoid him. Then again, Adrian had never been normal. He'd learned to accept his own idiosyncrasies, for the most part. He saw nothing wrong with holding out for a man who accepted him as he was.

The fact that his mind went straight to a man who'd been dead for over one hundred years strengthened Adrian's resolve. He would go to this damned party, and he'd have fun if it killed him.

Thus decided, Adrian pushed all thoughts of the next night

to the back of his mind, along with those of Greg, Lyndon and men in general. He had plenty of schoolwork to keep his brain occupied. At least physics never made him feel awkward, or sick with dread, or aching with unfulfilled need. Equations for his paper started clicking into place in his head, and he entered the dining hall with a smile on his face.

~ \* ~

Thirty-something hours later, Adrian sat wedged between a giggling sorority girl and the unexpectedly suave Scotty on Sigma Pi Sigma's stylish brown leather sofa, nursing a whiskey and soda and wondering why he'd ever thought this was a good idea.

Not that the party was objectionable, exactly, or the company less than engaging. In fact, Adrian had met more people in the past hour and a half than he had in the entire three years he'd been at Chapel Hill, and most of those people had been quite friendly.

*Some more than others,* he thought as Scotty slid close enough to press their bodies together. Adrian eased another inch to his left, enough to put some space between them. If he had to move again, he'd end up plastered against the girl sitting next to him, but he didn't know what else to do. He'd promised himself he wouldn't be rude to anyone tonight. However, as Sean always told him, he didn't possess the tact gene. So how was he supposed to extract himself from this situation?

"So. Adrian." Scotty twisted his upper body toward Adrian. His arm rested along the back of the sofa behind Adrian in a move a little too casual to be real. "How do you feel about Thai food?"

Adrian stared into Scotty's big, dark, admittedly sexy eyes.

They held the same hunger Greg's had that morning at Groome Castle. For a moment, Adrian's neck tingled with the memory of Greg's lips on his skin. He swallowed. "Thai? It's all right."

"Mmm." Scotty's fingertips traced the curve of Adrian's shoulder in a slow caress that made Adrian's skin spark. He bit back a moan, remembering the slide of Greg's hand over the small of his back. "How about Thai food in bed?"

The breath froze in Adrian's lungs. "What?"

"Come on, you heard me." Dipping his head, Scotty planted a light, openmouthed kiss on Adrian's neck. "I have leftover Pad Thai from Penang in my fridge. Let's heat it up and have a private party in my room, huh?" His hand slid up Adrian's thigh, dangerously close to the rising hardness in his jeans. "I'd love to wind some of those noodles around your cock and suck 'em off."

The heat simmering in Adrian's belly vanished like fog in the sunshine. Shoving Scotty's hand away, he jumped to his feet. "That sounds very, um, interesting, but I have to go."

"Hey, wait." Scotty grabbed his wrist, the movie-star smile still in place. "You're not really leaving, are you?"

"Yeah. It's late, and I have an early class tomorrow." Adrian tried to pull his arm free and frowned when Scotty's grip tightened. "I'm serious, Scotty. Let go."

Scotty's brows drew together. "But... You want it. I know when a man's turned on, and you *are*."

What the hell was he supposed to say to that? *Sorry, but I was thinking of someone else?* As much as he valued the truth, Adrian couldn't bring himself to be that harsh.

He shook his head. "I'm sorry."

Sighing, Scotty opened his hand. "Man. So close, and yet so far."

A smile tugged at Adrian's mouth. "That's just not my thing."

Scotty's eyebrows went up. "Noodles?"

"One-night stands."

"Ah."

Silence fell. The fact that Scotty said nothing about more than one night told Adrian all he needed to know. He cleared his throat. "Okay. Well. It was nice to meet you, Scotty. I'll, uh. I'll see you around. I suppose."

"Yeah. See you around."

With nothing more to say, Adrian turned and made his way through the crowded room to the hallway leading to the front of the house, his half-empty cup still clutched in his hand. Every square foot of space seemed to be occupied by couples making out or groups of people discussing some subject or other. Adrian had to stop every couple of minutes to greet a person he'd met earlier or talk to someone he knew from one of his classes.

By the time he stumbled out the front door into the October night nearly twenty minutes later, he felt wrung out and tense as a bowstring. How did the popular people stand this constant pressure to be pleasant, polite and personable? It was exhausting. It didn't help that someone had put on the latest rave music and turned it up so loud Adrian was hoarse from trying to talk over it. The only good part was, the adventure of getting out of the house had taken his mind off Greg long enough for his cock to deflate.

Draining the last of his drink, he tossed the red plastic cup into an overflowing trashcan and descended the steps onto the sidewalk. He started walking without much thought to his destination. He didn't care where he went as long as there were no other people there. What the hell had he been thinking? He should've known he would manage to feel uncomfortable even surrounded by a bunch of physics majors and assorted other scientific types.

He knew why. After all, how many people could say they'd accidentally opened an interdimensional portal with their mind at age eleven, nearly causing the deaths of everyone they loved? The horror and guilt of it had shaped him more than any experience before or since.

He aimed a savage kick at a particularly large chestnut in his path. It made him angry sometimes to think he'd spent so much time and energy keeping everyone around him safe from his abilities that he no longer had any idea how to connect to other human beings. Still, he wasn't sure he would change anything even if he could. He'd done what he had to in order to protect his family, himself and everyone around him from a very real threat. He didn't regret it, despite the damage to his personal life. A little hard work and the right partner could overcome that.

Right?

Lost in thought, he almost passed right by the Forest Theatre before the raised voices from inside registered. He stopped. It was none of his business, but a thread of fear laced through the anger in one of the voices. There was no harm in hanging around for a moment just to make sure everything was all right.

Moving as quietly as he could, Adrian retraced his steps until he reached the top of the wide, shallow stone steps leading to the stone archway that marked the entrance into the open-air theater. The voices were much louder here, angry words echoing off the surrounding rock. The thin sliver of new moon overhead lent minimal illumination to the scene, but Adrian could just make out two male figures standing face-to-face in the flagstone courtyard beyond the arch. One figure waved his arms in the air as he spoke, the sound of his frustration rising and falling in the night air.

Adrian frowned. The man's voice sounded vaguely familiar. Using the trees as cover, Adrian sidled as close as he dared. Did he know this person?

The other man growled out something with a distinctly threatening tone. The familiar man turned and walked away, striding toward the steps. "Leave me alone," he called over his shoulder. "If you ever contact me again, I'm taking out a restraining order."

This time, Adrian knew exactly who it was, and his stomach dropped into his feet. He scrambled to hide behind a tree. Getting caught was the last thing he wanted. Before he could move, though, the second man leapt forward, grabbed the first one, whirled him around and punched him in the face.

The sharp crack of a fist against bone changed Adrian's plans. Forgetting all about hiding, he sprinted down the steps toward the dark figure looming over the man huddled at his feet. "Hey! Leave him alone!"

The attacker straightened up. His face was a pale blur in the darkness. He spun on his heel and took off down one of the pathways leading from the theater into the surrounding woods.

Adrian shook his head. *Coward.*

Crouching on the cold stone, he laid a hand on the fallen man's shoulder. "He's gone. Are you all right?"

"Yeah, I'll be fine. Bastard can't land a decent punch anyway." The man pushed to a sitting position and felt gingerly along his jaw. "Thanks for chasing him away, I really appr—" He stopped, eyes going wide when they met Adrian's. "Oh, my God. Adrian?"

Adrian drew a deep breath and let out the sudden rush of resentment, lust and fear along with it. "Hi, Greg."

# Chapter Four

For a moment, Greg stared in silent astonishment. Then a slightly stiff version of his usual teasing smile spread across his face. "So, what're you doing out here at this hour? You heading someplace in particular or just looking for guys in distress to rescue?"

Adrian glared, irritated by Greg's nonchalant attitude. "Drop the act, Greg. That man just attacked you. It's okay to be a little shaken up."

Greg opened his mouth as if to argue, took one look at Adrian's face and let out a harsh laugh. "Yeah, okay, you're right."

"I know." Reaching into his jeans pocket, Adrian fished out his iPhone. "I'm calling the police."

Greg's hand shot out to curl around Adrian's wrist. "No."

The skin beneath Greg's fingers burned. Adrian drew a shaking breath. "Why not?"

"It'll just set him off."

Adrian shook his head. "Well, I'm sure he wouldn't like it, but so what? If he didn't want to go to jail, maybe he shouldn't have attacked you."

"No, it's just..." Sighing, Greg let go of Adrian's hand, pushed to his feet and walked over to the stone arch a few feet away. "I used to date him. I know how he is. I've already told him to leave me alone. If I let this go, he probably won't bother me again. If I call the cops and they arrest him, he'll be on my ass the second he's out, and not in a fun way."

"Oh."

Unsure of what to say or do, Adrian rose, shoved his phone back in his pocket and went to stand beside Greg. He watched Greg from the corner of his eye. They'd only known each other for a few days, but Adrian had grown used to the witty, outgoing boy he saw every day at Groome Castle. It bothered him to see this silent, hunch-shouldered Greg who stared into the trees as if he were being hunted.

*Maybe he is, no matter what he said about the guy leaving him alone if we don't call the cops.*

Heart thumping, Adrian laid a hand on Greg's shoulder. "Why don't you let me walk you home? Just in case."

Greg turned to look at Adrian. "Can we stay here for a few minutes? I mean, if I go back to my dorm now, he'll probably be waiting for me, but he'll give up pretty quick and it'll be safe soon, so..." He shrugged. "You don't have to stay with me if you don't want to, I know you probably need to get home yourself since it's so late and all. But I'm gonna hang out here for a while."

His tone was casual, but the scattered moonlight caught the pleading look in his eyes. Adrian couldn't have said no to that look, even if he'd been inclined to leave Greg alone with a violent ex out there in the night someplace.

"I'm staying with you. And once you feel like it's safe, I'm walking you back to your dorm." Feeling a little bolder in the face of Greg's vulnerability, Adrian slid his hand from Greg's shoulder down to gently grasp his arm. "Come on. Let's go sit down."

Greg let Adrian lead him through the archway and across the small flagstone courtyard to where the ground began to slope away in a series of wide, shallow stone seats toward the stage below. The two of them settled side by side on the top step.

They sat without speaking for several endless minutes. A couple of cars rolled past on the road behind them. In the surrounding woods, gusts of wind rasped the dying leaves against one another.

A visible shiver shook Greg's body. He rubbed his arms with both hands. "Wow. It's getting cold out here."

Adrian took a good look at the shirt Greg wore. It had long sleeves, but the material appeared to be a cotton far too thin to keep out the night's sharp chill. Another blast of wind moaned around the corners of the stone arch. Greg hunched over, teeth chattering, and Adrian wished with every fiber of his being that he'd worn a thinner shirt and a jacket instead of his favorite sweater.

Ignoring the wild hammering of his heart, Adrian scooted as close to Greg as he could and wound an arm around his shoulders. "I can't just sit here and watch you freeze to death," he said in answer to the startled expression in Greg's eyes. "And I don't have anything extra I can give you to wear, so..."

Greg's expression softened into a smile. "Thanks."

Adrian just nodded, unable to speak. Flirty, teasing Greg was eye-catching enough. Greg without his usual mask, however, was captivating. Adrian thought he could sit right there and stare into that open, unguarded face forever without tiring of it.

Unfortunately—or not, depending on how Adrian wanted to look at it—Greg sighed and rested his head on Adrian's shoulder. "So. You never said what you were doing out here."

49

"Um. I was walking home from a party." Adrian fought to hold still. It felt so damn good to have Greg's warm body cuddled against his side, soft hair tickling his neck. But he hadn't been this close to anyone since Christian, and he'd never in his life held a relative stranger in such an intimate way. The conflicting urges to press closer and run away played havoc with his equilibrium.

"Tell me about it."

For a terrifying moment, Adrian thought Greg had read his mind. "What?"

"The party. Tell me about the party." Greg nudged his shoulder gently into Adrian's ribs. "Sorry, is my extreme hotness scrambling your brains?"

In spite of Greg's teasing tone, the words were close enough to the truth that Adrian couldn't help laughing. Thankfully, the laughter broke his tension enough for him to realize that Greg simply wanted something to take his mind off what he'd just been through.

"It was a frat party," Adrian began, tightening his arm around Greg. "Sigma Pi Sigma."

"Oh my God, physics geeks."

"Hey, *I'm* a physics geek."

"I know. I *like* physics geeks. My cousin's actually a charter member of that fraternity. Alan Reed? You know him?"

"Oh, yeah. He's in some of my classes. Nice guy."

"Yeah." Greg squirmed into what Adrian assumed was a more comfortable position. "So. You were at a physics geek party. Continue."

Adrian grinned. Weird, that he was actually enjoying himself more now than he had at the aforementioned party. "So, I went to this party, even though I don't generally enjoy parties, because I've been turning into way too much of a hermit and I'd promised myself that I'd try to get out more."

"And?"

"And, I found out that frat parties, even physics-geek frat parties, are definitely not my thing."

"Yeah?"

"Yeah."

A leaf drifted over to settle on Adrian's right thigh. Greg brushed it off, his hand lingering just long enough to send Adrian's temperature shooting up several degrees. "Why not?"

Adrian licked his dry lips. "It was loud. It was crowded. I hate crowds. I had to make small talk with a bunch of people I don't know, and I'm terrible at that. And some guy I'd just met wanted to do perverted things to me with noodles."

Greg snorted with laughter. "Okay, you can't just say shit like that and not tell me more."

Heat flooded Adrian's face at the thought of repeating Scotty's words to Greg. "I am *not* telling you any more than that."

"Fine then, I guess I'll just have to imagine what exactly he wanted to do." Lifting his head, Greg grinned. "And believe me, I have a really good imagination."

Part of Adrian was glad to see the wicked gleam return to Greg's eyes, since it meant he'd recovered somewhat from the attack. A larger part didn't much like being on the receiving end of Greg's teasing. He scowled. "Leave it alone, Greg."

In an instant, Greg's smile vanished. He grasped Adrian's hand in a grip just short of painful and pinned him with a hard stare. "I'm sorry. You didn't deserve that, especially after everything you've done for me tonight. It's just...I do that, you know, I flirt and joke around and all, Mom says it's my coping mechanism, not that that's an excuse or anything, but..." Greg looked away, studying the play of light and shadow from the car headlights on the surrounding stone. "I'm sorry."

Greg looked young and lost, and Adrian's heart went out to him. "It's okay. You've had a pretty rough night. I'm sorry I'm so prickly about things."

The relief in Greg's face was clear when he turned to meet Adrian's gaze. "No big deal. I guess most people would probably agree with you about being teased like that."

Adrian doubted it, but he didn't say so. He saw no point in starting a petty argument when Greg was attempting to make peace between them.

Silence fell once more. The quiet felt companionable, though. When Greg leaned sideways, Adrian allowed their heads to rest together without much thought on the matter. Greg obviously needed the comfort of gentle human contact right now, and Adrian liked to think he wasn't a big enough bastard to deny such a need. He preferred not to dwell on the hot glow currently pulsing deep in his groin or the undeniable fact that the warmth of Greg's body and the clean scent of his hair lay at the root of it.

Adrian had no idea how many more minutes passed before Greg stirred, sighed and drew away. All he knew was he wished the tranquility they'd experienced between them tonight didn't have to end. He had a feeling it wouldn't be easy to get it back.

"Harrison ought to have given up on me by now," Greg said, sitting back and raking his fingers through his hair. "It should be safe for me to go back to the dorm."

"Harrison?" Adrian frowned. "Is that the guy who hit you?"

"Yeah." One corner of Greg's mouth tipped up in a bitter half-smile. "That sort of shit's why I broke up with him in the first place."

Adrian had no idea what to say to that. Pushing to his feet, he grasped both of Greg's hands and helped him stand. "All right. Which dorm are you in?"

"Winston."

Greg didn't try to hang on when Adrian let go of his hands, but he looked as though he wanted to. They climbed the steps and crossed the road in silence. Greg chose to cut behind the theater and through the old cemetery. Adrian wondered why, when there would surely have been a shorter route, but he didn't argue. Maybe Greg simply appreciated the peacefulness of the place. Or maybe he wanted to prolong the walk, in case Harrison hadn't given up yet after all. The thought made Adrian draw closer to Greg and cast uneasy glances at the dense shadows shrouding the trees and the taller headstones.

Adrian breathed easier once they reached the light and bustle of South Road. Even at near midnight on a Tuesday, students wandered the sidewalks in pairs and groups, and cars passed with enough frequency to lend an air of liveliness to the area.

"Do you see him anywhere?" Adrian asked as he and Greg strode down the sidewalk. "Harrison, I mean."

Greg glanced around. "No, I don't. Hopefully he'll just leave me the hell alone."

Adrian studied Greg's face. In the yellow glow of the streetlights, the developing bruise stood out deep red on his jaw. The sight made Adrian want to find Harrison and do painful things to him. It was a disturbing impulse, especially since Adrian had never felt the urge to physically hurt someone he didn't even know.

They made it to the South Road entrance of Winston Hall without incident. Greg stopped at the door and turned to face Adrian. "Thank you. For everything."

Adrian smiled, blushing. "No problem at all. I'm just glad you're safe."

"Me too." Greg glanced sideways and nodded to a couple of girls who thumbed into the dorm. Once the door swung shut behind them, he returned his attention to Adrian. "Would you go out with me?"

Adrian's heart lurched. "Go out?"

"Yeah." Greg moved closer, his gaze fixed on Adrian's face. "You helped me out tonight, Adrian. You didn't have to, but you did it anyway. I want to show you how much I appreciate that."

"I know you do. You don't have to take me out to prove it."

"How about if I take you out because I like you?"

The soft words made Adrian's head spin. He leaned against the dorm wall, trying to make the movement look casual. "You do?"

"Yes." Shoving his hands in his front pockets, Greg hunched his shoulders against a particularly vicious gust of wind. "Look, we got off on the wrong foot on Sunday, and I'd love to start over. I swear I won't...you know, try anything."

No matter how hard Adrian tried, he couldn't find a reason to turn Greg down. *And just how sad is it that you were looking for a reason not to go out with a guy you want this badly?*

"Okay." Adrian forced the word out past the mingled excitement and terror clogging his throat. "Sure. I'd love to go out with you."

Greg beamed. "Awesome. Does Thursday work for you? We get out of haunted house practice early, we could go get changed then head over to Top of the Hill after. I'll make reservations for seven, that sound okay?"

Adrian mentally rifled through his bank account. Could he afford to splurge on dinner? Would he even be expected to pay for his own meal or would Greg pick up the tab? He felt stupid for not knowing the rules, but he'd never really dated before. He and Christian hadn't gone on traditional dates, and there'd never been anyone before that. The few times he'd been out after Christian, he and his date had agreed beforehand to each pay their own way. Hopefully Greg wouldn't hold his lack of knowledge against him.

"Uh, yeah. That sounds great." Adrian watched from the corner of his eye as a group of three boys entered the dorm, deep in conversation. "Listen, why don't I come by here and pick you up? My apartment's off campus and I don't want you to have to walk there alone in case that crazy bastard's still stalking you."

"I'd appreciate that." Greg's wide smile mellowed into a softer expression that for reasons Adrian couldn't understand made his pulse race. "Okay. Well. I guess I'll see you tomorrow at the castle."

"Yeah. See you then."

Still watching Adrian's face, Greg backed the few steps to the door and pressed his thumb to the pad. The green light blinked and the lock clicked. He swung the door open and stopped just inside, the hall light illuminating his profile. "Good night, Adrian."

Adrian smiled at him. "Good night."

Once his knees stopped trembling, Adrian pushed away from the wall and began the trek back to his apartment. By the time he got home, the sense-memory of Greg's body curled against his side had turned the ache in his crotch into a full-blown erection.

He didn't even bother to strip, just yanked his jeans halfway down and fell backward across the bed. Eyes screwed shut, he jerked off to the mental picture of Greg's beautiful lips wrapped around his cock, Greg's naked body spread out beneath him, Greg's face flushed with orgasm. Adrian clamped his mouth closed and swallowed his cries when he came.

Afterward, he lay panting on the mattress with semen soaking into his sweater and trickling down his side and wondered if his fantasies would ever become reality, or if he'd manage to drive Greg away before they ever got that far.

*Don't think about it. Not yet. At least go on one date before you start worrying about how you're going to make him hate you.*

Adrian snickered. For once, his inner Sean was completely right. Forcing himself to his feet, Adrian headed into the bathroom to clean up before going to bed. He could worry—if necessary—later. Right now, he was determined to enjoy whatever happened with Greg while it lasted.

# Chapter Five

Wednesday's classes went by in a blur. Adrian gave himself a mental pat on the back for having read ahead in Quantum Mechanics, because otherwise he wouldn't have had any idea what they covered that day. All he could think of was Greg. What had happened last night, and what he hoped might happen tomorrow night.

At least he didn't have class with Ryan today. He wasn't sure he was up to explaining why he wouldn't be attending any more parties.

His last class didn't end until four. By the time he arrived at Groome Castle, most of the cast and crew were already there, huddled in the spacious foyer. He set his laptop bag beside the front door along with all the others and scanned the crowd.

He spotted Greg on the other side of the room, deep in conversation with Marisa. Adrian stood still, heart pounding. Things had changed since this time yesterday. How should he greet Greg? With a simple hello? A handshake? A hug?

And how sad was it that he was standing here frozen with indecision over how to say hello to someone?

Before he could overcome his paralysis, Greg turned his head and spotted Adrian. Even from fifteen feet away, Adrian saw the way Greg's eyes lit up. Cutting Marisa off mid-sentence, Greg jogged across the floor to Adrian's side, a wide smile on his face.

"Hi, Adrian." Greg took Adrian's hand and gave it a quick squeeze. "Where've you been?"

"Math class. It doesn't let out until four." Adrian reluctantly let Greg's fingers slip from his. "So. What are we doing today?"

"I guess you tech types are working on the effects. The rest of us are doing a dress rehearsal for the ghosts and such. Which means I need to go get the makeup on." Greg glanced over his shoulder to where his fellow actors were filing into the main hall. "Will you walk me back to my dorm again tonight after rehearsal? I know it isn't all that far, really, but the road back to campus is pretty dark and I'd rather not walk it by myself."

The sparkle in Greg's eyes told Adrian that fear for his safety wasn't the only reason Greg wanted an escort tonight. But the bruise on his face provided a stark reminder that, all flirting aside, Greg shouldn't walk alone after dark.

Before he could think about it too hard, Adrian lifted his hand and brushed his fingertips over the purplish swelling on Greg's jaw. Greg's breath hitched, and Adrian smiled. "I'm glad you asked, because I was going to walk you back anyway."

"Cool." Greg leaned into Adrian's touch for a moment before backing away. "I have to go. We can meet up in the foyer at eight if we don't see each other again before that, how about it?"

"Sounds good."

Greg's smile kicked up a notch. He turned and hurried across the room. Adrian watched him until he was out of sight. God, his ass looked good in those snug, faded jeans.

"Damn, he's got a great ass."

Startled, Adrian whipped around to face Chelsea, who stood behind him. "Oh. Uh. Hi, Chelsea."

"Hi." She flashed an evil grin. "You're aware that you were staring at Greg's ass like you wanted to eat it raw, right?"

Adrian lifted his chin and held her gaze in spite of his burning cheeks. "Yep. What's your excuse?"

Her jaw dropped open, then she burst out laughing. Hooking her arm through Adrian's, she pulled him in the direction Greg had gone. "Okay, you *have* to tell me what happened."

"What makes you think anything happened?"

"Hm, let's see. Maybe because yesterday you were ignoring each other, and today you're holding his hand and staring at his butt?"

Adrian laughed. "I see your point."

They walked into the main hall. Pushing open the black plywood door they'd built to cover half the opening into the room, Chelsea led him into the backstage area they'd created. "So?"

"So, what?"

"So what happened?"

Snickering at the frustrated growl in Chelsea's voice, Adrian followed her to the opening into the hallway leading to the back of the house. "I ran into him last night when I was leaving a party, and he asked me out."

*And I want to go out with him, God, do I ever, but I'm scared to death, because I want him to keep liking me as much as he does right now, and what if he doesn't once he gets to know the real me? The freak?* Adrian fought to keep the sudden flash of panic from showing on his face. He drew a deep breath, then another.

Chelsea's eyebrows shot up. "Really?"

"Yes, really." He nodded at Linda as she passed by on her

way to the foyer. "Is that so surprising?"

"Hell, no. I was starting to think he'd never do it."

He studied Chelsea's face. If she'd noticed his momentary agitation, she showed no sign of it. Relieved, he shrugged some of the tension from his shoulders. "What do you mean?"

"He's been drooling over you since day one." Chelsea pushed open the door of the bedroom the tech group had chosen for equipment storage. "Don't tell me you hadn't noticed."

Adrian grinned. "Well, I might have noticed a little bit of interest on his part."

Chelsea snickered, but didn't say anything else since Erin entered the room at that moment with two other tech team members at her heels.

Adrian turned to his work with a smile on his lips. For the first time in ages, it looked like he might actually be developing a social life. Sean would be thrilled.

~ \* ~

Adrian hadn't meant to go to the tower room that night. He had an actual date, with a real live man, in less than twenty-four hours. A date he was bound and determined not to be overly nervous about. Seeing Lyndon again, feeling the spirit's energy inside him, would only set him back.

Then he'd seen Greg in full makeup. The startling resemblance to the real thing loosened his tongue, and the resulting "you look exactly like him" set off a chain reaction of questions which ended up with Adrian, Greg and at least six other students climbing the narrow stairs to the little octagonal room which Lyndon Groome haunted.

At the top of the steps, Adrian paused and took a couple of seconds to calm his racing pulse. Part of him wanted very much for Lyndon to make an appearance. A larger part didn't want to share, even if no one but Adrian knew the ghost was there.

Squaring his shoulders, Adrian pushed open the heavy wooden door and walked inside. "Don't be disappointed if you can't see him. Not everyone can."

"But *you* can." Erin sidled a little too close, beaming up at him. "That's so cool, that you can see ghosts."

Greg insinuated himself between Erin and Adrian. Taking Adrian's hand, he led him across the floor to the window in a movement that managed to look casual even though Adrian knew damn well it wasn't. He raised his eyebrows at Greg and got a sly grin in return.

"Why is it that we all can't see the ghost? I mean, either it's there or it isn't, right?"

Shaking his head, Adrian let go of Greg's hand and turned to face Colin McCormack, one of the other actors. The boy was by far the most obstinately skeptical person Adrian had every met. He suspected the only reason Colin had come up here at all was because of Chelsea, who he put the moves on at every opportunity in spite of her obvious lack of interest.

"If an apparition is fully manifested, then yes, everyone would be able to see it," Adrian explained. "But if it isn't fully manifested, then only those who are sensitive to particular..." He fumbled for the right words. "Well, particular levels of energy, I guess you'd say, would be able to see it."

"And you're sensitive to those things."

The transparent scorn in Colin's voice stung, but Adrian ignored it. After the abuse he'd suffered in middle school and high school, this minor passive-aggressive ridicule was easily brushed aside. "Yes, I am."

Colin snorted. With a cutting glare at Colin, Chelsea moved to stand beside Adrian. "So, is he here? Lyndon, I mean. The real one."

Adrian shut his eyes and let his senses seep through the stone of the tower walls. The residual warmth of Lyndon's energy flavored the air all around, but it felt weak. Scattered. The potential crackled in the atmosphere, but it wasn't enough. Lyndon wouldn't manifest. Not right now, anyway.

Feeling strangely relieved, Adrian opened his eyes. "He's not here tonight."

"Well, dang." Susan Richards, one of the actors who'd been particularly anxious to see the phantom, let out a deep sigh. "Oh well. Maybe another time."

"Or not, since we're really not supposed to be coming up here at all."

Adrian shot Greg a surprised look. They didn't know each other very well, but he wouldn't have pegged Greg as a stickler for the rules.

On the other hand, keeping the rest of the cast and crew out of here meant keeping Lyndon to himself.

*You're not supposed to be coming up here either, remember? You promised yourself you wouldn't. And now you have a date with Greg to look forward to.*

The reminder made Adrian's stomach lurch with equal parts dread and excitement.

He forced himself to meet Greg's uncharacteristically hard gaze with a smile. "You're right. We really shouldn't be in here. We're going to get in trouble. Let's head back downstairs."

Greg tried to hide his relief, Adrian could tell. But his eyes lit up anyway, and Adrian wondered why he was so anxious to get out of the tower.

The whole crowd filed toward the exit, all talking at once. Adrian trailed behind Greg at the rear of the group. Just as he reached the door, he felt an electric surge behind him.

Heart pounding, Adrian spun around. Lyndon hovered in midair, wide eyes fixed on Adrian's face. The warm pulse of his presence slammed into Adrian's mind before he could shield against it. Images hit Adrian's cerebral cortex in a rapid-fire barrage that lasted only a second and stopped before he could make sense of it.

"Adrian?"

*Greg. I'm here with Greg. Gotta say something.*

Adrian blinked. In the time it took for his eyelids to sweep down and back up again, Lyndon had vanished. Shaking, Adrian turned to face Greg. "Yeah?"

Greg regarded him with mingled amusement and concern. "You totally zoned out just now."

"I did?"

"Yeah, you did." Moving forward, Greg laid his hands on either side of Adrian's waist. "You okay?"

"Yeah, I'll be okay. I just, uh…" Adrian laughed. "Lyndon showed up after all. Just for a second. He seems to like me."

Greg's expression went blank, and Adrian cursed for the millionth time his inability to lie. Why couldn't he have just said he was all right and leave it at that? Greg hadn't asked about the ghost. Why the hell had Adrian felt compelled to mention it?

"Let's get going. I need to get this damn makeup off." A smile softened Greg's face. "Then it's time to leave, and you did promise to walk me home."

Adrian's tension eased with the familiar curve of Greg's lips. "I did, yes. Let's go."

Still smiling, Greg started down the stairs. Adrian followed a few paces behind. He ogled the flex of Greg's muscles beneath his snug jeans without shame. After all, there was no one else to see, and he didn't think Greg would mind anyway.

~ \* ~

After a sexually charged walk with Greg followed by another fast and furious masturbation and a quick shower, Adrian sat hunched over his laptop attempting to study. It wasn't going well. Instead of concentrating on his Electricity & Magnetism homework, his mind insisted on replaying the images Lyndon had sent him. The few solid impressions Adrian could glean from the disjointed flashes—a man's face, a bolt of lightning, someone's embroidered collar—didn't make any more sense now than they had then, and Adrian wished his brain would let it go already and get back to work.

Frustrated, Adrian leaned back in his chair and shut his eyes. Maybe if he spent a few minutes focusing on what he'd seen, he'd be better able to pay attention to his studies.

He drew a long slow breath through his nose. As he blew it out, he imagined the solid world around him falling away, his mind shrinking inward toward a stack of photographs representing the mental images Lyndon had projected toward him. He took another breath, then another, until he'd reached a half-trance in which his conscious reasoning relaxed enough for his subconscious to take over.

Adrian's psychic projection of himself rifled through the snapshots in his head. He saw Groome Castle, new and resplendent with crystal, tapestries and expensive furniture. The corner of an old-fashioned classroom desk appeared in one photo, the leafy branches of an oak tree against a deep blue sky in another. One looked out across the old cemetery from the gazebo at night, the view tilted and partially obscured as if the observer had his head on someone's shoulder and that someone in turn rested a hand on his forehead. Most were faded and distorted, as if Lyndon couldn't quite remember how things had really looked so very long ago.

Only two of the images stood out stark and clear—the collar, and the man's face. A sense of finality and anger clung to the first one like an oily film. Around the vision of the dark-haired young man, however, Adrian felt a sadness so sharp and immediate it almost brought tears to his eyes.

*Cassius. His name is Cassius.*

Adrian had no idea how Lyndon had imparted that knowledge to him, but he felt the truth of it deep in his bones. The question was, why had Lyndon shown him these things?

Whatever had happened to Lyndon Groome, there must be more to it than what the stories said. Adrian swore to himself that he'd learn the truth, and put Lyndon's spirit to rest.

# Chapter Six

Thursday night arrived before Adrian was ready for it. He stood in front of Winston Hall at six forty-five, knees knocking and heart thumping so hard he thought he might throw up.

Never mind that he'd spent three whole hours that afternoon exchanging smiles and heated glances with Greg as they went about their work at Groome Castle. Never mind that they'd walked to Greg's dorm together only an hour and a half before, talking like old friends the whole time. It didn't matter. The dynamic between them had officially shifted from "hanging out" to "on a date", and Adrian had never been more nervous in his life.

When the front door swung open, Adrian nearly jumped out of his skin. A group of three girls and three boys spilled out into the night air. Adrian managed a smile and a nod when one of the girls gave him an odd look. She rolled her eyes.

Adrian waited until the group rounded the corner of the building, then pressed the intercom button beside the door. "Can I help you?" a girl's voice lilted.

"Yes, I'm here to pick up Greg Woodhall." Adrian sounded much calmer and more confident than he felt. Now if only some of that fake confidence would work its way inward.

"He'll be right out."

Was it his imagination, or did the girl on the other end of

the intercom sound amused? "Okay, thanks."

"Sure. Have fun!"

*She is definitely laughing.* Adrian stared at the intercom in bemusement. Before he had more than a few seconds to puzzle over it, however, the door flew open and Greg bounded out.

"Hi, Adrian." Greg walked over and stood beaming at Adrian. "Wow, you look amazing."

Adrian's cheeks flushed. He smiled at the appreciative gleam in Greg's eyes. "Thanks. So do you. Carolina blue's a perfect color on you."

"Thanks." Greg gave Adrian's jacket sleeve a tug. They descended the steps together and headed toward Raleigh Street. "Thank Christ for the gay fashion gene, huh?"

Adrian laughed, his nervousness evaporating. "I'm afraid I missed out on that one."

"What? No fashion gene?" Greg clutched at his chest in feigned shock. "How the hell do you dress yourself?"

"Maybe you haven't noticed, but normally I don't bother."

Greg shot him a fierce frown. "You've been running around naked and I didn't notice? Shit, I need to get my eyes checked."

Snickering, Adrian pushed the button for the "walk" signal at the intersection. "You know what I mean. I'm hardly fashionable most days."

"Point. Not that it matters. You could wear a trash bag and still be the hottest guy in the room." Greg plowed on before Adrian could let *that* process enough to embarrass him. "So how'd you put this smokin' outfit together? Luck?"

"This old thing?" Adrian ran a hand down the front of his deep burgundy silk shirt and snug black pants. "My brother picked out the shirt. Said it brought out my coloring."

"Is your brother gay?"

"No."

"What? A straight boy with good fashion sense?"

"He says he picked it up from shopping with girls. Which kind of makes sense, since he's been a serial monogamist since eighth grade." Adrian grinned at Greg as they crossed to the other side of the road. "Who knew you had all these preconceived notions about straights and gays?"

"Hey, everyone needs a flaw. This is mine." Greg stuck his hands in his jacket pockets and heaved a long-suffering sigh. "It's tough being almost perfect."

Adrian snuck a sidelong glance at Greg's ass, which looked far more than *almost* perfect in his form-fitting dark gray pants. "Almost."

The smoldering look Adrian got in return made it uncomfortable to walk, but he didn't care. It was worth it to be able to stroll through the cool fall evening with Greg by his side and know that, for tonight at least, he could have Greg all to himself.

They reached Top of the Hill with five minutes to spare. The place was packed, with people waiting at the bar and in the line of chairs beside the door. The hostess led them to the small table they'd reserved next to the window. Through it, Adrian saw the balcony—empty in the October chill—and beyond that, the lights of Franklin Street.

"Good thing you made us a reservation," Adrian observed as he settled into his seat. "Looks like the whole town's here tonight."

"It's always like this. Most popular date restaurant in town." Greg arched one fair brow over the top of the wine menu. "It's the romantic atmosphere."

Adrian didn't blush, for a wonder. *Must be getting used to his flirting.* "It certainly is romantic." He pinned Greg with his very best seductive look. "But I think that has more to do with the company than anything else."

To Adrian's delight, desire flared in Greg's eyes. He leaned forward, head tilting sideways just slightly. "Adrian, I do believe you're right."

Mesmerized, Adrian stared at the soft curve of Greg's mouth. God, those lips looked so enticing in the low light. The urge to lean over and kiss them pulsed through Adrian's blood.

*Not here. Not now. Later, maybe.*

The arrival of their waiter kept Adrian from dwelling on the possibilities of later, for which he was profoundly grateful. It wouldn't do to daydream about kissing Greg while sitting across the table from the man. Especially if he wanted a chance at kissing Greg for real. And God, he did, even though the thought made him sick with mingled anticipation and fear.

Greg ordered a bottle of Pinot Grigio. The two of them sipped the wine and talked while waiting for their dinner order to arrive. The anxiety Adrian had suffered earlier had vanished, and he felt completely at ease with Greg. Which amazed him, considering his usual difficulties when it came to connecting romantically with men.

Of course, they hadn't yet touched on any topic more difficult than classes, Chapel Hill and the haunted house.

*Stop borrowing trouble. You usually don't get this far, you know. Just relax and enjoy yourself for once.* Nodding to himself, Adrian drained his wineglass.

Greg gave him an amused look. "Okay there?"

"Yes. Fine." With a bright smile, Adrian planted his elbow on the table and plopped his chin into his hand. "So, you were gonna tell me about that weird play you were in last spring?"

Grinning, Greg picked up the wine bottle and refilled both

their glasses. "Yeah. It was written by a student who graduated year before last. It's called—"

"Oh my *God*. Greg?"

Frowning, Adrian straightened up and turned just in time to see a blur of blond hair and black clothes rush at Greg and throw a pair of long arms around him. Adrian tamped down the instant surge of anger and jealousy. It wasn't like he had any right to feel it. He raised his eyebrows in silent question.

With an apologetic look at Adrian, Greg pushed the boy gently but firmly away. "Hi, Trey. This is my date, Adrian Broussard. Adrian, this is Trey Grover."

Trey turned an ice-cold turquoise gaze on Adrian. "Oh. You're dating?"

*Do not rise to the bait.* Adrian forced himself to smile and hold out his hand instead of growling. "Hello, Trey. Nice to meet you."

"Hm, yes." Trey gave Adrian a brief, limp shake before swiveling around to beam at Greg like a lighthouse beacon. "So, where've you been hiding? I haven't seen you in a while."

"I've been pretty busy. Classes, the haunted house." Greg's gaze caught Adrian's, and the heat there was unmistakable. "Other things."

Trey glanced between the two of them. His lips thinned, and Adrian knew he'd caught Greg's meaning. Adrian found himself absurdly grateful for that.

"Yes. Well." Leaning far too close to Greg, Trey ran a fingertip up and down his forearm. "Call me, huh? I miss you."

Adrian watched Trey sashay off, narrow hips swaying, and shook his head. He was still angry, but mostly because the other man had obviously made Greg uncomfortable. "He's kind of clueless, huh?"

"You could say that. We went out once, and that was once too many for me." Greg touched Adrian's hand. "I'm sorry he interrupted us. He's a total self-centered prick."

"It's okay." Adrian stared into Greg's eyes, struck by a thought he'd had more than once in the past two days. "Why did you ask me out?"

Greg's eyebrows shot up. "This isn't about Trey, is it? Because trust me, he can't hold a candle to you in any way whatsoever."

"No, it's got nothing to do with him." Adrian glanced at the man in question, who was leaning against the bar flirting with a handsome man in a dark blue suit. "I've been wondering that ever since you asked me."

"I thought we cleared that up the other night." Greg took a sip of wine. "I asked you out because I like you."

Adrian smiled at the warmth in Greg's voice. "I believe you. But you're talented, good-looking and popular. And obviously there are dozens of guys who'd fall all over themselves at the chance to go out with you. Not all of them are like Trey, I'm sure. So why do you want *me,* in particular?"

Greg studied Adrian's face. "Truth?"

"Yes." Adrian's pulse sped up, but he held Greg's gaze without flinching. Always best to know the truth, however ugly it might be.

Setting his wineglass down, Greg leaned on his elbows. "At first, I just wanted you because you're ungodly hot. But when I told you I wanted you to fuck me, and you pushed me away? That did it. I couldn't stop thinking about you."

Adrian let that digest for a moment. It still didn't make any sense. He frowned. "What?"

"You wanted me as much as I wanted you. Any other guy

would've had us both in bed with his cock up my ass inside five minutes. But not you." Greg flashed a grin that made Adrian's insides turn somersaults. "What can I say? You're different. It intrigues the hell out of me. Makes me want to know more about you." Reaching across the table, Greg took Adrian's hand and wove their fingers together. "And here we are, out on a date. I'd say this is the perfect opportunity to learn all about each other, wouldn't you?"

Adrian made himself hold Greg's gaze and not stare at their intertwined hands. God, he was holding hands with Greg, *in a crowded restaurant*, where everyone could see. Everyone around them would know instantly that they were more than just friends. The knowledge excited and terrified him.

"You're absolutely right," he heard himself say, and the calmness in his voice surprised him. "What would you like to know?"

The sudden mischievous sparkle in Greg's eyes made the butterflies in Adrian's stomach—which had settled down during the walk to the restaurant—flutter to life. "What's your favorite sex toy?"

"Greg!"

"Sorry, sorry, I couldn't resist." Greg squeezed Adrian's hand, then let go and leaned back in his chair. "There's one thing I've been wondering, for real."

Adrian eyed Greg with caution. "What's that?"

"Well, don't take this the wrong way, but why're you here instead of State? Isn't that the place to go for physics?"

"I'm here on the Voltner Scholarship."

Greg's brows drew together. "The what now?"

"Dr. Voltner's a theoretical physicist working for NASA. He got his degree here, and decided to offer a full four-year physics scholarship each year in order to encourage other physics students to study here. I had to promise to go on to get my doctorate, but that fit right in with my plans so it wasn't any big deal." Picking up his wineglass, Adrian took a sip. He held the tart wine on his tongue for a moment before swallowing. "What about you? What're your plans for after graduation?"

"Broadway, what else? The roar of the greasepaint, the smell of the crowd." One shoulder hitched up in a careless shrug. "I think my parents are still hoping I'll change my mind."

"Why?" The second he said it, Adrian wished he could take it back. Sometimes he forgot that not everyone appreciated his bluntness. "Sorry. That's none of my business."

Greg looked surprised. "No, that's fine." He lifted his glass and swirled the wine around, watching the light glint in the pale liquid. "The theater's not an easy business to break into, and it's not an easy life. They worry, that's all."

"Oh." Adrian studied the angle of Greg's jaw, the curve of his mouth, the way his long lashes cast shadows on his cheeks. "I can see that."

Greg's gaze caught and held Adrian's. He smiled, gray eyes shining with something Adrian couldn't name but which started a warm glow deep in his belly. "Well, my dad worries. My mom thinks I'm subconsciously picking a career that's stereotypically gay because I'm unsure of my sexuality."

"Wow."

"You said it." Greg took a long swallow of wine. "Oh well, she's a psychiatrist. A banana's never, *ever* just a banana, you know?"

Adrian laughed. "What about your dad? What does he do?"

"He's a writer."

"Really? What does he write?" Adrian lifted his glass to his lips.

Greg waited until Adrian had a good mouthful before answering. "Romance."

Adrian just managed to swallow instead of spraying Greg with Pinot Grigio. He coughed into his napkin while Greg chortled.

"Very funny," Adrian wheezed once he got his breath back.

Greg flashed an unrepentant grin at him. "Hey, you're the one who thought it was so surprising for a man to write romance novels."

"Touché." Adrian drew a deep breath, which prompted another, albeit shorter, coughing fit. He rubbed at the center of his chest. "It *was* a surprise, but it's also pretty cool."

"I think so." Tilting his head sideways, Greg leaned forward in his seat. "So, tell me about your family."

Adrian smirked. "Well, I believe you already know about Sean."

Clasping his hands in front of him, Greg affected a high, feminine voice. "Oh my *God*, Sean Broussard is *soooo hot!*" Greg rolled his eyes. "No offense, but if Sandy doesn't shut up about your brother I might have to hurt her."

Sandy Ward wasn't part of the haunted house group, but she was a good friend of Greg's and a huge fan of Auburn football. Apparently she'd fallen head over heels for Sean and felt the need to tell Greg all about her feelings. Constantly. At great length. Greg was not best pleased by this and had already told Adrian so more than once. Adrian laughed out loud.

Greg leveled what was probably supposed to be a stern glare at Adrian. "All right, that's enough of that. Tell me about the rest of your family."

Adrian took a drink of wine to give himself a moment to

think. Although really, what was there to think about? He had nothing to hide when it came to his family. And there was no reason he would be obligated to tell Greg about his psychokinesis tonight.

He tried not to think of the fact that he and Greg were unlikely to be together long enough for the subject to ever come up. That was a negative thought, and he'd promised himself he'd remain positive tonight.

"My mom and dad got divorced when I was eleven," Adrian began. "Wasn't pretty, but it turned out to be a good thing. My mom's remarried to a very nice man. My dad's also remarried to a very nice man, finally."

Greg's eyes went wide. "Your dad's gay?"

Adrian grinned, pleased that he could surprise Greg so thoroughly. "Yes."

"And he's married to his partner?"

"Yeah. He and Sam have been together for ten years but Alabama only passed the law allowing gays to marry last year, so they've only been married a few months." Adrian saw Greg doing the math in his head and coming to the correct conclusion about what had prompted Adrian's parents' divorce. Adrian hoped Greg was too polite to bring it up, but decided to try and steer the conversation away from that topic just in case. "I know my dad and Sam didn't always have an easy time of it, but I'm lucky because they were always there to support me when I came out. I don't think I ever would've survived high school without them."

The sweet, open expression that made Adrian's stomach flutter softened Greg's face. Setting down his glass, Greg took Adrian's free hand in both of his. "I'm glad they were there for you, Adrian. And I'm glad you're here now, with me."

The feel of Greg's skin against his nearly overwhelmed

75

Adrian's senses. The room blurred until he couldn't see anything except Greg's face.

*And he's only holding my hand. God, what would sex with him be like?*

Adrian intended to find out. Not tonight. Not tomorrow night. Hell, probably not this week, or next week. He wanted to get to know Greg first. He had no intention of collecting notches on his bedpost, and he certainly did not want to be a notch on anyone else's. But if they kept seeing each other, if they continued to enjoy each other's company as much as they did now...

Oh yes. Adrian had every intention of learning what Greg sounded like when he came.

Twisting his hand in Greg's grip, he wound their fingers together. "So am I."


By the time they left the restaurant the temperature outside had dropped at least ten degrees, the predicted cold front slinking in on a stiff breeze. Remembering how good it had felt to hold Greg close before, Adrian used Greg's shivers as a reason to wind an arm around his shoulders as they walked. Greg pressed against him, left arm sliding around his waist. They both knew the cold was only an excuse, but for once Adrian didn't care. He liked the warmth of Greg's body at his side, the way Greg's hip bumped and swayed against his as they walked.

Turning his head, Adrian dared to nuzzle Greg's silky curls. They smelled fresh and clean, like he'd just washed his hair. Greg hummed and rubbed his head against Adrian's face like a cat. Adrian laughed. He had no idea whether to blame the wine, Greg or his resolve to let go of his own reins for a change, but he felt freer than he had in years. Possibly his whole life.

When Greg's dorm came into view, Adrian slowed his pace. He didn't want the evening to end. There would be other dates. He had no doubt about that. But Greg fit perfectly beneath his arm, and he didn't want to let go yet.

Greg pulled him aside into the shadows just before they reached the steps to the dorm door. His arms slipped around Adrian's waist, pulling their bodies flush against one another. "Adrian. I know I promised not to try anything, and I won't, but..." He brushed Adrian's cheek with his. "I want you so much right now. I don't want you to go."

Adrian swallowed against his hammering heart. "I...I want you too."

Greg's breath huffed against Adrian's ear. "Come inside with me. My roommate's staying with his girlfriend tonight." His palms splayed open on Adrian's back, fingers digging in. "God, I really want to be alone with you."

The naked desire in Greg's whispered words made Adrian's knees weak. He rested one shaking hand on Greg's hip and cupped his cheek in the other, forcing him back until they could look each other in the eye. Even in the near-dark, the fire in Greg's eyes came close to destroying Adrian's resolve.

"Not tonight." He traced the line of Greg's jaw with his fingers. "I'm sorry."

Greg let out a breathless laugh. "Can't blame a guy for trying, huh?"

Adrian ran his thumb across Greg's lips. They felt incredibly soft. Heart fluttering like a hummingbird's wings, Adrian leaned closer. Greg's gaze caught his, eyes heavy-lidded and full of heat. Sliding his hand upward, Adrian tangled his fingers into Greg's hair and brought their mouths together.

The instant their lips touched, Adrian's power flared inside him. Electricity licked the curve of his skull, skated along his skin and crackled in the air. His cock filled so fast it hurt.

On fire with a lust stronger than he'd ever felt before, Adrian licked at Greg's lips. Greg's mouth opened with a soft, needy sound. His head tilted, his tongue curled around Adrian's, and Adrian's tenuous control slipped another notch. His hair lifted and swirled in a wind that didn't come from the world around him.

Groaning into Greg's mouth, Adrian skimmed the hand on Greg's hip around to give his ass a hard squeeze. Greg responded with a low moan and a roll of his hips, and *God* he was hard already, as hard as Adrian, and *why* weren't they in Greg's bed right now?

*You know why. Get a hold of yourself.*

Summoning his years of hard-won discipline, Adrian planted both hands on Greg's shoulders and forced himself to break the kiss. Greg whimpered in protest, grasping at Adrian's arms with both hands. "No. Don't stop."

"Have to." Adrian's words emerged rough and breathless. He framed Greg's face in his palms and stared into Greg's wide, glazed eyes. "I told you before, I don't do casual sex."

Greg laid his hands over Adrian's. His gaze bored straight through Adrian's skull. "There was nothing casual about that kiss, and you know it."

Fear spiked through Adrian's blood. Did Greg know? Had he somehow figured out that Adrian possessed psychokinetic powers, and that Greg's touch caused them to rage out of control?

*No. Because if he knew, he'd understand that you can't possibly take him to bed until you can control what happens. If one kiss makes you lose it like this...*

Closing his eyes, Adrian leaned his forehead against Greg's. "I know. I just...I need more time. Please."

Silence. Adrian caressed Greg's cheeks with his thumbs. Overhead, the rising wind tossed the trees' branches and wailed around the corners of the building. Adrian could feel Greg's breath against his lips, warm and scented with the Kahlua cake they'd shared for dessert. Fighting off the urge to taste it straight from Greg's tongue took everything Adrian had. He licked his own lips instead, wishing he could kiss Greg again and do it right this time. Take it slow. Savor the feel and smell and taste of him.

"Okay," Greg whispered at last. His hands dropped to Adrian's chest and moved sideways to fist in his jacket. "But if you won't go to bed with me tonight, the least you can do is kiss me again."

Adrian couldn't help the laugh that bubbled up. Opening his eyes, he drew back enough to smile at Greg's frown. "You read my mind."

The corners of Greg's mouth turned up. "So get on with it, Casanova."

Maybe it was because he was prepared for his body's reaction. But this time, when Greg's mouth opened under his and their tongues slid together, the power that surged through Adrian's body no longer felt overwhelming. His heart still thumped too fast, his limbs still shook and his cock still felt full enough to burst, but he was able to disperse the excess energy harmlessly into the ground at his feet. He buried both hands in Greg's hair and drank in the sweet taste of his mouth, his tiny whimpers, the way he clung to Adrian as if he'd fall down otherwise.

*It was never like this with Christian,* Adrian thought, dazed, as he and Greg pulled apart several long, glorious minutes later. He stared into Greg's eyes, feeling as lust-drunk as Greg looked. "Wow."

"Oh, yeah. Wow." Greg fell forward with a groan, leaning against Adrian's chest. "I can't walk."

Adrian rested his cheek against Greg's head, hugged him close and breathed in his scent. *Just for a minute. Just a minute won't hurt.* "I know I'm amazing and all, but surely I'm not *that* good."

"You only think you're joking." Pushing himself upright again, Greg looped his arm around Adrian's waist. "Come on, Magic Man. Since you've incapacitated me, the least you can do is walk me up the steps to the door."

"Oh. Of course." Adrian gladly wrapped his arm around Greg's shoulders. They emerged from the shadows and started up the steps. "Magic Man?"

"It's your new nickname."

"It is?"

"Mm-hm."

"Okay." Adrian paused to give Greg a chance to explain. When no explanation seemed forthcoming, he decided to ask. "Why?"

Greg shot him a sly smile as they reached the door of the dorm. "No one's ever kissed me quite like that. It must be magic. Therefore, you are now Magic Man."

"Oh." Not knowing whether to be pleased that he'd affected Greg so strongly or scared that Greg had unknowingly hit so close to the truth, Adrian tried to cover his conflicted feelings with a smile. "I'm really glad you asked me out tonight, Greg. It was...wonderful. And I'd love to see you again. I mean, I know we see each other every day at Groome Castle, but I'd like to go out with you again."

"I knew what you meant." Greg smiled, his face alight with happiness. "Of course we're going out again. You can't kiss a guy like that and not keep going out with him."

Adrian's heart lurched. He knew his grin looked goofy as hell, but he couldn't help it. He took Greg's hand in his. "So, what's good for you? We've got the haunted house every night this weekend, but we could do something Saturday afternoon if you want."

"Oh my God, I know the perfect thing! Sandy's sorority's putting on a hayride for charity, you want to go?" Greg sidled closer. His eyes sparkled with excitement. "They're gonna have hot chocolate and everything, and we should be back in plenty of time to get to Groome Castle."

Adrian nodded in spite of the hard knot that formed in his belly at the thought of spending several hours in a hay wagon with a bunch of strangers. It would be fine as long as he was with Greg. "Sure. It sounds like fun."

"Fantastic. I'll get the details and let you know all about it tomorrow night." Beaming, Greg leaned forward and gave Adrian a quick peck on the lips. "See you tomorrow."

"See you."

Adrian let Greg slide out of his embrace and stood watching until the dorm door closed behind him, then turned and made his way down the steps and out to the sidewalk. His lips still tingled where Greg had kissed him.

*Oh, my God. Those kisses.*

Adrian lifted his face into the cold wind. It felt good. It focused his mind and eased his arousal to a bearable level. Good grief, he was going to have to work on keeping his abilities under control during sexual stimulation. He was out of practice.

Of course, he'd never had this much of a problem during sex with Christian. The fact that he had trouble keeping control with Greg and all they'd done was *kiss* worried him.

*Guess you'll just have to practice a lot.*

The idea frightened him almost as much as it excited him.

Pushing aside thoughts of Greg, Adrian forced himself to concentrate on his breathing and the rhythm of his heartbeat. By the time he reached Country Club Road, his pants no longer felt two sizes too small and he believed he might be able to think through this latest development with some degree of success. He turned down the road to his apartment, already planning in his head.

# Chapter Seven

Adrian arrived at Groome Castle before anyone else on Friday afternoon. With a thought, he turned the front door lock, went inside and headed straight for the tower room.

The place felt empty. He sat with his back against the wall to clear his mind and try to call Lyndon to him.

He knew he shouldn't. But he couldn't seem to help himself. If anyone had asked why he'd felt the need to come up here and seek out Lyndon, he wasn't sure he could've given a reason. All he knew was he'd woken with the burning need to tell someone all about the best night of his life, right down to the last delicious detail, and the only person he felt that comfortable with—other than the subject of his rhapsodizing—was the man whose spirit haunted this room.

Adrian drew a slow, deep breath and blew it out. As his body relaxed, he allowed his mind to open. "Lyndon? Are you here?"

For a moment, nothing happened. Then a tingle of energy raised the hairs on the back of Adrian's neck. Warmth washed through him, the air around him swirled and Lyndon's bloody form wavered into existence. The big, translucent eyes stared right at him, making him feel like he'd been pinned to the wall.

He smiled. "How do you do that? You're a ghost, I don't even know how aware of me you are, but it feels like you're poking through my brain with a stick."

Lyndon's mouth opened. Adrian sat forward, doing his best to stay relaxed and breathe normally.

The pale lips formed a single syllable. Adrian couldn't make it out, nor could he *hear* Lyndon's intent in his mind.

He shook his head. "I don't know what you're trying to tell me. Can you try again?"

If a ghost could have sighed, Adrian figured that's what he would have heard at that moment. Lyndon floated toward the southeast window and hung there, his form now so insubstantial Adrian could barely see it. An aching sadness weighed on Lyndon's energy, so that Adrian felt his own shoulders bowing under it.

*I guess maybe now's not the time to tell him about Greg.* Adrian let out a quiet laugh. As if it wasn't pathetic enough that he'd come up here to gush to a ghost about his hot date in the first place, now the ghost didn't seem to be in the mood to listen.

Planting his palm on the floor, Adrian pushed to his feet. He walked over to the window where Lyndon's barely visible outline hovered, leaned against the sill and peered out. A stretch of scruffy grass sloped away from the castle's outside wall toward the forest about thirty or forty yards away. Through the trees, he could just make out the nearby park. If he opened the window, he'd probably be able to hear the laughter of the neighborhood kids playing. He wondered if any of the children who surely snuck onto the castle grounds from time to time ever looked up here and saw Lyndon gazing down at them.

Adrian glanced at his watch and groaned. The cast and crew would begin arriving soon to prepare for opening night of the haunted house. He had about five minutes to get out of the castle and far enough away that no one would suspect him of breaking and entering.

Most likely no one would care. They might not even notice. After all, the three or four sets of keys changed hands often enough that the group sometimes had trouble keeping track of who had them on any given day. But the last thing Adrian wanted to do was draw attention to his abilities, so avoiding the possibility of discovery altogether seemed the best course of action.

He pushed away from the windowsill. "I need to go, Lyndon. I'll come see you again soon, okay?"

The silence in his head remained unbroken. Feeling unaccountably discouraged, Adrian cut himself off from the waning flow of Lyndon's energy and headed for the stairs.

*The haunted house is going to end in a couple of weeks,* he reminded himself as he descended the steps. *There won't be any reason to come back here after that. What if you haven't learned anything by then?*

Adrian stopped, one foot on the step behind him and a hand splayed flat on the stone wall. He pictured Lyndon's sorrowful specter in his mind and knew he wouldn't stop pursuing the truth just because he no longer had a legitimate reason to be here. Locked doors couldn't keep him out. He would have to be careful, that's all. He could do that.

*And to think, not so long ago you swore you'd never come up here again.* He let out a soft laugh. Funny how a taste of an old mystery could change his mind so completely.

Adrian took the narrow footpath winding through the woods behind the castle to the small neighborhood park a few minutes' walk away. With a quick glance around to make sure no one saw him, he climbed a short flight of wooden steps onto the sidewalk and started along the main road back toward

Groome Castle. Marisa's brand-new electric SUV passed him on the way. She stuck an arm out the window and waved. He waved back, smiling.

When he entered the castle again, several of the tech crew and actors had arrived and were helping Marisa set up. Adrian looked around, heart thumping. Just when he thought Greg hadn't gotten there yet, the man himself rounded the corner from the main hall. Their gazes locked, and Adrian's knees nearly buckled.

Greg's face lit up. He strode across the floor toward Adrian, grinning ear to ear. "Hi, Adrian."

"Hi." Adrian mirrored Greg's smile. Just the sight of him made Adrian's stomach flutter. "You ready for tonight?"

"Looking forward to it." Greg wound his arms around Adrian's neck and molded his body to Adrian's. "I missed you."

Before Adrian could process what was happening, Greg leaned in and kissed him. Adrian's psychokinesis flared in response.

Behind Adrian, the front door squeaked open and banged shut. "Hey, get a room!" a male voice bellowed.

Adrian broke the kiss, shooting a look at the boy who'd just entered. "Um. Not here, okay?"

Surprise and a bit of hurt shone in Greg's eyes for a moment before his usual teasing smile hid them. "Sure. Sorry." He dropped his arms and stepped back. "I should go start getting ready anyhow."

Adrian grabbed Greg's hand before he could go anywhere. "Wait."

Greg's eyebrows went up. He glanced at Adrian's hand clutching his. "What?"

What, indeed? Adrian had no idea. He only knew that he

longed to kiss Greg again, but he couldn't bring himself to do it right here where anyone might walk in and see. It made him feel like a sideshow exhibit.

What they needed was privacy. Turning his hand in Greg's, Adrian laced their fingers together and led Greg through the foyer toward the hallway to the bedrooms. He managed to avoid looking at any of the people they passed on the way.

Not that it mattered. After the show he and Greg had put on in the foyer, anyone who'd seen them knew where they were going and why. In fact, the couple of students who'd witnessed that kiss probably thought Adrian and Greg were finding a nice, quiet place to have sex. Adrian winced at the thought. God, if his cheeks turned any redder his face might burst into flame.

He didn't turn back, though. His entire body ached with a desire stronger than any he'd ever felt, and he intended to slake what he could of it now. If a kiss was all he could allow himself yet, then that's what he'd take. So far he'd found kissing Greg orders of magnitude more exciting than even the best sex with Christian, so the prospect was hardly a disappointment.

As they passed the bathroom, Greg yanked Adrian inside and kicked the door shut behind him. Adrian didn't even bother to argue with his choice of private space. Dropping Greg's hand, Adrian slid one arm around Greg's waist, fisted the other hand in his hair and let Greg pick up where they'd left off. Greg's head tilted, his mouth opened wide and his tongue twined with Adrian's. He grabbed Adrian's ass in both hands and thrust his hips forward, and Adrian felt Greg's hardness push against his own.

Adrian's powers, already roused and quivering, exploded like a silent bomb. It took every ounce of his severely strained concentration to channel the wild energy into something harmless and pleasurable so it didn't shatter every window in the castle. He managed, barely. Invisible fingers caressed his face and neck, twisted in his hair, slipped beneath his shirt and down his pants to glide a delicate touch up the sensitive skin of his cock. Greg whimpered, and Adrian knew he'd felt it too.

Through the haze of need in his brain, Adrian wondered what Greg thought of the mysterious touches, if he connected them with Adrian at all or if he believed some unseen but lustful entity inhabiting this room had decided to molest them.

They jumped apart when someone pounded on the door. "Hey, hurry up! Other people need to get in there too, you know."

"Yeah, just a second," Greg called back. His voice sounded rough and breathless. He gazed up at Adrian with a sly smile. "So. I guess you're not much for PDA, huh?"

"Not really." Cupping Greg's face in both palms, Adrian kissed his forehead, his nose, his chin. "Even if I was, I couldn't kiss you in public. You get me too excited for other people to be watching, if you know what I mean."

Greg laughed. "Yeah, I noticed. And it's mutual, by the way, which is pretty amazing because it's been a long time since any guy's been able to get me hard with just a kiss." He gave Adrian a swift, chaste peck on the lips, then pulled out of his arms. "I don't suppose it would do me any good to ask if we could just suck each other off real quick?"

The idea tempted Adrian more than he liked. The scary thing was, he might've said yes if whoever was waiting for the bathroom hadn't chosen that moment to bang on the door again and demand that they come out *right now*. Greg glared daggers through the door, and Adrian let out a silent sigh of...relief? Annoyance? He couldn't decide, and how weird was that?

Adrian let his arms drop. "We need to go."

"I know." Greg's voice emerged sharp and tense. His

expression softened when Adrian flinched. Reaching up, he raked his fingers through Adrian's hair. "I know," he repeated in a gentler tone. "Just...please promise me that if we keep seeing each other, you'll eventually take me to bed. I can't take getting these little tastes without knowing I can have the whole enchilada at some point, you know?"

Adrian blushed, shocked in spite of himself. "Oh. Um. Wow."

"I'm sorry. I know that probably sounds crude to you, but I'm just being honest here." Greg stared into Adrian's eyes with an openness that Adrian found at once refreshing and uncomfortable. "I like you, Adrian. A lot. That's why I'm willing to wait for you. But I desperately want to have sex with you, and I want you to promise me you'll be ready eventually. If you can't promise me that, please tell me now."

*Because if you never want to have sex with me, I won't keep seeing you.* Greg didn't go so far as to actually say it, but the words were there between the lines. Adrian thought he should feel indignant about that. Trapped, maybe. After all, he could argue that Greg was trying to coerce him into sex when he didn't want it.

There was only one problem with that argument—he *did* want sex with Greg. Wanted it so badly his blood sang with it.

*So do it*, the Sean-faced demon in his head goaded him. *For once in your miserable existence, just damn well do what makes you happy. What are you so afraid of? Your powers? Look how well you controlled them just now. Practice makes perfect, and how are you gonna practice if you never do anything?*

Adrian smiled. Scary how much sense Sean-demon made sometimes. Even scarier how the possibility of sex with Greg seemed so much more important than any of Adrian's fears and neuroses.

Looking Greg squarely in the eyes, Adrian nodded. "I can definitely promise you that."

The movie-star smile that already had Adrian hooked lit Greg's face. "Good." Leaning in, he planted a soft, lingering kiss on Adrian's mouth. "I can't wait," he whispered as they drew apart.

"Neither can I." Clutching Greg's hand in his, Adrian flung the bathroom door open, lifted his chin and stalked out past the line that had formed while they'd been inside. With any luck, no one would notice the swelling in the front of his jeans or the loopy grin on his face.

# Chapter Eight

Throughout his six-month relationship with Christian, Adrian had become accustomed to sex whenever the mood struck. The thing was, the mood didn't strike all that often. For the first few weeks, sure, they'd screwed constantly. Then the novelty had worn off, familiarity had set in, and they'd settled into a once or twice a week pattern more like that of a long-married couple than a pair of teenage boys.

The experience had led Adrian to believe he simply didn't have much of a sex drive. Aside from the mild irritation of discovering yet another way in which he was different from everyone else, it hadn't bothered him much. He had big plans for his life, and those plans didn't include a relationship. Not being burdened by the hormonal urges that plagued most men his age could only be a good thing.

Then along came Greg. Greg, who could turn Adrian's legs boneless and his cock stone hard with nothing but a single smoldering look. Every time they kissed, every time Greg's hands slid beneath Adrian's shirt to spread across the bare skin of his back, Adrian's powers surged into a savage whirlwind of crackling energy. It terrified him, yet at the same time he found the feel of all that raw power pulsing inside him almost unbearably exciting.

Unfortunately, that excitement appeared inextricably linked

to Adrian's intense sexual attraction toward Greg. And how ironic was it that he'd made up his mind to give in to his need and take Greg to bed, yet in the two weeks between the first haunted house show and today—Halloween, the day of the final show—they hadn't had more than a few minutes alone at once?

Greg, only half joking, called it poetic justice. Adrian just called it hell.

"Tomorrow night," Greg declared as he and Adrian walked hand in hand to Groome Castle. "We are holing up in your apartment and spending the entire night fucking like bunnies."

Adrian cast a furtive glance around them. "Not so loud."

"Oh, for God's sake, Adrian, give it a rest." Greg shot him an irritated look. "Nobody cares, okay? Everybody is having sex. Nobody's gonna get their panties in a wad just because somebody else is talking about the sex *they* want to have. Eventually."

A planter shattered as Adrian walked past it. He clenched his jaw. Those sorts of things had been happening disturbingly often lately.

"I promised we'd...you know...when I was ready. You were fine with that. I don't understand why this is different."

"When you said that, you weren't ready to *have sex*." Greg enunciated the last two words far more than was strictly necessary. Adrian groaned. Greg plowed on with a determined glint in his eyes. "Now you are, and I know we *could* be fucking, if only life would cooperate. And *that* is the goddamn difference."

Adrian sighed. "Okay, I see your point."

"So. Tomorrow night? Your place? I'll bring the rubbers and lube."

Someone brushed past on Adrian's other side. He whipped

his head around, heart in his throat. Theo Smathers grinned and waved as he jogged past. "Hey, guys. See you at the castle."

"Yeah, see you." Adrian turned back to Greg, who wore a smug expression. "Okay, so obviously he heard you, and obviously he didn't care. Point taken."

"Uh-huh." Greg elbowed Adrian in the ribs. "Answer my question."

Adrian laughed out loud. "Yes, okay? Yes. Tomorrow night. My place. You bring the necessary...things. I'll supply the bed."

"Thank *Christ*." Letting go of Adrian's hand, Greg bounded in front of him, flung both arms around his neck and planted a hard, hungry kiss right on his mouth.

Fire raced through Adrian's veins. His arms slid around Greg's waist, his mouth opened and his tongue sought Greg's without his brain's permission. It was like this every time. One touch, one kiss, and pure instinct knocked propriety and the desire for privacy sideways.

In fact, it seemed to have gotten worse lately. In the past two days, he'd come to his senses to find himself on the verge of groping Greg in public no less than three times.

*And this makes four.* Snatching his hand out of the back of Greg's jean, Adrian broke the kiss and pushed Greg away. "Stop. Please. Not here."

Greg let out a frustrated growl. "For fuck's sake, it's just a *kiss*, okay? I swear I'm not going to sully your virtue in public."

"It's not just a kiss," Adrian snapped. On the porch of the house they'd just passed, a potted fern fell and broke. Scowling, Adrian stuck his hands in his pockets and stalked up the sidewalk as fast as he could go, leaving Greg scrambling in his wake. "Every time we kiss, it *does* things to me, and I...I can't control it. And I don't like not being in control of myself."

"Yeah, well, in case you didn't notice, it 'does things' to me too."

Some of the sharpness had leached out of Greg's voice, but the sarcasm that remained wasn't much of an improvement, in Adrian's opinion. He kept his gaze trained on the Groome Castle tower, just visible through the trees ahead, because he really didn't want to see the mulish expression he knew would be on Greg's face right now.

"That's not exactly what I meant." Adrian kicked a horse chestnut so hard it bounced off a nearby trashcan and into the street. "But in any case, even if it was nothing but a kiss, why isn't it enough for you that I don't feel comfortable kissing like that in public? Why do you have to keep pushing it?"

Silence. Adrian cut a surreptitious glance to his left. Greg caught his gaze and held it, gray eyes glittering in a blank mask of a face. "That's what you think? That I'm pushing you? Trying to make you do things you don't want to do? On *purpose*?"

"Um. Well." Adrian tripped over a crack in the sidewalk, stumbled and recovered. He stared at his feet, grateful for the excuse to look at something besides Greg's eyes. As much as he liked Greg, as much as he enjoyed his company—entirely aside from the physical attraction—he had a knack for twisting Adrian's words so that even *he* wasn't sure what he meant anymore. Biting down on his frustration, Adrian shrugged. "I don't know, Greg. You tell me. *Is* that what you're doing?"

Greg snorted. "See you at the castle."

He strode off without looking back. Torn between hurt, anger and sheer irritation, Adrian stood there and watched him go.

Once Greg turned the corner onto the gravel road leading to Groome Castle, Adrian started walking again with a sigh. This was how it started when his relationship with Christian went bad. Things had become complicated. Frustrating. Infuriating. They'd started fighting more than talking, they'd stopped listening to each other, and by the time it ended neither had even cared anymore about making the other happy.

*Is that already happening to Greg and me? After only two weeks together? Am I already sabotaging it by turning minor annoyances into major problems?*

Adrian's stomach clenched. In spite of the short time they'd been seeing each other, Adrian had grown used to having Greg around. The thought of a day without his company filled Adrian with a terrible desolation.

He reached the corner and made the turn onto the gravel road. Up ahead, Greg swiveled and looked over his shoulder. Their gazes locked for a moment before Greg whipped around again, but Adrian caught the heat—and the hope—in Greg's expression.

*I'm not letting this end,* Adrian decided, watching Greg's golden brown curls twist in a sudden breeze. *I'm not going to let my stupid hang-ups ruin this thing with him.*

Not when being with Greg made him feel so damn *alive*.

He started jogging up the road, passing several other students on the way. "Hey, Greg!"

Greg stopped and half-turned. "Yeah?"

"Wait up."

Greg waited in stony silence, hands in his jacket pockets. Adrian skidded to a halt in front of him, grabbed his face in both hands and kissed him. Greg stiffened, then relaxed. His hands rested on Adrian's hips, but he let Adrian control the kiss. Adrian was profoundly grateful for that. His powers flared briefly before settling into an easily controlled simmer. Adrian figured sheer nerves had a lot to do with that. He could practically feel everyone watching them. It was horribly uncomfortable, but he ignored it.

*You can do this. Just this once. For Greg.*

They drew apart after a couple of minutes. Greg pulled away and smiled up at him. "What brought that on? I thought you didn't like public kissing."

"Yeah, well." He shrugged, feeling somewhat like a zoo animal on display with all the passersby staring at him. "I thought I owed you one."

Greg's brows drew together. "Not that I don't appreciate it, 'cause I do, but why would you think that?"

"Because, I know you wouldn't deliberately push me into doing anything I wasn't comfortable with, and I shouldn't have insinuated that you'd been doing that." Taking Greg's hand in his, Adrian wove their fingers together. "I'm sorry, Greg. Forgive me?"

A strange expression fleeted through Greg's eyes and vanished before Adrian could grasp it. "There's nothing to forgive." Greg squeezed Adrian's hand. "C'mon, let's get a move on. We're gonna be late."

They started up the road hand in hand. Adrian smiled. He'd just gotten past his first serious disagreement with Greg, and tomorrow night he'd *finally* get to take Greg to bed. Life was looking up.

~ ✳ ~

Lyndon Groome—the real one—appeared in the middle of the main hall an hour before the haunted house was supposed to end for the night. And this time, lots of people besides Adrian saw him.

Hidden behind one of the gauze screens, Adrian gaped as a

trio of teenage girls squealed in terrified delight at the grisly spectacle of Lyndon hovering in midair to one side of their path. Adrian's psychokinesis had been acting up for days, but until now he'd been able to channel it into relatively inconspicuous things like cold drafts and objects moving in the dark where no one would see them. Had his powers reached critical overload? Or had Lyndon simply decided that the anniversary of his death—if today indeed marked that event—was the perfect time to leave his tower and scare the crap out of all the people who'd taken over the castle for the better part of a month?

Guilt prodded at Adrian's insides. In spite of his vow to solve the mystery of Lyndon's fate, Adrian hadn't returned to the tower room even once in the last two weeks. Between the haunted house, classes and Greg, he simply hadn't found time. He wondered if he imagined the spark of hurt in the ghost's translucent eyes.

*Cassss,* Lyndon sighed in Adrian's head. At least Adrian *thought* it was only in his head. Between the sound effects and the crowd, it was kind of hard to tell.

Adrian wished he could leave his post, open his mind to Lyndon and find out what was going on. But there wasn't time. The haunted house was still in full swing, and since it was Halloween they had the largest crowd yet. Lyndon faded and vanished in between a couple of high school kids on a date and a group of UNC basketball players, and Adrian still had no idea why the ghost had appeared here tonight, why he'd been visible to others this time, and whether or not Adrian's psychokinesis had been responsible.

*Sorry, Lyndon. I'll visit the tower tomorrow. I promise.* Adrian hoped Lyndon heard him, somehow.

The story of Lyndon's unexpected appearance started spreading almost immediately. By the time Marisa locked the castle door behind the last customer, Adrian had caught enough furtive whispers and sidelong glances to know that most of the cast and crew had heard about it.

"That was an amazing effect," Erin said, sidling up to him at the drinks table just as the cast party was getting into full swing. "How'd you do it?"

Adrian snorted into his half-finished cup of chardonnay. "I assume you're talking about the ghost." He shot a surreptitious look around the room. Where the hell was Greg? He'd gone to take off his costume and makeup over half an hour ago, and Adrian felt horribly alone without him.

Erin nodded. "Everybody's talking about it. They're all saying it must've been you, because you're the smartest person we've got." She tilted her head sideways, a curious expression on her pale face. "So? How'd you do it? And why didn't you *tell* anyone you were gonna?"

Before he could answer, something poked him hard in the ribs. Startled, he jumped, turned and came face-to-face with Greg's teasing grin. "Greg. What took you so long?"

Greg laughed. "Sorry, Susan and I got to talking." He took Adrian's hand in his and gave it a squeeze. "Please continue."

Adrian blinked at him. "Huh?"

"The lady there asked you a question." Greg blew a kiss at Erin, who laughed and shook her head. "I interrupted you before you could answer her. Please continue." He aimed a thoughtful look at Adrian. "I'd kind of like to know the answer to that one myself. In fact, that's what Susan and I were talking about just now. Wondering how you'd pulled off that trick. I didn't see it myself, but I sure heard enough about it."

Adrian glanced around. It seemed as though everyone had picked now to come get a drink, and every ear was inclined his way. He rubbed his thumb nervously over the back of Greg's hand. "It wasn't me. That was really Lyndon Groome's ghost."

Surprised silence met his declaration. Across the room, someone dialed up The Shins' *Oh! Inverted World* on the iPod connected to the portable speakers Marisa had brought. Chelsea, Conor and Ashwin struck up an impromptu singalong to "New Slang", and Adrian had to fight off a sudden urge to run and join them. He couldn't carry a tune with a handle, but he'd take any excuse he could get to avoid talking about Lyndon in front of all these people.

Susan broke the quiet with an excited squeal. "That's so *cool!* But I thought he only appeared in the tower room? I wonder why he came down here?"

"Maybe he always appears down here, just nobody knew about it before now." Erin stuck a finger in her Sprite and stirred, her expression thoughtful. "I mean, this is the first time anybody's spent any real time here in decades. This could've been happening all along, every Halloween."

"Or maybe the ghost never appears at all, unless there's someone here to see him," Theo piped up. He grabbed a plastic cup and filled it with red wine from one of the boxes on the table. "Think about it, dude."

Greg shook his head. "You people have all lost your collective minds. There's no such thing as ghosts."

Susan and Theo both scoffed. Erin's eyes went wide. "Greg, Adrian just said he didn't create the effect. I believe him. But I saw an extremely realistic-looking ghost tonight. I didn't imagine it, and neither did all those other people who saw it. It had to come from somewhere. We all know Adrian's the best effects person we have, by far. So if he didn't do it, how do you explain it?"

Greg didn't say anything, but Adrian saw the answer in the way his gaze dropped and the faint tightening of his jaw.

*He thinks I'm lying.*

Setting his cup carefully on the table, Adrian tugged his hand free of Greg's grip. "Excuse me."

Greg's brow furrowed. "Adrian? You okay?"

"Fine, I'm fine, I just...I have to. Um. Go. To the bathroom."

He fled down the hallway before Greg could talk him out of it. He needed to be alone, if only for a few minutes. Just get away from all those people watching him. It hurt that Greg believed him capable of telling such blatant lies, and he knew his feelings showed on his face for anyone who cared to look. He hated that.

*Why are you letting this get to you?* he wondered as he slipped into the bathroom and locked the door behind him. *You've only known him a few weeks. You've been dating him exactly sixteen days. Why have you let what he thinks of you become this important?*

Leaning his hands on either side of the sink, he stared at himself in the mirror. His eyes brimmed with the fear and confusion roiling inside him. He shook his head, disgusted with himself. Keeping people at a distance had become a survival mechanism for him over the years. How the hell had Greg managed to get around that in such a short time without Adrian even noticing?

A soft knock sounded on the door. "Adrian, it's me. Come out of there. Let's talk."

Adrian watched his reflection light up in spite of himself at the sound of Greg's voice and thought of his vow from a few hours ago—to make this thing work. To not let his insecurities ruin it. So what if they'd only dated a couple of weeks? Having had a taste of real intimacy for the first time in his life, Adrian couldn't go back to the lonely half-life he'd had before. And that meant he was by God going to open that door, go sit down with

Greg and talk. About ghosts, and truths, and lies, and...

*And hopefully not about why everything I touch lately breaks, or why he and I feel electricity all around us every time we kiss.*

Adrian let out a quiet laugh. If Greg didn't believe in a ghost so many of his friends had seen with their own eyes, what in the world would he think if Adrian said he could move things with his mind?

Greg knocked again, harder this time. "C'mon out. Please. I'm sorry, okay?"

Shaking himself, Adrian pushed away from the sink, unlocked the door and swung it open. "You're right. We should talk."

"Yeah." Greg laid both hands on Adrian's cheeks, a solemn expression in his gray eyes. "I just think you deserve credit. That's all."

Adrian frowned. Before he could ask what that meant, however, Greg dropped his arms, took Adrian's hand in his and led him down the hallway.

To Adrian's surprise, they entered the last room on the left. No one was certain what its purpose had been in Groome Castle's heyday, but since it was too small to be useful for the haunted house it had ended up as the default make-out room. Some enterprising soul had even brought a futon.

Adrian's heart thudded hard enough to make him dizzy when Greg shut the door behind them. "Um, Greg? I thought we were...I mean, tomorrow..."

Greg looked startled for a moment, then laughed. "Yeah, we are. I brought us in here because we won't be interrupted. When this door's closed, everybody respects that. Other rooms? Not so much."

"Oh, okay. That makes sense." Relief, disappointment and insistent lust overcame Adrian's muscle control and he plopped onto the futon. Kicking off his sneakers, he curled his feet beneath him. He figured he might as well be comfortable before the fighting started. "Why didn't you believe me, Greg?"

"Hmm." Greg lowered himself to the futon beside Adrian. "Because there are no such things as ghosts. And because I know for a fact that you're more than capable of creating a visual effect as good as the one I've been hearing about all night."

Adrian drew a couple of slow, deep breaths and blew them out. It wouldn't do to let his irritation get away with him. Across the room, a pile of school newspapers fluttered in an impossible breeze. "Yes, I am capable of creating that visual effect. *If* I had the right equipment to do it. Which I don't, not here tonight. Besides which, I don't lie."

That got him a skeptical look. "Everyone lies."

"Not me."

"Never?"

"Never."

"Not even by omission?"

*Shit.* Adrian studied his hands. "That's not exactly the same thing, is it?"

Greg shrugged. "Okay, not really." Turning sideways, he pinned Adrian with a calculating stare. "So you say you don't lie."

"I don't!"

"You say. But ghosts don't exist, Adrian. They *don't.* So where does that leave me? What am I supposed to think?"

Impotent fury swelled in Adrian's chest. Overhead, the dim bulb buzzed and flickered behind its old-fashioned cream-colored glass shade. He shoved to his feet and walked to the other side of the room, arms wrapped around himself, his back to Greg. "You could try opening your mind a little bit and believing me."

Behind him, Greg sighed. Cloth rustled, muted footsteps paced across the floor, then Greg's arms slid around Adrian's waist and Greg's chin rested on Adrian's shoulder. The touch brought a rush of energy that blurred Adrian's vision and prickled over his skin. He covered Greg's hands with his and hung on for dear life.

"I don't think you're a pathological liar or anything," Greg whispered, his breath tickling Adrian's neck. "I think you mostly *do* tell the truth. I think you only lied this time because you hate having the spotlight on yourself. You don't like people noticing you. You'd rather be in the background. So instead of taking credit for that fantastic special effect, you claimed it was the ghost everybody already thought was here anyway. I don't know why you did the effect in the first place, when we already had me playing the ghost, but whatever. I think you only lied because you're too modest to claim the credit. But, Adrian, you deserve the credit for what you did. Can't you see that?"

Adrian didn't know whether to be touched that Greg wanted to see Adrian's achievements recognized or aggravated that Greg still refused to believe him. He felt guilty for his continued anger in the face of Greg's desire—however misguided—to give credit where he thought credit was due. But he couldn't help it. Adrian's childhood and adolescence had taught him the value of truth. He hadn't been less than honest with anyone, including himself, in years. Being accused of deliberate lies *now* felt like a knife in the heart.

Gathering his scattered wits, Adrian broke out of Greg's arms, spun and faced him with as much calm as he could muster. "Whatever you might think, I am not lying, for any

103

reason. I did *not* create any sort of special effect tonight. What everyone saw tonight was the ghost of Lyndon Groome. Whether you believe it or not doesn't make any difference. It's the truth. I can't tell you anything else. I am not going to start lying now just because the real world doesn't fit into your mental box."

"Adrian—"

"No, let me finish." Adrian raked both trembling hands through his hair. "I like you. I want...I want to keep seeing you. But not if you can't trust me to tell the truth."

Greg stared, eyes wide in a face as pale as Lyndon's. "Are you serious?"

"Completely." Adrian shoved his hands into his jeans pockets. His pulse raced, and his breath came short and harsh. "So. That's it. What do you say?"

"I don't know." Greg shook his head, his expression stunned. "You're asking me to switch my own beliefs around just because you want me to."

"What? No, that's not what I'm asking at all."

"Oh, really? Because it sounds like it to me."

Frustrated, Adrian clamped his mouth shut and counted to five in his head before he allowed himself to answer. "Explain to me how I'm asking you to do that."

Greg shot him a withering look. "You want me to believe that everything you tell me is the truth, right? So you want me to believe ghosts are real. And I can't just make myself believe that all of a sudden, just because you want me to."

Staring into Greg's stony face, Adrian felt his barely controlled anger tip and spill. It was almost a relief to grab Greg by the shoulders, shove him across the room and slam him against the wall hard enough to tear a sharp cry from him. A surge of guilt made Adrian wince, but he didn't loosen his grip.

"I don't care what you personally believe about the stupid fucking ghosts," Adrian growled, his nose inches from Greg's. "All you have to know is that *I* believe they're real, and that *I* am telling the truth about what *I* did and did not do." He gave Greg a shake, hard enough to hopefully get his point across but not hard enough to hurt him. "Listen to me. I will never. *Ever.* Lie to you. That's a promise. Got it?"

Greg just stared without answering, his breathing fast and harsh in the thick silence. Adrian's stomach plummeted into his feet. He'd screwed everything up. It was bound to happen eventually, he'd known that all along, but still, he'd hoped...

A pained whimper was the only warning he got before Greg snatched a double fistful of his hair and yanked him into a hard, hungry kiss.

# Chapter Nine

In an instant, all Adrian's anger and frustration melted away in a firestorm of pure lust. Clamping one hand onto the back of Greg's neck and grabbing his ass with the other, Adrian plunged his tongue deep into Greg's mouth.

Adrian's psychokinesis, already unstable, erupted into a cascade of miniature explosions inside his mind. The air around him heated until his skin began to burn with it. His control hanging by a thread, Adrian gathered the crackling energy to him and twisted it until it became a vague, sensual caress sliding along his torso. The soft not-quite-touch felt so damn *good*. Adrian shuddered, the hand on Greg's neck climbing upward to tangle into his hair.

A rough groan bled from Greg's throat. His hips rocked against Adrian's, one leg bending up in an awkward attempt to wrap around Adrian's waist. Adrian moved his hand from Greg's butt to his thigh, holding it against his hip.

Tightening the hand in Greg's hair, Adrian tore his mouth from Greg's and yanked his head back. Greg sucked in a hissing breath when Adrian's teeth dug into his neck. "God. Adrian. Fuck me."

*Oh, my God.* Even though they'd talked about it, even though they'd planned it, something about standing face-to-face with the raw reality of finally being inside Greg made Adrian's legs shake and his chest hurt.

He shut his eyes. Greg's pulse fluttered like a captive moth against his lips. Fine tremors shook Greg's body. Dropping Greg's thigh, Adrian slid his hand beneath Greg's shirt to trace the delicate ridges of his vertebrae. "What about tomorrow?"

"What about it? Those plans don't have to change." Greg loosened half his death grip on Adrian's hair and shoved his free hand down the back of Adrian's jeans. His fingers were cold and shaking against the bare skin of Adrian's ass. "I can't wait 'til then, Adrian. Please don't say no this time. Please don't."

Adrian's heart gave an odd little thump. Eyes still shut, he bit the spot on Greg's neck that always turned him pliant and quivering. Greg moaned and arched in his arms.

Opening his eyes, Adrian pushed back until he could see Greg's face. Greg's eyes glittered from beneath half-closed lids. His cheeks glowed pink in the dim light, his hair stuck up at odd angles, and his shirt was rucked up nearly to his armpits. Adrian thought he'd never seen anything more enticing in his life.

Unable to help himself, Adrian leaned in and brushed his lips against Greg's. "We don't have any supplies."

"I do." Greg's tongue darted out to tease the corner of Adrian's mouth. "In my pocket."

The mental picture of Greg walking around during the party with a condom and packet of lube in his pocket struck Adrian funny, but the laughter dissolved into a moan when Greg latched his mouth onto Adrian's neck and sucked.

*You and Greg can finally have sex. Right here, right now. There's nothing to stop you anymore.*

The realization hit Adrian like a brick to the skull. He planted a palm on the wall behind Greg's shoulder to steady himself against a sudden rush of dizziness.

Greg unwound his other hand from Adrian's hair and clutched at his shirt instead. "Let's go lie down now, okay?"

*Lie down?* For a moment, Adrian couldn't think what Greg meant. Then he remembered the futon. "Oh. Yeah."

Greg snickered. Adrian shut him up with a kiss and hauled him across the floor toward their temporary bed. A quick thought cleared their path of any potential obstacles. Adrian had already tumbled to the thin navy blue pad with Greg on top of him before he realized, with a thrill of fear, that Greg could've easily seen the old papers, plastic cups and Adrian's sneakers skittering aside all by themselves. *That* would've killed the mood pretty fast.

*But he didn't see. Just this once, focus on what's right in front of you instead of worrying about what might have happened or what might still happen in the future.*

He tugged on the hem of Greg's long-sleeved UNC T-shirt. "Off."

Greg sat up, pulled the T-shirt off and tossed it aside. Adrian allowed him to take the condom and lube from his pocket before pulling him to the futon again and rolling on top of him, insinuating himself between Greg's spread thighs. Greg yanked Adrian's sweater up to his shoulders just as Adrian started to fumble one-handed with the button and zipper of Greg's jeans. The sweater caught Adrian's arm and knocked it violently sideways. Adrian tore the sweater off, bent and dug his teeth into Greg's right nipple.

Greg gasped, his back arching. "Oh, fuck. Yeah."

Encouraged, Adrian licked the flesh he'd just bitten, then moved to give the other nipple the same treatment. Greg moaned and squirmed beneath him. The movement slid their bare torsos together enough to send tiny shockwaves spilling down Adrian's spine. He used the resulting flare of psychokinetic energy to smooth an invisible palm over Greg's chest alongside his own hand.

"Oooh, my God," Greg moaned, grasping at Adrian's hair. "Adrian. Please."

Planting both hands on the futon at Greg's sides, Adrian wriggled further down his body. "Please what?" He bent and kissed the soft skin just above Greg's navel, then swirled the sparse blond hairs with his tongue. He'd never felt so powerful—or so confident—during sex before. It felt wonderful, and he wanted to draw it out as long as he could. Considering the insistent throb in his jeans, he'd be lucky to hold out ten minutes, but he was going to damn well do his best to make it last.

"Please *fuck me* already."

Adrian glanced up. The desperation in Greg's eyes matched the growl in his voice. Adrian's power responded with a pulse so strong it left him struggling to breathe. By the time his conscious brain realized there was no reason not to do what Greg wanted because they could go as slow as they pleased tomorrow, his baser instincts had already taken over his motor function enough to get Greg's snug jeans unzipped.

Greg bent his right leg up, almost knocking Adrian in the head with his knee. He pulled off his shoe and let it fall to the floor, then hooked his thumbs into the waistband of his jeans and wormed them over his hips. As soon as Adrian figured out what Greg was doing, he grasped the right leg of Greg's jeans and managed to wrench that side free.

With Greg finally naked—except for the jeans crumpled around his left calf—Adrian planted both hands on Greg's splayed legs and held him still so he could get a good look. God, the sight of all that smooth, pale skin exposed just for him made him want to lick, to bite, to taste. Especially Greg's cock, lying flushed and rock hard against his belly. Fine golden hairs downed the balls drawn up tight against Greg's body.

Adrian dipped his head, nuzzled between Greg's thighs and breathed deep. The sharp musk of sexual arousal shot straight to his groin. Pushing Greg's legs farther apart, Adrian sucked one testicle into his mouth, rolling it with his tongue to savor the taste of warm skin and dried sweat.

The wail he got as a result had him fighting to keep from coming, and he knew he'd better hurry if he wanted to actually get inside Greg before he lost it. With a quick swipe of his tongue up the length of Greg's cock—because how could he resist?—he sat up on his knees, undid his jeans and shoved pants and underwear down over his hips. His prick sprang free to sway in front of him. His damp skin was so sensitive even the brush of the air nearly undid him. He bit his lip and hung on with every ounce of his hard-won control.

"Turn over," he ordered, his voice trembling almost as much as his fingers.

Greg folded both legs up and rolled onto his knees and elbows. He shot Adrian a fevered look over his shoulder. "Hurry."

Adrian stared at the tiny pink whorl of Greg's anus. It always amazed him that something the size of an erect human penis would actually fit in there.

*But it does. And you're wasting time thinking when you could be fucking.*

This time the voice in Adrian's head sounded so much like Sean it was disturbing. Shoving the thought to the back of his mind, Adrian retrieved the condom packet from the floor and tore it open. He managed to roll the rubber over his erection on the first try in spite of the way his hands shook. He ripped the lube packet open with his teeth. There didn't seem to be much in it. Dropping the packet, he slicked a finger with saliva and pushed it inside Greg in one slow, smooth motion.

"Oh, fuck yes." Greg's hands clenched the fabric of the futon. His spine bowed, his hips rocking backward to force Adrian's finger deeper. "More."

A great fist took hold of Adrian's insides and squeezed. Leaning forward, he lapped at Greg's hole where it stretched around the invading digit. Once he had the entire area dripping wet, he pulled his finger out enough to slip a second one in beside it. Resting his cheek against Greg's ass, Adrian pumped his fingers in and out, in and out, twisting and scissoring. If he didn't get his cock inside Greg soon, he thought he might explode. He was certain Greg would, considering some of the barely coherent threats being hurled at him in between the moans and wails and pleas for more. But he'd never forgive himself if he rushed things and ended up hurting Greg. So he worked Greg open with as much patience as he could muster, stroking Greg's cock with his free hand and trying to ignore the ache in his crotch.

Finally, after what seemed like ages but probably wasn't more than a few seconds, Adrian felt the tightness in Greg's muscles ease. He stuck the tip of his thumb in and spread his fingers apart, just to be sure. The little opening fluttered and stretched, and Greg let out a pitiful mewl. "God, Adrian, please?"

"Yes."

Adrian pulled his fingers from Greg's body and sat back on his heels. He picked up the lube packet. It fell from his shaking hand. He scooped it up again and squeezed the contents into his palm before his violent tremors could dislodge it from his grip again. A couple of swift strokes spread the slick gel along the length of his cock.

Heart hammering, Adrian rose to his knees and scooted forward until the head of his cock rested against Greg's loosened hole. His head swam with an excitement so intense he felt dizzy and sick. He hoped he didn't ruin the moment by throwing up.

Adrian wiped the sweat from his brow with the hand not wrapped around his shaft, then planted his damp palm on Greg's hip. "Ready?"

"Yes." Greg pushed backward. "C'mon. Move."

Brow furrowed in concentration, Adrian pressed forward. After a second's resistance, the head of his cock popped past the ring of muscle and into Greg's ass. One more thrust drove Adrian root deep. He whimpered as a wave of psychic energy blasted through him. His hair lifted and swirled around his head. Static electricity crackled in his ears.

With a groan, he fell forward onto his hands, his chest plastered against Greg's back. Adrian's power seethed around and between them like a living thing. It was wonderful and terrifying, and Adrian had no idea whether or not he could rein it in. Squeezing his eyes shut, he buried his face in Greg's neck and let his psychokinesis drive his cock just a little bit deeper into Greg's body, fuck him a little bit harder. When he lifted one hand to stroke Greg's cock, his power gave his touch an extra sizzle it didn't ordinarily have.

He just hoped Greg would chalk up the sensation to heat of the moment and not expect it to be that good every time.

*Unless I'm this out of control every time we have sex.*

He let his conscious mind dance out of reach of the uncomfortable thought and sink back into the pure pleasure of the here and now—the hot living grip of Greg's ass on his cock, the sweet sound of Greg's cries, the smell of their sweat-slick skin, the way their bodies slid together when they moved. He didn't want to *think* right now, only feel. It had been far too long since he'd had sex, and it had never been this good before. He wanted to enjoy every single second.

Adrian had no idea how much time had passed when Greg's moans changed pitch and his legs began to shake. "Oh, oh God, oh God, ohGodohGod..."

Opening his eyes, Adrian nipped at the back of Greg's neck. He angled his hips to hit Greg's gland, jerking Greg's cock as hard and fast as he could. *Come on. Come on. Let me see you come. Let me feel your ass grab my cock and squeeze it hard.* Part of him wanted more than anything to actually say it, but he'd just couldn't. It felt dirty enough to think such things inside his head. He could never bring himself to voice them out loud.

As if reading Adrian's mind, Greg came with a great full-body shudder, sobbing Adrian's name. Semen spilled in a warm, slippery flood over Adrian's hand and pattered onto the futon. The feel of Greg's insides undulating around his cock sent Adrian tumbling over the brink. He came with his prick buried deep in Greg's ass and one hand still cupping Greg's privates. His lips shaped a silent litany of *yesyesyesyesyes* against the hot, flushed skin of Greg's back while his hips pumped out too many months' worth of pent-up need.

When his strength gave out, Adrian cinched his arms around Greg's waist and took him down to the futon with him as he collapsed. They lay spooned together, panting, in a silence that didn't feel at all uncomfortable.

Neither moved until Adrian's cock softened enough to slip from Greg's hole. Greg snickered. "Feels weird."

"Mm." Rolling onto his back, Adrian removed the condom, twirled it enough to keep the semen from spilling, then placed it carefully on the floor beside the futon before resuming his former position on his side. He snaked his arm around Greg and pulled him close. "This feels nice, though."

"Very." Greg squirmed onto his other side, facing Adrian. He wrapped his arms around Adrian's neck and threw a leg over his hips. A lazy, satisfied grin curved Greg's lips. "Man, that was fantastic. Totally worth waiting for."

Adrian smiled, his cheeks heating. "Thank you. I agree, by the way. Sex has never been anywhere near that good for me before."

"Yeah? Cool." Greg raked a hand through Adrian's hair. "You did all the work, though. All I did was lie there and beg like a slut."

Laughing, Adrian shook his head. "Stop that. You were amazing."

Greg snorted, eyes sparkling. "Liar."

Adrian cupped Greg's chin in his hand. "Didn't I just promise I'd never lie to you?"

"You did." Greg studied Adrian's face. "How many guys have you been with? Sexually, I mean."

*Damn. Here it comes.* They hadn't discussed their sexual histories, aside from each proclaiming themselves to be disease free and agreeing to use protection anyway. In Adrian's admittedly limited experience, most guys loved to brag about their prowess between the sheets and expected their partners to be just as experienced as themselves. Adrian knew he didn't measure up, and he'd dreaded what might happen if Greg preferred a man with lots of notches on his bedpost.

Adrian sighed. "One."

Greg's eyebrows shot up to his hairline. "One?"

"Yes."

"Seriously?"

"Yes." Adrian gnawed his bottom lip. "Is that a problem?"

Greg gaped at him for a moment, then burst out laughing. "No, it's not a problem," he gasped when he got himself under control. "I just can't believe someone as good at sex as you are has only had one partner. You must've done nothing but fuck."

"Not really, no." Adrian hunched his shoulders, feeling his face turn bright red as Greg's grin widened. "Can we please not talk about that anymore?"

"Okay, sure." Scooting closer, Greg planted a gentle kiss on Adrian's lips. "It's so cute how you're embarrassed by your natural talent."

"Shut up." Adrian gave Greg's butt a smack. "Not everyone has a natural talent they can be proud of." He ran an invisible hand over the palm print he'd left on Greg's rear and wondered if he'd ever be able to openly share that part of himself with Greg. He'd certainly never shared it with anyone else. Had never believed he'd be close enough to anyone outside his family to trust them with his greatest secret.

"Mmmm." Greg wiggled his ass against Adrian's corporeal hand. "Speaking of which, I'm auditioning for the lead in the school production of *Sweeney Todd* week after next, will you come with me?"

Surprised, Adrian nodded. "Of course."

"Great. Thanks." Greg snuggled close, tucking his head beneath Adrian's chin. "I just need the moral support, you know? I mean, I think I'm perfect for the part, acting-wise, but I'm nervous about having to sing. I know my voice isn't the greatest. I've been working with a voice coach, and I've been practicing a *lot*, but still. I'm really nervous."

Adrian nuzzled Greg's hair. "I've heard you sing a couple of times. You sounded fine to me." It was true. Adrian had no idea what was involved in the role Greg was trying out for, but from what little he'd heard he saw no reason to think Greg couldn't do it. And he knew for a fact Greg was a fantastic actor.

"Thanks." Greg kissed Adrian's throat. The tip of his tongue dug into the hollow at the base, then traced the pulse point. "You know what, I think we'd better get dressed and go back to the party before I have to molest you again."

Adrian swallowed. Already, desire had his cock filling again. "I think you're right."

Lifting his head, Greg covered Adrian's mouth with his. The kiss went deeper this time, and it was all Adrian could do to keep himself from shoving Greg's thighs apart and gulping his cock whole.

Greg broke the kiss an endless time later. He stood and held his hands down to Adrian. "Come on. Let's go."

Adrian let Greg haul him to his feet. They dressed in silence. Adrian tossed the used condom in the trashcan in the corner, then turned the futon over so the semen stain wouldn't show. Greg laughed, but didn't argue. They left the little room hand in hand and returned to the party, to the inevitable ribbing of their friends.

It took Adrian nearly an hour to notice that the random power surges he'd been living with for the past couple of weeks appeared to have vanished, and he felt far more in control of his psychokinesis than he had at any time since he first met Greg.

The revelation made him smile. He didn't *need* a scientific reason to have sex, but it sure didn't hurt.

# Chapter Ten

The next afternoon, Adrian took advantage of the hectic post-haunted-house clean-up at Groome Castle to slip away and visit the tower room. It had been far too long since he'd felt Lyndon's presence in his mind. He missed it. Besides, he'd made a promise to himself—and to Lyndon—to solve the mystery of Lyndon's disappearance and bring peace to his restless spirit. Adrian couldn't even begin to do that unless he made an attempt to reconnect with Lyndon's ghost.

Rain had rolled in that morning, shrouding the tower in watery gray gloom. Adrian chuckled as he walked into the room. The place had never really looked haunted to him until now.

Of course, it didn't *feel* haunted at the moment, which could be a problem. He wouldn't have very long before Greg figured out he wasn't anywhere downstairs and came looking for him. Not that he minded being found, especially if it meant a kiss like the one he'd gotten at Greg's dorm when he went to pick him up earlier.

The thought of it started a hot glow deep in Adrian's belly. He pushed the memory of Greg's mouth and hands and warm, pliant body ruthlessly to the back of his brain. Being found by Greg might be very nice indeed, but instinct told him that if Greg found him *here* it would be decidedly less than nice.

A brief surge of guilt made his stomach roll. Sneaking away

like this without telling Greg where he'd been felt a lot like lying.

*But it isn't. Not really. Do you know every single place he goes every day? Of course not. And he doesn't have to know every place you go either. You're just dating, you don't own each other.*

It was a logical enough argument to settle his disquiet somewhat. In any case, he didn't have time to think about it right then. He needed to get a move on if he wanted to contact Lyndon and leave the tower before Greg could find out he'd been up here.

Closing the door, Adrian moved to the center of the room and settled cross-legged on the floor. He took a moment to center himself, then relaxed his control over his psychokinesis. Lyndon's welcoming energy eddied around him and flowed through his mind.

Adrian smiled. "Lyndon? Are you here?"

The air in front of him shimmered. He felt a pulse of power, but he knew right away it wasn't strong enough. He forced back his disappointment. So what if Lyndon couldn't manifest? Adrian was going to do his damnedest to communicate with him anyway. It would just take a little extra concentration.

Shutting his eyes, he cleared his mind of all thought and let the patter of the rain ease him into a light trance. Lyndon's warm energy pulsed in his skull. Adrian opened himself to it without trying to shape or direct it. Either Lyndon would talk to him, or he wouldn't. Adrian had done all he could to establish a connection. The rest was up to Lyndon.

For a while, nothing happened. Adrian waited, counting out three seconds for each inhale and three more for each exhale. His pulse beat a shade too quickly against his eardrums. He willed it to slow.

118

The minutes passed, and Lyndon remained present, but silent. With time running out, Adrian allowed his conscious self to sink a bit deeper while his subconscious rose closer to the surface. It had the potential to make his psychokinesis stronger and therefore unpredictable, but he didn't think it would be dangerous. He had no intention of letting himself fall *that* far from conscious control.

Soon enough, it became clear that the whole thing was a moot point, since Adrian's attempt to connect with Groome Castle's resident spirit wasn't working. The more Adrian reached out for Lyndon, the more he felt Lyndon's presence slipping away. Frustrated and inexplicably sad, Adrian let himself emerge from his trance. He opened his eyes...

...And cried out as a savage burst of energy slammed him flat on his back on the hard stone floor. He lay there gasping for breath and staring blindly into the middle distance as a series of images seared themselves into his brain...

...*The tower room, white and hunter green and pale gold in the early morning sun. A huge bed with the covers balled in the middle. The smell of sex, a feeling of happiness as vast as the Carolina sky...*

...*Rain. Wind. Wet earth all round. So cold...*

...*Cold, God, cold enough to freeze skin from bone. Powder-white covering the ground between the trees. Gray sky, low and threatening overhead. Handful of snow, molded into the perfect missile, tossed right into the center of a broad, black-wool-covered back. He turns, pale cheeks pink with cold, and the snowball in the face is worth it just for that beautiful smile and the sparkle in those blue eyes...*

...*Blue flowers embroidered on a white collar...*

...*White walls, narrow cot with a thin blue blanket, a wooden cross on the wall. Spare, Spartan, unlike the Castle, but it's okay because it's his room and that means privacy and entire glorious days alone, naked, in bed. Like now. He rolls over, smiles, opens his arms. He's so lovely like this, his dark hair mussed with sex and sleep. One kiss, and the whole universe lights up in kaleidoscope colors...*

The vision ended as suddenly as it began, leaving Adrian blinking away a haze of tears. He'd seen the tender light in Cassius's eyes via Lyndon's memories of him, and he'd felt the answering swell of emotion in Lyndon's heart. He knew what it meant, despite having never felt it himself.

"Oh, my God," Adrian whispered to the stained and chipped stone ceiling. "They were in love."

Two men. Lovers. In Chapel Hill, North Carolina in nineteen-oh-five, a time and place when such a thing would definitely have been frowned upon. It may have even still been illegal back then, Adrian wasn't sure.

He sat up, heart pounding. Could this explain why Lyndon vanished that night? Did he and Cassius run away together? No one talked about a boy named Cassius going missing, but that didn't necessarily mean anything. If Cassius had no family to raise the alarm, or if he told them he was leaving town—though probably not *why*—his disappearance might have passed more or less unnoticed.

Of course, the existence of Lyndon Groome's ghost made a happy ending to that scenario unlikely. Lyndon had died young and violently, and his phantom still haunted the Groome Castle tower room over a century later. That meant either he'd died right here in the tower, or something about this place had been important enough to him in life that it kept his spirit anchored here even after death. Judging by the visions Adrian had just experienced, he guessed the latter. Lyndon and Cassius must have spent enough time together in this room that it became a place of emotional importance to Lyndon. Adrian wondered if the rumor of Lyndon's murder by thieves in the forest was true, and if Cassius had been killed along with him.

The sound of high-pitched laughter from outside startled him out of his thoughts. He glanced at his watch and was surprised to see he'd been up here less than fifteen minutes. It felt like much longer.

Rising to his feet, he shuffled across the floor on legs that felt weak and rubbery. His throat still ached with the threat of tears. What a terrible thing, to find the kind of love so many people only dream of, only to have it all torn away. No wonder Lyndon radiated such heartbreaking sadness.

At the door, Adrian paused a moment to get hold of his rattled emotions. If Greg saw him looking like this, there would be awkward questions, and Adrian didn't want that. He smoothed his rumpled shirt, raked his fingers through his hair and blinked rapidly until the lingering moisture dried from his eyes. As soon as his cheeks cooled and he felt in control of himself once more, Adrian descended the steps.

A quick glance around showed the back hallway to be empty. Relieved, he hurried into the main hall. A steady stream of students moved in and out of the tremendous space, hauling the wooden frameworks outside to load onto the flatbed truck Marisa's boyfriend had brought. Spotting Chelsea across the room struggling to lift one of the frames by herself, Adrian hurried over.

"Hi, Chelsea." He lifted the trailing side of the bulky structure. "Need some help with that?"

"Oh my God, yes!" She beamed at him. "You're a lifesaver, thank you."

"No problem."

They fell silent as they made their way through the foyer

and outside. The rain soaked through Adrian's clothes in seconds. As soon as they'd swung the frame onto the truck, Adrian retreated to the meager shelter of the doorway, shivering. "Damn. I wish I'd thought to wear my raincoat today."

Chelsea grinned. "Want to borrow mine?"

He suppressed a shudder at the mental image of himself in Chelsea's green-and-white polka-dotted jacket with the tiny bows decorating the sleeves and the rounded collar. "No thanks."

She laughed. "Fine, let male pride give you pneumonia."

"You don't get pneumonia from getting wet. You get it from bacteria or viruses."

"Yeah, whatever." She patted his dripping head. "I'm gonna go grab some coffee. You want some?"

"No, thanks. I was just looking for Greg, actually." Adrian frowned, realizing for the first time that he hadn't seen Greg since well before he'd headed upstairs to the tower room. "Have you seen him?"

"He was out on the back porch a little while ago, I think."

"Oh, okay." Adrian gave Chelsea a warm smile. "In that case, I think I'll come with you and get a cup of coffee myself, since it's on the way."

"Cool." Chelsea looped her arm through his. They went back inside, heading for the large kitchen where the group had set up coffee and snacks to keep themselves fed and caffeinated while breaking down their haunted house and putting Groome Castle back to its normal state. "I think it's so awesome that y'all are together now."

"So do I." Adrian glanced at her as he led her into the narrow hallway branching off the foyer. "How did you know we'd...um, gotten together?"

"Please, *everybody* knew the second you two walked out of the Love Room last night."

Adrian groaned, his face going red in spite of his attempts to keep his blush at bay. "Oh, hell."

She gave his arm a squeeze. "Don't worry, I seriously doubt anybody thought anything of it other than 'it's about damn time.' Well, except Erin, but c'mon, she already knew she didn't have a chance with you."

Sighing, Adrian pushed open the kitchen door. "I swear, I'll never get used to other people discussing my love life. It's weird."

"Well, then, let's discuss mine." Chelsea let go of Adrian's arm and made a beeline for the big metal urn on the counter. She took two Styrofoam cups from the stack, handed one to Adrian and began filling the other. "I asked Theo out, and he said yes."

"Seriously? That's great!" Adrian gave her a one-armed hug before filling his own cup. "You doing anything special?"

"Depends on what you call special, I guess. We're gonna go to T.J.'s for dinner tomorrow, then go see Doombunny at Cat's Cradle." She stirred three sugars and two packs of creamer into her coffee, lifted the cup and took a sip. "We both *love* that band. It's fate, I tell you."

Adrian laughed. "Colin's going to be jealous."

"Pfft. Maybe he should've bought a clue earlier." Chelsea glanced through the back door window. Her eyes widened, and she grinned. "Here comes Greg. I'm just making myself scarce now." Grabbing her cup, she turned and scampered across the kitchen to the hallway she and Adrian had just come from. "See you later, Adrian."

"Yeah, see you."

Smiling, Adrian took a sip of his coffee. It tasted a little burnt, but the heat felt good going down. He cradled the warm cup in both hands, leaned against the counter and waited. A moment later, the door opened and Greg stomped inside, looking put out.

He stopped when he saw Adrian. A guarded expression flitted through his eyes swift as thought before his face lit up and he smiled. "Adrian. Hi." He bounded across the room. Adrian barely had time to set his coffee down before getting a double armful of Greg. Still grinning, Greg pressed a light kiss to Adrian's lips. "Jesus, you're soaked. What happened?"

"I was helping carry stuff out to the truck, and of course I didn't have a raincoat or anything." Since no one was around to see, Adrian ran his tongue over the purple bruise on Greg's neck. A quick movement at the back door window caught the tail of his eye. Lifting his head, he saw something shift out of sight. He frowned. "Greg? Is someone else out there?"

"Just someone I know." Greg kissed the corner of Adrian's jaw. "Mmm. Wanna get out of here?"

Adrian opened his mouth to question Greg again—because clearly the person on the porch was more than "just someone"—but Greg's lips on his throat convinced him it didn't matter so much right then. He ran his hands up underneath Greg's shirt, seeking the warmth of his bare skin. God, it was so hard to think straight with Greg's body molded to his. At least his psychokinesis wasn't going haywire anymore. "Are you sure that's all right?"

"Sure. Most of the work's done. You need to get out of those wet clothes, then you need a warm bath, and *then* you need to get in a warm bed with a nice, warm man. Namely, me." Fingers traced the line of Adrian's spine and wound into his hair. Greg licked along the shell of Adrian's ear. "C'mon, let's head on back to your apartment. I really, really want to suck your brains out through your cock."

"Oh. Oh, my God." Adrian's knees wobbled. He clutched Greg tighter. "Yeah. Okay."

Greg let out a low, lustful laugh that raised goose bumps on Adrian's arms. "Thought you might like that." He pulled away, taking Adrian's hand in his. "Come on."

Adrian grabbed his coffee and let Greg lead him out of the kitchen. By the time they reached the main hall where several of the other students still congregated, he'd managed to rid himself of his semi-erection.

He didn't realize he'd forgotten his umbrella until he and Greg were halfway to his apartment, but he didn't mind. Greg had an extra-large one to share.

Besides, Adrian knew he'd go back to the castle soon enough. He still had the mystery of Lyndon Groome's death to solve.

~ ✳ ~

"And therefore, when one considers the concept of simultaneity as it applies to subatomic particles, one can only conclude..."

Adrian glanced at his watch. Five minutes had passed since the last time he checked. He swallowed a frustrated sigh. The lecture had already run overtime, and he was supposed to be at the Paul Green Theater for Greg's audition ten minutes ago.

Just when Adrian thought he couldn't take another second, Dr. Perez strode up to the lectern to thank the guest lecturer and dismiss the class. Adrian jumped to his feet, swung his laptop bag onto his shoulder and jogged out of the hall while most of his classmates were still in their seats.

"Adrian, wait up!"

With a frustrated groan, Adrian slowed down to a rapid walk. "I'm late meeting someone, Ryan. What's up?"

Ryan matched his pace, grinning ear to ear. "I heard through the grapevine that some lucky man finally captured the enigmatic Mr. Broussard. More specifically, I heard you were dating Greg Woodhall."

Surprised, Adrian glanced at Ryan. "You know Greg?"

"Not personally, no. But I know who he is. My friend Isobel was in theater classes with him last year, and she had a *huge* crush on him. All to no avail, of course." Ryan nudged Adrian's shoulder. "So, it's true? You and Greg are an item, for real?"

Adrian rolled his eyes. "Good grief, doesn't anyone have anything better to talk about than my love life?"

"It's your own fault. You wouldn't be nearly as interesting if you hooked up all the time like a normal person." Ryan leaned closer with an exaggerated squint. "Nice hickey, by the way."

Heat flooded Adrian's cheeks. He covered the mark on his neck with one hand. "Shut up."

Ryan laughed. "Sorry, it's just weird to see you walking around with love bites, you know? I was starting to think you were asexual."

"I dated Christian for six months in freshman year. Did you forget that already?"

"Dude, Christian never once left you looking like you'd been sexed up by a mountain lion and liked it."

It was true, which irritated Adrian beyond belief. He shot a glare at his friend. "Change the subject or go away."

Ryan held up a placating hand. "Actually I did have a real reason for stopping you. I wanted to ask you if you had Dr. Orson's lecture from last week. I got held up at computer lab and missed it, and they've already taken it down off the website."

"Oh. Yeah, I have it on my hard drive. I'll email it to you."

"Cool, thanks." Ryan dodged around a slight young man and a tall, rangy girl making out in the middle of the sidewalk. "I *tried* to ask you about it last night, but you ignored me in favor of gazing soulfully into Greg's eyes." Folding both hands beneath his chin, Ryan batted his eyelashes.

Adrian frowned. "What're you talking about? I didn't see Greg last night. I was home alone all night working on a paper."

"Really?" Ryan's eyebrows went up. "Huh. Must've been someone else I saw."

*Someone else. With Greg. Last night.*

*Gazing into his eyes.*

Adrian shook off the instant surge of jealousy. Any number of perfectly legitimate reasons existed for what Ryan had seen.

"Someone else. Yeah." Adrian forced a laugh. "I would've thought you'd be able to recognize me by now, though."

"Hey, it was dark, and I only saw him from the back. And the guy had on a knit cap or something. I just assumed it was you because whoever it was, he was alone under a tree at night with Greg, and I'd heard y'all were dating. It was definitely Greg, though." Ryan pointed a finger at Adrian. "If I were you, I'd find out who this dude is. Looked to me like he was trying to put the moves on your boy."

A trickle of unease ran up Adrian's spine. He didn't believe Greg would cheat on him. But something felt off. Maybe he should ask Greg about it.

*No. Ryan probably just saw him talking to a friend of his. If you start asking questions, it'll look like you don't trust him, and he'll get angry. Just keep it to yourself.*

Easier said than done. But Adrian *did* trust Greg, and he was determined not to let his insecurities turn something innocuous into a potential source of contention between them. He wouldn't ask Greg about the man Ryan had spotted him with last night, no matter how badly he wanted to.

Adrian glanced at his watch and cursed under his breath. "Shit. I need to hurry. I'll send you that lecture later this afternoon, all right?"

"Sure." Ryan gave him a narrow-eyed stare. "You okay, man?"

Adrian answered his friend's obvious worry with a smile. "I'm fine. Talk to you later."

"Yeah. Later." Ryan clapped Adrian on the shoulder, then veered off across the quad.

Drawing a deep breath to steady himself, Adrian picked up his pace and hurried toward the theater as fast as he could without actually running. He had an audition to get to.

~ ✳ ~

"Well, crap."

Adrian glanced over the top of his MacBook at Greg, who sat on the other side of the library table staring at his own laptop as if it had just told him his favorite grandmother died. "What's wrong?"

"I didn't get the part." Shutting his laptop, Greg dropped his chin into his hands. "Ms. Halstead said my monologue was excellent, but my singing voice wasn't very good."

Greg's expression was so forlorn it tore at Adrian's heart. He reached across the narrow table to touch Greg's arm. "I'm sorry. For what it's worth, I thought you were great."

A faint smile touched Greg's lips. "Too bad you're not casting the play."

Adrian shook his head. "I don't understand why she said that about your singing. I didn't see anything wrong with it."

"Yeah, well. 'Nothing wrong with it' wasn't enough to beat out Jon Hudson."

"Which one was he?"

"The really tall guy with the ponytail."

"Oh." Adrian studied the document open on his laptop. He remembered the man now. His acting ability hadn't been quite as good as Greg's, but it hadn't been far off, and his singing had been truly impressive. Adrian had no idea if saying so would hurt Greg's feelings, however, and he'd just as soon avoid finding out.

Apparently luck was not with him. Greg leaned forward, watching Adrian's face. "You can't tell me you thought I sang as well as Jon."

*Damn.* Steeling himself for whatever might happen next, Adrian met Greg's gaze. "No, that's true. He's definitely the better singer."

Greg looked startled for a second, then let out a quiet laugh. "Well, you did tell me you'd never lie to me."

"Yeah." Adrian bit his lip. "I'm sorry. I don't mean to hurt your feelings. I know I can be really blunt."

"No, that's okay. You didn't hurt my feelings. I want to hear the truth." Greg raked a hand through his hair. "They're casting for *Wicked* in February. I'll try out for the part of Fiyero. That'll be my goal." He pinned Adrian with a bright, fierce gaze. "I can do this. I can."

Adrian took in the determined gleam in Greg's eyes and felt an odd flutter in his chest. Pushing his laptop aside, he reached across the table and took Greg's hands in his. "I know you can."

Greg beamed at him. Shooting a glance toward the librarian—who was frowning at them—he lowered his voice to a whisper. "You want to go grab some dinner, then go back to your place?"

"Sure." Adrian peered at the clock on his Mac. It was only five thirty, early enough that nothing on Franklin Street should be too crowded yet, even on a Saturday. "I could go for Pita Pit, how about you? I'm not in the mood for the dining hall tonight."

"Me neither. Pita Pit sounds perfect, let's go."

They gathered their laptops, pulled on their jackets and exited into the mid-November twilight. Greg produced a Tarheels toboggan from one pocket of his coat and tugged it over his ears. "Damn, it's cold out here."

"I know. They've been predicting an unusually cold winter this year."

Greg stuck his hands in his pockets and hunched his shoulders. He didn't say anything else, but he didn't have to. Adrian knew what he was thinking—he wanted Adrian's arm around him, like the night of their first date.

Adrian stifled a sigh. He couldn't deny that it would feel good to walk down the sidewalk with Greg's body warm and solid against his side. But he just couldn't do it. Even though his psychokinesis had settled down a lot since he and Greg started having sex, it still tended to react unpredictably when Greg pushed his comfort zone in public. And walking through the Chapel Hill crowds with their arms around each other definitely pushed Adrian's comfort level. It made him feel rather like a bug pinned to a piece of cardboard.

*I have known the eyes already, known them all.* He laughed.

Greg shot him a sharp look. "What?"

"Nothing. Just thinking of something I read once." *And thinking that if I ever get that pathetic I hope someone smacks some sense into me.*

"Fine." Hoisting his laptop bag farther up onto his shoulder, Greg started walking faster. "Let's hurry. I'm freezing my ass off."

Adrian shook his head and picked up his pace to match Greg's. It amazed him that someone with as much professional drive and determination as Greg could be so childish at times.

They'd just emerged onto Franklin Street when a man Adrian didn't know stepped out in front of them. He wore black jeans and a red wool coat. A brown knit cap covered his hair.

*A knit cap. Ryan said the guy Greg was with the other night wore a knit cap.*

*Yeah, and so do a million other people. Greg's wearing one right now. You're being paranoid.*

The logical argument didn't help. Adrian studied the stranger's face with growing suspicion.

Eyes as pale as a Husky's stared at Greg with unnerving intensity. He ignored Adrian completely. "Hello, Greg."

"Um. Hi." Greg moved closer to Adrian. "Uh, 'scuse us."

He tried to go around the stranger, but the man moved in front of them again. Alarmed, Adrian looked the man up and down. Physically, he didn't seem very intimidating. He was about Adrian's height, and not much bulkier. But Adrian didn't like the hard glint in his eyes at all.

Adrian took Greg's hand and stared at the side of the stranger's head. "If you'll excuse us, we really need to go."

The man cast a baleful look in Adrian's direction. "Who's that?"

Greg sighed. "This is Adrian. We're dating now."

The man whipped around and pinned Adrian with a narrow-eyed stare. "No. You stay away from him."

"Harrison, you can't—" Greg clamped his mouth shut so fast his teeth snapped together with an audible *clack*. He met Adrian's gaze for a second, then looked away, but not fast enough to hide the expression in his eyes.

A rush of pure fury drew the dead leaves at Adrian's feet into a miniature whirlwind for a moment before he got it under control again. He couldn't decide which made him angrier—the fact that Harrison seemed to be stalking Greg still or that Greg obviously hadn't wanted Adrian to know.

Not that it mattered right then. Adrian hadn't felt this kind of rage in years, and if he didn't do something with it, he thought it might eat him alive.

He stepped between Harrison and Greg and met Harrison's livid gaze. "No, Harrison. *You're* the one who needs to stay away from Greg. He doesn't want to see you anymore. And if I ever catch you bothering him again, I will make you very, very sorry. Are we clear?"

Behind him, Greg let out an exasperated noise. "Adrian, goddammit—"

"Shut up, Greg." Harrison bared his teeth. "I'd like to see you try to keep me away."

An idea popped into Adrian's head, and he went with it before he could overthink it. Gathering his anger to him, he used it to sharpen and focus his psychokinesis. It was surprisingly simple to compress the air around Harrison's neck just a bit. Not much. Not enough to really *hurt* him. Just enough to make his eyes go wide and his hand fly up to his throat.

Simple to start. Not so simple to continue. After a couple of seconds, Adrian's control unraveled. Harrison sucked in a deep lungful of air. The malice in his eyes was gone. He stared at Adrian with fear stamped into every line of his face.

*Oh, my God. He knows what I can do. He knows. All because of my stupid temper.*

*And who's to say you couldn't have hurt him? Maybe you could. Maybe you could even have killed him, if you wanted it.*

Neither were exactly pleasant thoughts. But Franklin Street wasn't the place to have a crisis about it. Adrian arched an eyebrow and tried to look as if he didn't feel like throwing up. "You okay, Harrison? You don't look so good."

Shaking his head, Harrison backed up. "You stay away. You stay *away* from him, demon! He's *mine*, you can't have him!" He fled across the street, narrowly avoiding being hit by several cars, and blended into the crowd on the other side.

"Jesus fucking Christ," Greg groaned. "I swear, if I knew how to get in touch with his parents, I'd call them. He's gone off his nut."

"Yeah." After a quick look to make sure Harrison had really gone, Adrian turned to Greg and laid both hands on his shoulders. "Are you all right?"

"I'm fine. He didn't even touch me, in case you didn't notice."

Adrian frowned at the peevish tone in Greg's voice. "Well, obviously he's still been bothering you, even after you told him not to."

"Yeah, so?" Greg started down the sidewalk, his laptop bag bumping against his side and Adrian at his heels. "He never does anything but this. Just keeps trying to get me to come back. He's just being a pest."

"Are you kidding me? He's already hit you once." Adrian gestured in the general direction of the Forest Theatre. "And according to you, he's hit you before, when you were dating. That's why you broke up with him."

Greg's shoulders tensed. "He's only hit me that once since we broke up, and that was because I pissed him off. As long as I don't make him too mad, he doesn't do anything but talk. I can deal with that."

"Jesus, Greg." Adrian rubbed a hand over his face. "Listen to yourself. You're making excuses for his behavior."

"They're not excuses. I *know* him, Adrian. I know what he's like, and I know how to handle him."

The steel in Greg's voice brooked no argument. Adrian gritted his teeth and switched tactics. "Fine. He's just pestering you. What happens when it escalates like it did before?"

"It won't."

"But what if it does?"

Greg shot an irritated look over his shoulder. "I'll handle it."

"Really? Like you've been handling it up until now?" Adrian swerved around a woman pushing a stroller. "He's the one you were talking to at Groome Castle the day we were taking down the haunted house, wasn't he?"

"What if he was?"

"What if—" Adrian's bag slipped off his shoulder. He heaved it back up again. "Ryan saw you talking to some guy under a tree the other night. He thought it was me, but it wasn't. Obviously. It was Harrison, wasn't it?"

He got a barbed glare in return. Greg set his jaw and walked faster.

The angry silence was answer enough. Adrian sighed.

"Dammit, Greg. Why didn't you tell me about all this before?"

Greg stopped walking and turned around so fast Adrian almost ran into him. "Yeah, that was him at Groome Castle, and it was him your fucking loudmouthed friend saw me with the other night. And he's found me and talked to me several other times that you never knew about. And I didn't tell you because I was afraid you would do this if I did."

Adrian blinked, surprised. "This? What do you mean, 'this'?"

"*This.* Interfering. Trying to rescue me." Greg pointed at him. "I don't need rescuing."

Adrian gaped at him. "I didn't mean—"

"Do I look like a damsel in distress to you?"

"No! I was just—"

"I can handle him, okay? Just stay out of it."

"Wait, okay, just wait a minute—"

Greg held up a hand. "No. I'm done for tonight. I'm going back to my dorm. Call me when you're ready to apologize."

Anger spiked through Adrian's brain again. "Shit. I'm sorry, okay? But it bothers me that you didn't trust me enough to tell me he was still stalking you."

"I just told you why."

"I know. But I've never given you any reason to think I'd treat you like a...what, a damsel in distress? So why would you think that?"

Greg's mouth curved into a bitter smile. "Does it matter? I was right."

Adrian had no rebuttal to that. Feeling utterly defeated, he walked the few steps to the closest bench, sank onto it and dropped his bag beside him. "I'm sorry. I don't know what else to say. I'm sorry."

"I know." Greg fiddled with the buckle on his laptop bag. He wouldn't look at Adrian. "I'm sorry too. Just... Yeah. Okay. I'll talk to you tomorrow."

Greg walked away without looking back. Adrian sat and watched him go. At least Harrison didn't seem likely to harass him any more tonight. Which was a good thing, because in spite of what Greg had just said, Adrian had to fight the urge to get up and follow him to make sure he got home okay.

Adrian ran a frustrated hand through his hair. Would he *ever* be able to get this relationship thing right?

He waited a few minutes, then pushed to his feet and started the trek back to his apartment. His stomach rumbled, and he felt a moment of irrational anger at himself for still being hungry after what had just happened with Greg.

As he passed the neighborhood leading to Groome Castle, he stopped and peered up the empty road. The streetlights shed pools of soft yellow illumination on the pavement at intervals until the road curved out of sight. He couldn't see it, but he knew that a ten-minute walk would bring him to the old home.

When he veered off his path and onto the sidewalk toward the castle, he told himself he only wanted to look at the outside of the place in the moonlight, that he wouldn't go inside.

He believed it until he touched the stones of the castle wall and felt the pull of Lyndon's energy.

Unlocking the front door with a thought, he strode inside and headed straight for the tower. Maybe he and Lyndon could help each other. God knew he could use a friend tonight.

~ \* ~

Adrian crouched in the blackness at the rear of the Forest

Theatre, watching the vague blur where he knew the stage lay. His heart galloped so fast he thought it might fly straight up his throat and out of his body, but he didn't move. He had to wait. For what, he wasn't sure. He only knew he mustn't move, mustn't even blink, or he'd miss it.

Hours later—seconds? Minutes? He had no way of knowing—a spotlight switched on. The white light illuminated a single figure which floated weightless in midair, bare feet hanging several inches above the stage, arms spread wide as if secured to an invisible cross. The figure wore old-fashioned black breeches and a white linen shirt, untucked with the laces open. Blood matted the golden brown curls, splattered the pale neck and dripped into the gray eyes. As Adrian watched, a long, ragged wound opened the exposed chest from one side to the other. Blood poured out, more blood than Adrian had ever seen, a bright red waterfall that ran down the man's legs and pattered onto the stage.

Adrian tried to cry out, tried to run to the stage and sweep Greg into his arms. But he couldn't move, couldn't make a sound. Even his tears solidified before they could fall, sealing his eyelids open so he'd never have to look away.

Greg's gaze locked onto Adrian's. "I, oh, I can handle it," Greg sang, each word drawn out over several lilting notes. "You, whoa, oh, you don't need to rescue me... No, you don't... You don't... Oh, whoa, whoa, Adrian..."

Adrian sat straight up in bed, panting. The dream still seemed horrifyingly real. He could even hear the tune Greg had been singing. Though it appeared to have been reduced to a less robust version, without Greg's voice.

*Shit, it's my phone.* Adrian snorted. He was going to kill Chelsea for reprogramming his ringtone to Mariah Carey when he wasn't looking.

Reaching over to the bedside table, he grabbed his iPhone and checked the display. His stomach clenched when he saw the name. He answered before Greg could change his mind.

"Hi, Greg." He lay back against the pillows, willing his pulse to slow down. "What's up?"

Greg let out a humorless laugh. "I'm calling you at four in the morning, Adrian. You don't have to pretend it's okay."

"I'm not pretending. You can always call me if you need me." Silence. Adrian could hear Greg's ragged breathing. "Are you all right?"

"Yeah. Well, no, not really. Fuck, I don't know."

Greg's voice sounded rough and thick, as if he'd been crying. Adrian's brow furrowed. "Greg—"

"Look, I just...I think I just need to explain why I acted like I did earlier. So, I'm gonna do that, and it'll be easier if you just listen. Is that okay?"

"Of course it is. Anything you need."

A sharp exhale hit the receiver. "Okay. So, the thing is, when I was with Harrison, I was nothing but a thing to him. That's still all I am to him. Just something he had and lost and wants back. And then when you started getting in his face..."

Greg trailed off. Adrian bit his tongue and waited.

When Greg started talking again, his voice had gone quiet and sad. "When the two of you were fighting over me, I could've walked away, and neither of you would've even noticed, because what I thought or felt or wanted didn't matter right then. Y'all were involved in your pissing contest, and I might as well not have even been there. Do you have any idea what that feels like? It feels like I'm not even a person. And I know you didn't mean it like that, I know you don't see me as a possession like Harrison does. It just... For a minute there, it *felt* that way. And

I'd promised myself I'd never let that happen again, and...well. I know I acted like an ass, and I'm sorry. I guess I just freaked out a little. And I don't know if any of this is even making any sense to you, but I had to at least try to explain."

*It all makes sense now. Jesus. No wonder he was pissed.* Adrian's stomach rolled. He'd always despised men who treated their partners like property. It made him sick to realize he'd turned into one of those men, however briefly or unintentionally.

Adrian rubbed his free hand over his forehead. "I'm glad you did. It makes perfect sense, and I don't blame you for being upset. I'm so sorry."

Soft laughter floated through the receiver. "I'm just glad you're not too pissed off at me. Most guys aren't as willing to listen as you are."

"Hell, I'm glad you're not too pissed off at *me.*" Adrian tucked a hand behind his head. "Besides, you're worth holding onto. What we've got going here is worth holding onto. Of course I'm going to listen to what you have to say. Especially when I clearly screwed up."

The hitch of breath on the other end of the line tugged at Adrian's heart. "Thank you," Greg whispered. "You know what, I think I'm a lucky guy."

The line went dead before Adrian could answer. He set the phone down and smiled. "So am I."

# Chapter Eleven

"Happy Thanksgiving, sweetheart! We miss you!"

Adrian smiled at his mother's image on his laptop screen, his whole family crowded around and behind her at the dining room table in the big, rambling house on Mobile Bay where his mother and her husband, Lee, lived. His heart ached to see them all together without him, but there was no help for it. Dr. Perez had offered him a coveted spot as an assistant on an ongoing research project for the physics department, which required him to stay on campus over at least one holiday through the remainder of the school year. He'd chosen Thanksgiving and Easter. The opportunity was too good to turn down, no matter how difficult it was to be away from his family right now.

"I miss you guys too." Adrian snagged a cookie from the tin on the table and held it up. "Thanks for the pumpkin cookies, by the way. They're great."

"You're welcome." His mother turned to grin at his father, who sat in a chair he'd pulled up just behind her right shoulder. "Your dad made them, of course. You know I can't bake."

"I helped," Sean interjected from his spot leaning on the back of his mother's chair.

"Yes, Sean, and you did a great job." Adrian's father patted

Sean's arm, the dark eyes so like Adrian's own shining in amusement. "So, Adrian. What are your plans for Thanksgiving dinner? And please don't tell me anything about a sandwich alone in front of your computer while working, because I have no desire to nurse your mother through a stroke today."

Adrian laughed. His dad knew him far too well. Probably because Dr. Bo Broussard was a scientist himself and therefore knew the lure of a compelling project. Sam had had to pull him away from more than one of them during Adrian's teen years.

"Actually, I'm heading over to Dr. Perez's house in a couple of hours." Adrian nibbled the edge of the cookie he still held. "He invited all his research assistants over for Thanksgiving dinner with him and his wife."

Beside Adrian's father, Sam smiled, the corners of his eyes crinkling. "Well, good. That was nice of them to invite y'all over."

"Yeah, it was. I'm looking forward to it."

*For more reasons than a good meal.* Greg was spending the holiday with his family a couple of hours down the road in Goldsboro, and Adrian was surprised by how much he missed him. Even the considerable work of the research project hadn't kept Adrian busy enough to drown out the ache of loneliness. His smile slipped a fraction.

His mom's brows drew together in a worried frown. "Honey, are you okay?"

To her left, Lee shook his head. "Sweetheart, don't hound the boy. Of course it's difficult for him to be away from home, but I'm sure he's managing fine."

Sean flashed an evil grin. "He misses his boyfriend."

Instantly, Adrian's face went beet red. It had become a Pavlovian response lately to his brother's teasing. He dropped his head into his hands. "Shut up, creep."

Sean snickered. Their father gave him a stern look. "Sean, please."

He didn't have to say anything else. Sean's expression softened. Leaning closer to the screen, he lowered his voice to a whisper. "Sorry, bro. You know I love you."

Adrian's throat went tight. He grinned. "Yeah, I know. I love you too. Hey, what about that girl you've been seeing lately? Maia? How's that going?"

A wide, goofy smile spread over Sean's face. His eyes shone in that particular way they always did when he talked about the young woman he'd been seeing for the past few weeks. "It's going great. She is soooo fantastic."

Everyone at the table laughed. Sean just shrugged and joined in.

For a second, a familiar jealousy clawed at Adrian's insides. He squashed it before it could take root and grow. During their childhood and teen years, Adrian had spent a lot of time consumed with resentment over his brother's ability to shake off both friendly ribbing and real ridicule and laugh at himself. They were adults now. It was about time Adrian accepted his own sensitive nature and stopped envying Sean's more easygoing one.

Adrian forced a chuckle. "That's great. I hope I'll get to meet her one day."

Excitement lit Sean's face. "You will! Unless you don't come home for Christmas either."

Adrian's mouth fell open. "She's coming home with you for Christmas?"

"Yeah, isn't it great? Mom said I could invite her, and her family was totally cool with it." In the background, the oven beeped. Sean glanced at it. "That's dinner. I'll get it, Mom." He favored Adrian with a beaming smile. "Talk to you later, bro.

Love you."

"Love you too. Bye."

Sean dashed out of frame. Their mother shook her head, chuckling. "My God, that girl's got him wrapped around her little finger."

"Does not!" Sean protested off screen.

Lee arched an eyebrow. "I'll go help Sean. It's good to talk to you, Adrian. Take care of yourself."

"You too, Lee. Talk to you later." Adrian waved at him.

Pushing back his chair, Lee rose to his feet and went to join Sean in the kitchen.

Adrian's mom planted an elbow on the dining room table in front of her and rested her chin in her hand. "Speaking of Christmas, honey, when are you coming home? And where are you planning to stay, here or your dad's? I don't want to rush you or anything, and there's certainly no pressure, since we're all planning to spend plenty of time together, I was just curious."

Behind her, Adrian's father leaned sideways to whisper something into Sam's ear. Sam nodded in response, and Adrian thought he heard "I don't know why not" or something like that.

"Um, I don't know yet," Adrian answered when his mother frowned. "I mean, classes end on the tenth, but beyond that I'm not sure. It kind of depends on where we are on Dr. Perez's project. I don't have to stay over Christmas, but I might need to hang around just for a day or two to catch up on reports before I go."

*And why didn't you invite my boyfriend to stay? We've been dating longer than Sean and Maia.* Adrian bit his tongue to keep himself from asking out loud. He was surprised, not only by his mother's discrimination—which he had to admit had probably been subconscious on her part, considering her lack of visible guilt—but by how much it stung.

"Oh, okay." She nodded. "Well, just let me know when—"

"Mom!" Sean interrupted from the kitchen. "Where's the cranberry sauce?"

She sighed. "In the fridge."

"I don't see it."

"Second shelf, behind that heart-healthy margarine."

A silent moment passed. Sam hid a wide grin behind his hand, as if he knew what was coming. Sure enough, after a couple of seconds, Lee called out, "It's not there, honey."

"Lord, help. I love them dearly, but those two should not be allowed in the kitchen." Shaking her head, Adrian's mother smiled at him. "I'll talk to you soon, sweetheart. I love you."

"Love you too, Mom. Bye."

She blew him a kiss, stood and hurried to help her husband and youngest son sort out dinner. Adrian's dad exchanged a look with his husband, then scooted his chair closer to the table where their laptop sat. "Adrian, Sam and I were wondering if you'd like to invite Greg to spend Christmas here in Mobile with you."

Adrian stared at the both of them, wondering if they'd learned to read minds. "What?"

"Only if you want to, of course." Sam leaned forward, his expression open and earnest. "Look, I know it embarrasses you to talk about this relationship, so I'm not going to make a big deal out of it. But it's pretty obvious that being with him makes you happy, and even though Sean shouldn't have teased you I think what he said was accurate. You miss Greg right now. Which is only normal."

"Anyone who's important to you is important to us as well,"

his father added. "Greg is welcome in our home any time, and we'd love to have him here for Christmas if you want to invite him."

To Adrian's horror, the backs of his eyelids prickled. He forced the impending tears away by sheer willpower. "I'd really like that. I don't know how he'll feel about being away from his family, but I'll definitely ask." Watching his father and Sam on screen, he felt a wash of gratitude for these two men who had loved and supported him through his torturous teenage years and helped him emerge on the other side sane and whole. "Thank you both. For everything."

His father studied his face with the patented Dad Look that seemed to see straight through flesh, bone and pretensions to Adrian's core. "Your mother loves you, Adrian. Every bit as much as she loves Sean. She didn't intend to leave you out."

Adrian nodded in agreement, even as the still-bitter child inside him screamed about the injustice of it all. This wasn't the time or place to complain about excusing unintentional discrimination. His dad and Sam understood that issue far better than he ever could anyway. Besides, he knew his mom. She'd changed since the old days. The second she realized what she'd done, she'd be overcome with remorse, and a new champion in the fight against subconscious homophobia would be born.

Which might or might not be such a good thing. Being a pragmatic woman, Adrian's mother rarely got caught up in causes, but when she did she was relentless to the point of maddening.

Adrian's dad glanced toward the kitchen. "I guess we'd better sign off now, they're bringing the food in. But either Sam or I will be on the chat anytime we're online, and we pretty much have our phones on all the time, so call us whenever you want to talk, okay?"

"Sure, Dad. Happy Thanksgiving. I love you." Adrian turned to Sam. "You too, Sam."

Sam smiled. "Love you, Adrian. Happy Thanksgiving."

"And Happy Thanksgiving from me too." His father gave him a wide smile. "Let us know about Greg. I love you, son."

The picture froze. Adrian stared thoughtfully at it. In the hazy still, his dad leaned forward, one arm reaching toward the laptop. A bit behind him and to his right, Sam sat gazing at his husband as if he formed the center of the universe. Maybe for Sam, he did.

Adrian had caught his father and Sam looking at each other that same way many times in the past. For years, witnessing such unabashed affection pass between them had made Adrian feel very peculiar, like he had a nest of live worms squirming in his stomach. Now he finally realized *why* the naked emotion had bothered him so much as a youngster—he'd wanted that kind of love, so badly it rubbed his insides raw, yet he'd had no way to recognize such a thing in himself or to articulate it even if he had.

*I still want that. I want someone to look at me the way Sam's looking at Dad right now. I want to have someone I can look at like that.*

He refused to wonder if Greg could be that person. It was far too soon to be thinking such things, no matter what his heart tried to whisper to him in his more vulnerable moments.

# Chapter Twelve

Adrian pulled his Toyota hybrid into the shaded drive and cut the engine. "Well. Here we are."

Beside him, Greg gazed at the two-story cottage with naked terror in his eyes. "What if they hate me?"

"They're not going to hate you."

"But, what if—"

"Greg. Stop."

Greg turned and regarded Adrian with a solemn trust that warmed him right to his toes. Smiling, Adrian reached out to cup Greg's cheek. "Relax, okay? My family is going to love you."

"I hope you're right."

"I am."

"You better be." Greg unbuckled his seat belt, leaned across the console and wrapped both arms around Adrian's neck. "Kiss me before we go in there."

Chuckling at the nervous quaver in Greg's voice, Adrian undid his own seat belt and tilted his head to press his lips to Greg's. The soft moan Greg let out set off a minor explosion of lust deep in Adrian's belly. He wound one arm around Greg's shoulders and buried the other hand in his hair, pulling him as close as possible with the console in the way. Greg's mouth opened, Greg's tongue slid against his, and something in the dashboard rattled in response to the spike in Adrian's powers. Adrian whimpered, his hand clenched in Greg's hair.

They both jumped when someone rapped on the driver's side window. Adrian tore himself from Greg and whipped around, heart in his throat. Sean grinned from the other side of the glass. "Hey. I'm not interrupting, am I?"

Adrian groaned. "Jesus Christ, I'm going to kill him."

"So that's the famous Sean Broussard, huh?" Greg leaned over and peered out the window. Sean waved at him. Greg waved back.

"The one and only."

"Uh-huh." Plopping back against the seat, Greg drew a deep breath and blew it out in a slow, steady stream. "Okay. Let's go before I lose my nerve."

Adrian gave Greg's hand a quick squeeze. He popped the trunk, then opened his door and climbed out into the sharp chill of the Alabama December evening. Sean enveloped him in a bone-crushing hug before he could even shut the car door behind him. Laughing, he wrapped both arms around his brother and clutched him tight.

"It's great to see you, bro," Sean declared, his voice suspiciously shaky in Adrian's ear.

Adrian swallowed the sudden lump in his throat. He remembered vividly how much it had affected him to see his family again when he first came home for the holidays freshman year. This was the first time he and Sean had seen each other since August.

He patted Sean's back. "Great to see you too, Sean. Videochats just aren't the same, are they?"

"No way." Sean drew back. His wide smile remained firmly in place, but the faint redness edging his eyes gave him away.

He held out a hand to Greg, who walked up at that moment. "You must be Greg. I'm Sean, Adrian's brother."

"I know." Greg grasped Sean's hand and they shook. "It's nice to meet you, Sean."

"You too." Letting go of Greg's hand, Sean moved toward the trunk of Adrian's car. "Come on, I'll help y'all get your stuff inside. You must be worn out after that long trip."

"Ten hours." Greg trailed Adrian and Sean to the back of the car. "And Adrian wouldn't even let us take a real lunch break."

"We stopped at Krystal." Reaching past his brother, Adrian heaved his suitcase out of the trunk. "That only took fifteen minutes. If we'd gone to a sit-down restaurant, we'd still be on the road right now."

Sean laughed. "Get used to it, Greg. Adrian inherited the tyrannical driving gene from our dad." He lifted Greg's suitcase and a bag stuffed with presents and stepped back. "Adrian, you can get that last bag, can't you?"

"Sure." Adrian grabbed the large backpack containing odds and ends that hadn't fit anywhere else. "Greg, will you shut the trunk for me?"

"Yeah." Greg pushed the trunk closed. He reached for the suitcase Sean held and frowned when Sean swung it out of the way. "Hey, I can carry my own stuff."

"Obviously. But you're our guest." Sean strode toward the porch, throwing a grin over his shoulder. "My mom would *kill* me if she found out I let a guest carry his own bags in."

Greg glowered. Adrian leaned over and kissed his cheek. "He's right. Our mom's kind of weird about stuff like that, and one of the neighbors would definitely tell on us. But my hands are full, so could you grab my keys and lock the car for me, please?"

"Yeah." In a shockingly sudden move, Greg grabbed Adrian's hair with both hands and kissed him hard. "Thanks for that."

Adrian grinned. "You're welcome."

The shine in Greg's eyes made Adrian's heart thump hard against his sternum. He followed Sean on wobbly legs. Behind him, the car door slammed. Greg caught up to him just as he got to the porch stairs. They climbed the four shallow steps together.

Just as Sean reached the front door, it swung open. Adrian's father stood on the other side. His face broke into a wide smile. "Hello, boys. Come in."

He stepped back. Sean walked into the hallway that ran from the front door to the back. Adrian followed, with Greg beside him. The spicy scent of chicken gumbo permeated the room, making Adrian's stomach rumble. The minute they were inside, Adrian set the bags on the floor at the foot of the stairs and swept his dad into a hug.

"It's good to have you home, son," his father's voice rumbled against the side of his head. "I've missed you. Sam and I both have."

Adrian's eyes stung. He swallowed against the lump in his throat. "Me too, Dad." He pulled back and reached for Greg's hand, drawing him forward. "Dad, this is Greg Woodhall. Greg, this is my father, Dr. Bo Broussard."

"Please, call me Bo." He held his hand out, smiling. "It's wonderful to finally meet you, Greg. We've heard a lot about you."

"It's great to meet you too, sir. Um, Bo." Greg shook the offered hand. He seemed much more at ease than he had in the car. Adrian doubted anyone but him would've noticed the too-wide eyes or the rapid pulse fluttering in Greg's throat. "Thank

*Love, Like Ghosts*

you for inviting me here for Christmas, I really appreciate it."

"We're happy to have you." Adrian's father let Greg's hand slide out of his grip. He walked a few steps toward the kitchen door on the left at the other end of the hall. "Sam!" he called. "They're here. You and Maia come on out."

"They're making blackberry cobbler with some of those berries Dad froze this summer," Sean explained. "Maia wanted to make dessert and made the mistake of letting Sam help."

"Sean, that was ugly." Their father glared, but the corners of his mouth twitched.

Adrian stifled a laugh. Sam liked to help in the kitchen, but he really wasn't much of a cook. Dad had learned subtle ways to keep him out years ago.

The kitchen swung open and Sam strode down the hallway toward them, followed by a petite, curvy girl with a wild halo of dark curls and big amber eyes sparkling behind a pair of cat-eye glasses. Sam trotted up to Adrian, laughing, and hugged him hard. "Adrian. God, it's good to see you."

"You too, Sam." Adrian coughed when Sam thumped him on the back. He hugged Sam back, grinning. "Sam, I'd like you to meet Greg Woodhall." He pulled back and nodded toward Greg. "Greg, this is Sam Raintree, my step-dad."

Sam took Greg's hand and shook. "It's great to meet you, Greg."

"You too, Sam." Greg returned Sam's smile. "I was just telling Bo how much I appreciate y'all inviting me to stay here. I want to thank you as well."

"We're happy to have you. The more the merrier, as they say." Sam dropped Greg's hand and took his husband's, weaving their fingers together. "Sean?"

"Yep." Sean walked over and slung an arm around the

151

young woman's shoulders. "Greg, Adrian, this is Maia Marchand, the most beautiful and talented woman on the planet. Maia, this is my brother Adrian and his boyfriend Greg."

A pink blush stained Maia's mocha cheeks, but the look she shot Sean was a fond one. She held out her hand. "Nice to meet y'all."

"Same here." Adrian shook her hand. "Did Sean say something about blackberry cobbler?"

"I hope so, because that's my favorite." Greg took his turn shaking hands with Maia. "And speaking of food, whatever's cooking smells amazing."

Adrian's dad laughed. "Chicken gumbo, dirty rice, cornbread and green beans. Nothing fancy."

Leaning against Adrian's shoulder, Greg let out a moan that had Adrian fighting off a surge of lust. "Man, that sounds fantastic. Especially after nothing but a granola bar and coffee for breakfast and a couple of Krystal burgers for lunch."

"You ate seven," Adrian muttered, but he doubted anyone heard him over the explosion of laughter.

"Why don't you two go ahead and put your things up in your room?" Sam suggested. "We should have dinner on the table by the time you get back downstairs."

"Okay." Adrian gave Greg's shoulder a squeeze. "I'll give you the grand tour too, after we drop our bags."

"Sounds good to me."

They moved apart. While Greg crossed to where Sean had set his luggage, Adrian slung the backpack over his shoulder and lifted his suitcase. He allowed Greg to take his own bag and the sack of presents without saying anything. Greg might take that sort of pampering from Sean, but Adrian knew better. He didn't much feel like hearing the choice words it would earn him later if he tried to carry Greg's things for him.

Adrian led Greg up the stairs and to his room at the front corner of the house, overlooking Carlen Street. They both set their bags on the floor in front of Adrian's closet. Adrian gazed around at the familiar earth-toned walls, burgundy bedding and matching drapes with a smile. Ever since they moved here when he was fourteen, this room had been his sanctuary. He'd never shared it with anyone before. The idea of sharing it with Greg made his heart beat faster with a mix of anticipation and fear.

"So." Sauntering up to Adrian, Greg wrapped both arms around his waist. "This is your room, huh?"

"It is." Adrian settled his arms around Greg's neck and kissed the end of his nose. "What do you think?"

Greg grinned. "I think your dad's hot."

Adrian was shocked into laughter. "Oh my God, don't even talk about my dad like that."

"Why not? He's a good-looking man. Him and Sam both, actually, but yeah. Your dad's definitely hot." Greg's fingers traced up and down Adrian's spine, creating a wave of gooseflesh in their wake. "He looks just like you in thirty years."

*Good grief, my boyfriend's lusting after my dad.* Adrian had no idea how to react to that. He fought the urge to squirm. "Okay, so I know what you think of my dad. Which I really, *really* didn't need to know, thank you very much. So why not answer my *real* question now?"

Greg snickered. "Yeah, so, I also think I wish we had more than a few minutes, because I'd sure as hell like to try out that bed."

Adrian smiled, pleased to see Greg looking so relaxed. "Trust me, we're giving the bed a workout later."

Desire flared in Greg's eyes. "Good." He tilted his head up

to catch Adrian's lips in a brief but sizzling kiss. "Come on and give me that tour, before I drag you to bed right now."

"Yeah, I guess that's a good idea."

Stealing one more swift kiss, Adrian took Greg's hand and led him into the hall to begin the tour of the house. Voices and laughter drifted from downstairs, along with the mouthwatering smells of dishes Adrian had been eating all his life. God, it was good to be home.

He glanced at Greg, who smiled and squeezed his hand. Warmth blossomed in Adrian's chest. Yes, it was good to be home. Better than ever, now.

~ \* ~

"And then, Mr. and Mrs. Van Housan *both* scream like a couple of little girls, and she says, 'That's her, that's our Miss Puffy Pants!'"

Adrian snorted into his coffee. "Seriously? Did you see it?"

Sam nodded. "Yep. One toy poodle ghost, hovering as dramatically as you please right over the dog bed just like they'd claimed it did."

"I don't believe it."

"Neither did we." Sam sipped from his cup. "And we were right. David found some state-of-the-art projection equipment set up behind the Japanese screen Mrs. Van Housan had in the corner of the room. It turned out to be the granddaughter doing it."

Adrian shook his head. "For Christ's sake, *why*?"

"Who knows? Brand-new degree from Cal Tech, no job, living with a couple of folks as gullible as those two? Hell, she probably did it for the sheer entertainment value."

Laughter bubbled up from Adrian's chest. It was nice being able to spend some time alone with Sam. Sean and Maia had gone back to their mom and Lee's place last night after dinner, and Dad and Greg were both still sleeping. Adrian had woken before dawn to find Sam already up and making coffee. They'd sat down together at the kitchen table and talked, just like they had so many times during Adrian's teen years, when fear and bitterness kept him up late and woke him early.

So far, their conversation had been much lighter this time. Adrian was glad.

Setting down his coffee mug, Sam yawned and stretched. "Anyway, enough about the adventures of BCPI. What've you been up to, other than studying and going out with Greg?"

*And there goes the light conversation.* Adrian had thought about how and when to approach Sam about the subject of Lyndon. In fact, it was the main reason he'd woken so early that morning. He'd been out to the castle several times in the last month or so, and had continued to make contact with Lyndon, but he kept getting the same images over and over again. He was stuck. If anyone could help him make the breakthrough he needed to solve Lyndon's case, it would be Sam. However, the discussion would be anything but superficial.

Resting his elbows on the kitchen table, Adrian gazed at the steam rising from his red and green mug. "Actually, I've been kind of doing an unofficial investigation of one of the campus buildings. I wanted to ask you about it."

"Oh, yeah?"

"Yeah." Adrian chewed his lip, thinking hard. He didn't want to lie to Sam, but he also didn't want to tell him all the details. What Sam knew, Adrian's dad eventually knew as well, and he was nothing if not a stickler for the rules. He'd tear Adrian a new one if he found out Adrian had been basically breaking and entering in order to communicate with a ghost.

Sam's hand touched Adrian's. He looked up to meet Sam's concerned gaze. Sam frowned. "Adrian, what's wrong?"

"The building's definitely haunted," Adrian answered after a moment, deciding on the SparkNotes version of the truth. "I've been able to establish communication with the spirit several times. I know he died young, and he died in some sort of violent manner. But I can't get any further than that. I've been there four times in the last few weeks, and he keeps sending me the same images every time." Adrian sighed. "I'm stuck, Sam. I want to figure out exactly how he died, maybe find his body so he can move on, but I can't seem to get any further than I've gotten already, and I don't know what to do."

Sam listened with an unreadable expression. When Adrian finished, Sam grunted, lifted his mug and drew a long, thoughtful mouthful. Adrian squirmed in silence while Sam studied his face.

Finally, he couldn't take it any longer. "So? What do you think I should do?"

Sam's eyebrows lifted. "First off, I wonder why this is so important to you." He raised a hand, halting the protest on Adrian's lips. "But it clearly *is* important, and you're an adult now, so I suppose the why of it is none of my business."

Adrian stared at the table and said nothing. His cheeks burned under Sam's unrelenting scrutiny. After a few seconds that dragged on forever, Sam began speaking again.

"I think the problem may be that you're holding yourself too much in check when you're communicating with the spirit."

Startled, Adrian raised his head. "No, that can't be it. I'm opening my mind as much as I can." *So much it scares me sometimes.*

Sam gave him a gentle smile. "I don't doubt it. But I know

you, Adrian. After all you went through as a child, and as hard as you worked for so many years to get your psychokinesis under control, keeping a tight rein on yourself is second nature to you at this point. I think being able to let your guard down and open yourself up completely would take some hard work and a deliberate effort in the other direction. I don't think it's something you'd be able to just *do* with a few quick and dirty relaxation and meditation exercises."

Resentment kindled in Adrian's gut. Years of practice kept it off his face. "I was able to establish communication with him easily enough that way. I've done it that way before too. Entities have always been attracted to my abilities. You're the same way, you've said so yourself."

"Yes, that's true. Ghosts and other paranormal entities have always been drawn to me. Whether because of my psychokinesis or my other psychic abilities, who knows. Those abilities seem to be linked in you and me both." Sam set his mug on the table, his fingers still curled around the handle. "But your psychokinesis is several orders of magnitude stronger than mine. You were forced to exercise a level of control at an early age that I don't have to use even now. When you have to build up such a strong subconscious control over something like that, of course it's going to be more difficult for you to let go of that control. But it sounds to me like this spirit of yours has given all he's going to give, or all he *can* give, in the situation the way it stands now. If you want to break through the barrier you've reached with him, you're going to have to work on letting go. Letting down all your shields, and letting him into your mind completely." Sam's gaze sharpened. "Either that, or let this one go."

Adrian swallowed hard. The idea of relinquishing even a little bit of the control he'd worked so hard to achieve terrified him. What would happen if he couldn't get it all back? What happened if something angered him while his guard was down? Even worse, what if repeatedly loosening his grip on his powers meant they slipped away from him while he and Greg were making love? Christ, he'd never forgive himself if his need to help Lyndon ended up hurting Greg.

*Maybe you should give up.*

He shook off the thought before it could take hold. He wouldn't give up. Couldn't. Leaving Lyndon to the mournful twilight existence he'd suffered for over a century wasn't an option.

He gripped his mug until his knuckles paled. "It's the only way?"

"Well, obviously you know this ghost better than I do. But from what little you've told me, it sounds like it." Sam laid a hand on Adrian's arm. "Can I give you one more piece of advice?"

"Sure." Adrian forced an anemic smile. "I can use as much as I can get."

One corner of Sam's mouth hitched upward. He dropped his hand, lifted his mug and sipped from it. "Tell Greg about this."

Astonishment made Adrian's pulse speed up. "Um. What?"

Sam snorted. "Don't pretend you don't know what I'm talking about. You haven't told Greg about this ghost hunt of yours."

*Shit.* Adrian hunched his shoulders and studied the scratch on the wooden table. "What makes you say that?"

"Other than the fact that it's true? Because if Greg already knew about it, you would've asked this question last night, when we were talking about Bay City Paranormal and Greg was asking a million questions."

Adrian let out a humorless laugh. "He doesn't believe in ghosts. In fact, he's pretty disapproving of the whole ghost-hunting business. I still can't believe he was asking all those questions."

"He didn't seem very disapproving. In fact, he seemed pretty interested."

"Yeah, well, he's never been very interested when it was *me* talking about it." Adrian couldn't keep the bitterness out of his voice. Sam chuckled, and Adrian shot him a glare. "I don't see what's so funny."

Sam smiled. "Did you ever consider that maybe he's jealous of your time? That maybe he sees how much interest you show in this subject, and he's afraid it's something that might take you away from him?"

Adrian blinked. He'd never considered that before. Not that it made any difference, when the result of telling Greg his secret would be the same, but still. It certainly put Greg's attitudes at school versus last night in perspective.

"Yeah," Adrian said, sounding as surprised as he felt. "I can see that."

"Good." Sam regarded him with a solemn expression. "I know why you don't want to tell him, Adrian. You're afraid he's going to be angry. And you're probably right. But you need to do it, soon, before he finds out some other way and the fact that you kept it from him causes trouble you can't fix."

Something in Sam's eyes spoke of hard experience, and Adrian knew with gut-wrenching certainty that Sam was right.

The question was, could he do it? Could he look Greg in the eye and tell him the truth, knowing it might mean the end?

"I can't." The words came out in a barely audible whisper. Adrian stared into Sam's eyes, pleading with him to understand. "Not yet."

Sam nodded, but his expression was sad. Rising to his feet, he clapped Adrian on the shoulder. "Think it over, okay?"

Adrian nodded as Sam gathered the coffee mugs and carried them to the sink, but he knew he wasn't going to think about it. He wouldn't tell Greg.

*Oh, my God. I just lied to Sam.* Even though he hadn't spoken, even though he wasn't even sure Sam had seen him nod, even though Sam was probably well aware of what Adrian was and was not going to do with regard to telling Greg the truth about Lyndon. It didn't matter. Ever since that night at his mother's house when he was eleven, he'd never told a direct, deliberate lie.

Until now.

Pushing back his chair, Adrian hurried from the room as fast as he could and stumbled out onto the front porch. He leaned against the railing and gulped the icy winter air until he no longer felt the urge to vomit.

~ \* ~

At least a dozen times over the next twenty-five days, Adrian almost talked himself into telling Greg. But he never did. Greg would push him against the wall and kiss him breathless, or laugh at one of Sean's corny jokes, or simply flash the smile that always made Adrian's knees weak, and somehow he just never got past the "thinking about it" stage.

Adrian snorted. Yeah, sure. "Somehow." *Don't bullshit yourself, Adrian. You were right before. You told Sam you'd think about telling Greg, but you knew damn well you wouldn't.*

"Did you say something, son?"

Adrian turned and smiled at his father, who'd just entered

the dining room through the adjoining kitchen door. "No. Just laughing at myself."

"Oh. Okay." Setting the pile of napkins he carried in the middle of the table, Adrian's dad planted both hands on his hips and studied the room with a critical eye. "Well, I guess there's nothing else we can do here until Sam gets home with dinner. When's Greg getting back from shopping?"

"He said Maia would be dropping him off around six." Adrian glanced at his watch. "It's almost five forty-five now, so he should be here soon."

"All right." Dad wandered into the living room, with Adrian trailing after him. "I'm really glad the two of them hit it off so well."

"Me too." Adrian plopped into his favorite chair, kicked his sneakers off and curled his legs beneath him. "He hit it off with all of you, right from the start. I can't tell you what a relief that was."

One dark brow lifted. "For you or for him?"

Adrian grinned. "For both of us."

Laughing, his father sank onto the sofa next to Adrian's chair. "He's a wonderful young man, Adrian. I'm glad you found each other."

Adrian nodded his thanks. Though they'd never said so—except for Sean, who'd said so a lot—he knew his family used to worry about him being alone. They'd all been happy when he started dating Greg. He knew all of them had to be as thrilled as he was that Greg liked them, and that the feeling was mutual.

His dad leaned forward, elbows on his knees and a serious expression on his face. "You two seem pretty serious, though. I hope..." He paused, as if searching for the right words.

Adrian's stomach churned with a sudden attack of nerves.

161

That sober look in his dad's eyes never preceded anything he wanted to hear. "What?"

A pensive smile curved his father's lips. "I just don't want to see you getting too serious too fast and end up getting hurt. That's all."

Adrian squelched the swell of indignation inside him before it could make him say anything he'd regret later. He just had to remember that anything his dad said came from a desire to protect him.

"Don't worry, Dad. I'll be careful." Adrian picked at the place where the cuff of his sweater sleeve had begun to fray. He studied the dark blue threads so he wouldn't have to look his father in the eye. "I care about Greg. A lot. And I want this thing with him to last. But I know we're still young, and I know how different we are. I'm trying not to count on anything."

"Oh. Son."

The quiet heartbreak in his father's voice brought Adrian's head up again. "What? What's wrong?"

His father shook his head, dark eyes sorrowful. "You've gotten so used to being alone, you think that's how it has to be. Sometimes I think you actually believe you *deserve* to be alone. But you don't. You're such a loving, wonderful person, Adrian. You deserve to have someone special love and cherish you. And if Greg turns out to be that person, then I'll be happy for you both." Leaning forward, he took one of Adrian's hands in both of his and gazed straight into his eyes. "When you decide to let someone into your heart, you don't do it by halves. I don't think that's a bad thing. I just don't want you to get hurt if Greg's feelings wane over time and yours don't."

Adrian's heart lurched. His father was right, and he knew it. Had known it since the beginning. Hadn't he been waiting for the end—preparing for it, steeling himself for it—ever since his first date with Greg? Of course, he'd expected to bring it on himself via some subconscious sabotage. As time went on and their relationship became a part of his day-to-day life, the expectation of disaster had drifted to the back of his mind. But it still waited there, lurking like a spider. Maybe it was time to learn precisely where he and Greg stood now, and whether or not they had a future together.

He opened his mouth to answer his dad—though what he would say, he had no idea—but the sound of a car pulling into the drive stopped him. His father shot a swift glance at the front door, then pinned him with a fierce stare. "You deserve to be happy, Adrian. Don't ever let anything stop you from fighting for your happiness. Remember that."

Footsteps sounded on the front porch. Jumping to his feet, Dad pressed Adrian's hand once before letting go and hurrying over to open the door. Adrian stood and turned in time to see his dad greet Sam with a tender kiss and take two of the three fragrant paper sacks he carried.

Adrian flashed a quick smile and started toward the door to close it while his dad and Sam walked into the dining room. Almost a month after his miniscule lie, Adrian still had trouble looking Sam in the eye sometimes, even though he was now positive Sam knew perfectly well he'd been less than truthful. Sometimes Adrian wished he could tell little white lies like normal people without it twisting his gut into knots.

Before Adrian could take more than two steps, Greg walked in behind Sam, arms laden with bags from the mall. His gaze caught Adrian's, and his face lit up like the twinkling white lights on the Christmas tree still standing in the living room's big bay window.

Adrian's breath caught. Thoughts of his sins, major and minor, flew out of his head. Crossing the room in a few swift

163

strides, he cupped Greg's face in his hands and pressed a soft, chaste kiss to his lips.

Greg let out an almost soundless gasp. The bags thudded to the floor. Adrian could practically taste Greg's shock, and no wonder. Public affection still made Adrian uncomfortable. Until now, the most he'd done in front of his family was hold Greg's hand. This kiss must be as big a surprise as a public groping would be to anyone else.

When he drew back a few long, glorious seconds later, Greg stared up at him with glazed eyes. "Wow. What was that for?"

"Because I wanted to." Adrian glanced over his shoulder, where his father and Sam were busy setting the food out on the table and ignoring Adrian and Greg so pointedly that the attempt at giving them a little privacy was obvious. "Because if I can't be affectionate with my boyfriend in front of my own family, then I'm a completely hopeless case, and I don't want to be a hopeless case."

Greg's mouth curved into the sweet, open smile that always made Adrian ache inside. "C'mon, let's go eat. Whatever Sam had in those bags, it smelled absolutely out of this world."

They linked hands and walked into the dining room together. Adrian didn't mind Greg's lack of effusive thanks for what was, for Adrian, a tremendous public expression of his feelings. Greg might not have Adrian's directness with words, but Adrian had learned long ago to read even the subtlest nuances of Greg's moods in his expressive eyes. Right now, there was nothing subtle about the grateful joy shining there.

Adrian hoped a discussion about where their relationship was headed wouldn't quench that light. If he even had the balls to start it.

~ ✳ ~

That night, Greg clamped his legs tight around Adrian's waist and stifled his soft cry in the curve of Adrian's neck when he came. The rhythmic clenching of his ass wrenched Adrian's release from him a moment later. He screwed his eyes shut and whimpered into Greg's hair as the orgasm tore through him. The window rattled faintly in its frame, and the tiny still-rational corner of Adrian's brain hoped that if Greg noticed, he'd think it was the wind.

When his tremors subsided and Greg's feet slid off his back, Adrian reached between them and held onto the condom while he eased his limp cock carefully out of Greg's hole. He reached up to drop the used rubber into the plastic bag on his headboard, then collapsed onto his side and hauled Greg into his arms. "Wow."

Greg laughed, his breath soft and warm against Adrian's lips. "You said it." He slung a leg over Adrian's hips, buried a hand in his hair and planted a kiss on his mouth. "I kind of wish we didn't have to go back tomorrow. This bed is way better than the one in your apartment."

"And let's not even talk about the bed in your dorm room."

"Oh, my God." Greg snuggled closer, grinning. "I think the only reason those damn things exist is to discourage students from having sex in the dorms."

"I think you're right." Adrian brushed the damp hair from Greg's brow. "I'm really glad you got to come home with me, Greg."

"So am I. Your family's terrific." Greg ran his fingertips over the line of Adrian's jaw. "Besides, I would've missed you too damn much if we'd been apart for a whole month."

The tender shine in Greg's eyes made Adrian's throat feel raw and tight. Resting their foreheads together, he wound both arms around Greg's waist and splayed his open palms flat on Greg's bare back. "Me too," he whispered, his voice rough with all the things he didn't quite know how to express.

Frowning, Greg drew back enough to look into Adrian's eyes. "Adrian, is something wrong?"

Adrian's pulse tripped, stumbled and resumed its rhythm in double time. He licked his lips. "Wrong?"

"Yeah. You've been a little off ever since I got home tonight. Like something was bothering you." Greg stroked a hand through Adrian's hair in what Adrian suspected was an entirely subconscious gesture of comfort. "Look, I know I'm not very good at talking about stuff, but if there's ever anything you want to talk to me about, you know you can. Right?"

*And there's your perfect segue.* Adrian's heart slammed against his sternum. Confronted with the opportunity to actually talk to Greg about their relationship, Adrian wasn't sure he could do it.

"It's just something my dad said earlier." Adrian drew Greg closer and kissed a droplet of sweat from his forehead. This would be so much easier to say if he didn't have to look Greg in the eye while he said it. "He told me how much he and Sam liked you, and how glad they are that we got together, but he was worried that maybe we were getting a little too serious too fast."

Greg's hand stilled at the back of Adrian's neck. He didn't say anything in response to Adrian's confession. A cold, sick feeling curled in the pit of Adrian's stomach. He wasn't sure what he'd expected Greg to do, but lying there in awkward silence wasn't it. What did it mean?

*God, maybe he thinks I want to break up with him.*

Adrian rubbed his cheek against Greg's. "I *am* serious about you. Very much so. But I don't think it's too serious at all. I think it's just perfect."

The tension in Greg's back eased a little, but his silence continued unbroken, and the knot in Adrian's gut twisted tighter. Did Greg see this thing between them in a more casual way than Adrian did? Was he going to think Adrian was too clingy now? Too needy? Would *he* want to break up now?

Adrian swallowed hard. The thought of Greg leaving him set off a bright spark of panic deep in his chest.

*Get a hold of yourself. You know Greg's not one for heart-to-heart talks, especially if it involves how he feels instead of how someone else feels. Don't jump to conclusions.*

Closing his eyes, Adrian nuzzled Greg's throat. God, he smelled good. Skin and sweat and sex, with a bare hint of the musky cologne he wore still detectable some fourteen hours after he'd put it on. His body fit perfectly against Adrian's. The faint stubble on his cheek scraped the shell of Adrian's ear. Adrian could feel the steady thud of Greg's heartbeat against his own. He held Greg tight and hoped it wouldn't be the last time.

Eventually, Greg stirred in that unmistakable "I'd like to move now" way. Sighing, Adrian loosened his grip so Greg could roll over. Greg flopped onto his back and dipped a finger into the semen coating his stomach. "I guess we should go clean up."

*Okay. So we're going to ignore this issue.*

Adrian bit back the urge to roll his eyes at himself. He hadn't even had the guts to *make* it an issue. All he'd said was that his dad was worried about them getting too serious too fast, and that he himself didn't think that was so. Chances were the implications of that statement had flown right over Greg's head.

*You know that's not true. You felt him react. He knew what you were saying, he just didn't want to deal with it.*

Adrian knew he should press the issue. He should ask Greg point-blank where he saw their relationship going. Whether it was just a casual fling to him or if he saw a future for the two of them. But his silence had killed Adrian's courage more thoroughly than anything else could have, and Adrian knew there would be no such discussion tonight.

Forcing a playful grin, Adrian leaned over and pecked Greg on the lips. "I'll clean you up."

"What do you—oh!" Greg squeaked when Adrian scooted down and swiped his tongue through the rapidly gelling semen. "Fuck, that tickles."

Adrian chuckled, his morose mood lifting with the sound of Greg's half-stifled laughter. "You big baby." He lapped up another salty-bitter mouthful, swallowed it and licked the residue from his lips. Greg tried to squirm away. Adrian held him down with an arm across his hips. "Be still. You don't want to go to sleep sticky, do you?"

"No. Wait, yes!" Greg clamped his hand over his mouth just in time to muffle a burst of what sounded suspiciously like giggles. The other hand attempted in vain to keep Adrian's tongue from digging into his navel. "OhGodpleasestop, stop, you're killing me!"

Adrian ignored Greg's pleas and increasingly wild thrashing long enough to clean every trace of come from his belly. When he lifted his head at last, Greg gave him an indignant, red-faced glare, but allowed Adrian to roll him over and spoon against his back without an argument. He laced his fingers through Adrian's and pulled Adrian's arm snug around his waist.

"If you get spooge all over my back after all that, I'm gonna kill you," Greg muttered, wriggling his butt until it sat firmly against Adrian's groin.

Adrian smiled. "Don't worry. Whatever was on me either dried up or got rubbed off on the sheets."

"Good." Turning his head, Greg pressed a soft kiss to Adrian's lips. "Night, Adrian."

"Good night."

For a moment, they just lay there, staring at each other. In the muted blend of moonlight and streetlight from the window, Adrian thought he saw something he couldn't quite name flicker in Greg's eyes, something that made Adrian's pulse quicken in response. Then the whatever-it-was vanished. Greg smiled, curled up in Adrian's arms and closed his eyes. Adrian lay awake for a long time, lost in thought.

# Chapter Thirteen

Greg was unusually quiet the next morning. Adrian wanted to blame the early hour—five a.m., dark and cold as the grave—but he knew that wasn't it. The pensive expression on Greg's face at the breakfast table spoke volumes. He was still thinking about what Adrian had said last night. Adrian knew it, deep in his bones.

If only he knew in what direction Greg's thoughts ran.

If only he had the courage to ask.

By six, he and Greg had said their goodbyes to Adrian's family and were on the road back to Chapel Hill. Greg sat with one leg curled beneath him, staring out the passenger side window at the headlights zooming by on the other side of the interstate while Adrian drove. Adrian frowned at the road ahead and wished he could read Greg's mind.

Normally, silence didn't bother Adrian. However, silence between him and Greg wasn't normally this uncomfortable. Or maybe Adrian was the only one uncomfortable. It wasn't like Greg was going out of his way to let Adrian know how he felt.

*Get a grip. You know he gets moody sometimes. Maybe this is just one of those times.*

Adrian worried his lower lip between his teeth, thinking hard. What could he say that would draw Greg into conversation without being too serious?

When it hit him, Adrian grinned. "Hey, don't you have auditions for that other play soon?"

Greg gave him a blank look. "Other play?"

"Yeah." Adrian glanced sideways, his confidence slipping. Had he remembered wrong? "You know, you were talking about it just the other day. The one you mentioned right after the other audition, back in November?"

Comprehension lit Greg's eyes. "Oh, you mean *Wicked.*"

"Yeah, that's it." Relieved, Adrian shot Greg a smile. "You have auditions for that one soon, right?"

"Couple of weeks."

"Which part are you trying out for again?" Adrian's cheeks heated. "Sorry, I know you told me already, but—"

"But your theater brain is about the same as my physics brain." Greg grinned at him. "It's okay. I'm trying out for Fiyero."

The name meant nothing to Adrian. Not that he was about to let on. "Right. I remember now." He darted a sidelong glance at Greg. At least he wasn't staring out the window anymore. "Do you want me to come with you again?"

Greg shrugged. "You can if you want."

He didn't seem very enthusiastic. Adrian's heart sank, but he nodded and forced a smile. "I'd like that, if you don't mind."

"Any time." Greg slouched in his seat and planted both feet on the dash. "You know what, let's not talk about that. Let's talk about something else."

"Okay, sure, if you like." Adrian switched on his signal, moved into the left lane and hit the gas to pass a puttering old Buick. "What do you want to talk about?"

Tilting his head, Greg studied Adrian's face. "Tell me about this research project you've been working on."

Surprised, Adrian cast a wide-eyed look in Greg's direction. "Huh?"

Greg laughed. "C'mon, Adrian. You've been all over this thing for weeks now, but I don't have the first clue what it's all about."

Adrian straightened and flexed his fingers around the wheel. "You really want to know?"

It wasn't that Greg never showed any interest in Adrian's academic life. He'd asked several times how the project was coming along and always knew what was going on in Adrian's classes. But the fact remained that upper level college physics wasn't easy. It tended to make most people's eyes glaze over, and Greg was no exception. Adrian didn't blame Greg for not wanting to talk about the research project. The fact that he'd asked—no, flat-out insisted on details—shocked Adrian to his core.

"What, you think I'm stupid? You think I won't understand what you're talking about?"

"What? No, God, I don't—" Adrian caught Greg's grin and let out a long breath ending in a laugh. "Smart ass."

Greg snickered. "You're too easy."

"Yeah, yeah." Adrian slid the Toyota back into the right lane in front of a delivery truck for a local grocery store chain. "All right. Basically, what we're doing is working on possible practical applications of quantum mechanics to interdimensional travel."

"Seriously?"

"It's more complicated than that, but yeah, that's the gist of it."

"You could really travel between dimensions?"

Adrian smiled. "That's what we're trying to figure out."

"Wow." Greg shook his head. "Have I ever told you that you're scary smart?"

"Not today."

"You're scary smart."

Adrian pulled the "scary" face he'd taken to using whenever Greg teased him about being abnormally intelligent. Greg laughed, and some of Adrian's tension melted away. He reached across the console and squeezed Greg's knee. Maybe things were getting back to normal.

~ \* ~

A week later, Adrian had begun to wonder if he was wrong.

He and Greg talked, teased and laughed just like always. They still held hands everywhere they went. Greg still stayed at Adrian's place most nights. Each time they kissed, each time they made love, Adrian felt branded deep inside, just like he had the very first time.

In other words, everything was exactly as it had been before the Christmas holiday.

At least on the surface. Underneath, though, something had changed.

Adrian couldn't put his finger on the difference, but he knew it was there. He felt it. Something in the way Greg looked at him. Something small. Subtle. Furtive, even, caught in glimpses from the corner of his eye and gone when he tried to look at it directly. He had no idea what to make of it, and even less of an idea what—if anything—to do about it.

"It's not that he's distant," he explained to Chelsea as the two of them huddled over their closed laptops in a sunny corner of Davis Library. "He isn't, exactly. It's just that sometimes I'll catch him watching me with this really strange look on his face. Really intense. Like..."

Chelsea raised her eyebrows. "Go on." She slouched in her chair, watching him with the calm curiosity that always drew the words from him with such ease.

His brow knitted. "That's just it. He only does it when I'm not looking, and when I catch him, he stops, so I can't pin it down. I've never had anyone *look* at me like that. It's..." He shook his head. "I don't know. I have to be honest, it excites me a little, but it scares me a lot, because I don't know what it means."

"Hm." She tapped a fingertip against her chin. "Have you tried just asking him?"

Adrian laughed, softly so any passing librarians wouldn't get them in trouble. "I know that seems like the obvious answer, but I can't, Chelsea."

"Why not?"

*Yeah, Adrian. Why not? Why can't you ask your lover—your boyfriend, the man you've been in a relationship with for over three months now—what's bothering him? Why can't you have an honest conversation with the person you should be closer to than anyone else, when you've always prided yourself on your honesty?*

He had no answers for himself, or for his friend. He gave her a rueful half-smile. "I'm scared of what he might say."

Chelsea's eyes filled with sympathy, but she didn't ask Adrian to elaborate. He was grateful for that, mostly because he couldn't put his finger on what exactly frightened him so much, and it bothered him to admit it.

A movement caught the edge of Adrian's vision. He glanced to his right. Theo was strolling toward them, hands in his jacket pockets, his usual half Mona Lisa, half miscreant grin on his face. He lifted a hand and waved. "Yo, Adrian!"

The Rocky impression, loud and startling in the quiet of the library, drew more than a few stares and barely stifled laughs. Adrian winced, but waved back. "Hi, Theo."

Jogging the last few feet, Theo swooped down and planted a kiss on Chelsea's lips. "And hello to you, my little sweet potato."

She shook her head, brown eyes sparkling with mingled humor and affection. "You're nuts."

"What about 'em?" Theo cupped his groin and waggled his eyebrows at her before plopping into the empty chair on the other side of the small round table beside the window. "So, what're you two discussing with such seriousness over here?"

Adrian shot Chelsea a look he knew she would understand. She bobbed her head in a tiny nod, and he breathed easier. He and Chelsea had become fast friends in the past few months. In that time, he'd gotten to know Theo as well. He liked Theo a lot, but he didn't feel comfortable with anyone other than Chelsea being privy to his relationship problems.

If they even *were* real problems and not just figments of his imagination. Which remained to be determined.

"Nothing much." Chelsea took Theo's hand and wound their fingers together. "So what's up? I thought you had your improvisational theater class right now."

"Yeah, but Leander had an emergency, so she canceled for today." Theo traced the bones in the back of Chelsea's hand with his thumb as if they fascinated him. "I was thinking if you're done studying for now, we could go get a coffee or something." He looked up and grinned at Adrian. "You can come too, if you want. No offense or anything, man, but you look like you could use some caffeine."

Adrian let out a grim laugh. "No offense taken. I *am* tired." He glanced at his watch. Plenty of time for a cup of coffee before he was supposed to meet Greg. On the other hand, he'd been meaning to search through the library's UNC yearbook archives ever since he learned they existed a few days ago. This would be the perfect time to do that. "Thanks, but I think I'll have to pass. I'm meeting Greg at the dining hall at six, and I need to get some things done before then."

"It's cool." Theo nudged Chelsea's leg with his foot. "What about it, Bugaloo? Coffee?"

"Yeah, okay." Leaning over, she pecked him on the lips, then pried his hand off hers and stuffed her laptop into her green and yellow bag. She stood and slung the bag over her shoulder. "See you later, Adrian."

"Tell Gregorio hi," Theo added, pushing to his feet. He wound an arm around Chelsea's shoulders.

Adrian chuckled. "I'll tell *Greg* you said hello. See you both later."

They strolled off with their heads together, whispering. Adrian watched them with a smile on his face. They seemed like an odd match—rational, level-headed Chelsea and Theo who seemed to live in a bubble of his own personal reality—but it worked.

*Kind of like Greg and me.*

If they still worked.

The possibility that they might not made Adrian feel cold and sick.

Pushing the thought to the back of his mind, Adrian opened his laptop and went to the UNC library website. A quick search took him to a free digital archive of UNC yearbooks dating back to the late eighteen hundreds. He found the nineteen-oh-five yearbook, downloaded a copy and settled down to search through the document for any students with the first name of Cassius.

It seemed like such an obvious piece of research, he could've kicked himself for not thinking of it sooner. Adrian blamed overwork and fatigue, since it hadn't even occurred to him to search Lyndon Groome's fellow students for the mysterious Cassius until halfway through Christmas Break. As soon as he and Greg returned from Mobile, Adrian had made a trip to the registrar's office to try and find out if any students with the first name Cassius had attended UNC in nineteen-oh-five. He'd learned that student records weren't available to the public, but an acquaintance on work-study there had told him about the online yearbook archives. Adrian had made up his mind to search the nineteen-oh-five yearbook at the first opportunity. If Cassius had been a student here, hopefully Adrian would be able to learn more about him, which might eventually lead to information useful to solving the mystery of Lyndon's death. If Cassius hadn't attended UNC, well, that knowledge could be helpful in its own right.

Cassius turned out to be a surprisingly popular name at Chapel Hill in that particular year. Adrian eventually found eleven students with that name—five seniors, two juniors, and four freshmen. Not one of them matched the picture in his head, however. He also discovered a faculty member among the ranks of the Cassiuses—Dr. Hilliard, a professor of divinity. That one gave Adrian a moment's serious thought, remembering the vivid mental picture of the cross on the wall over Lyndon's lover's bed. But Dr. Hilliard, though young and dark-haired in the old photo, proved on closer study to have dark eyes, not light. He also possessed a crooked, angular jaw and a nose that looked to have been broken at some point. Definitely not the man whose image still haunted Adrian's dreams.

With a deep sigh, Adrian stretched his arms over his head and arched his back against the chair's cushions. Vertebrae cracked, loud as a gunshot in the quiet. A girl with two pencils pinning her hair up glared at him over the tops of her glasses from a nearby table. He gave her his best cold stare until she colored and dropped her gaze to the book open on the table in front of her.

Turning his attention back to his laptop, Adrian studied the neat rows of faded black and white pictures without seeing them. He wasn't certain what to do now. Sure, it was good to know that Cassius apparently hadn't been a student here. But it left Adrian very neatly at a dead end. If Cassius hadn't been a UNC student, who was he? And if Adrian couldn't follow the one lead he had in Lyndon's case, then where was he to go from here?

He shook his head. "I have no fucking idea."

The two-pencil girl let out an annoyed huff. "Can you *please* keep it down over there? Some of us are trying to study."

Several scathing retorts flashed through Adrian's mind. He dismissed them as childish and ultimately beneath him. He gave the girl a tight smile. "I was just leaving."

"Good." She bent over her book again.

Closing his laptop, Adrian slid it into his bag and stood, his bag over his shoulder. A swift twist of his thought sent the girl's pencils clattering to the floor. She dove after them with a squeak. He grinned as he walked to the stairs.

Outside, the unseasonable warmth of the afternoon had begun to fade into the hard cold of a normal January evening. Adrian squinted against the setting sun and considered what to do now. Searching the yearbook hadn't taken as long as he'd been afraid it might. He still had over an hour before he was supposed to meet Greg.

*You could go to the castle*, his inner voice whispered. *Talk to Lyndon. You haven't talked to him since before Christmas. Maybe you can learn something new from him by now. Besides, don't you miss him?*

Adrian almost laughed out loud. *Miss him? A ghost?*

The idea was ridiculous.

*But it's true.*

Adrian frowned at a crack in the sidewalk at his feet. Could it be true? Could he really have gotten so attached to Groome Castle's resident spirit that he actually missed talking to him? Even after he'd started a relationship with Greg?

He thought about it. And realized he did.

This time, Adrian didn't try to hold back his laughter, in spite of the strange looks it earned him from the people passing by. Somewhere along the way, he'd developed a friendship with a man who'd been dead for over one hundred years. It was either laugh at himself or go crazy, and he'd balanced on the precipice of mental breakdown enough for one lifetime.

At least his early desire to be Lyndon's lover had vanished when he started seeing Greg. He didn't think he could handle being at the center of a romantic triangle in which one party wasn't even alive.

Stuffing his hands into the front pockets of his jeans, Adrian started across campus toward the road to Groome Castle. He needed to hurry. He would likely require several minutes of quiet meditation before he could connect with Lyndon, and it was imperative that he arrive at the dining hall before Greg tonight.

*So he won't find out what you're doing. So you can keep the truth from him.*

Adrian picked up his pace and kept his head down to hide the guilt in his eyes.

Lyndon had nothing new to say, or to show. Just the same

images, over and over and over again, as tantalizing and frustrating as ever. By now, Adrian had memorized the way Cassius's eyes crinkled at the corners when he smiled, the gilded quality of the light on the bed in the tower room, the blinding surge of anger and finality that always accompanied the embroidered collar.

Adrian had come to believe the collar related somehow to Lyndon's death. Had his murderer worn it? Had that collar been the last thing Lyndon had seen before he died? The need to know burned in Adrian like nothing else ever had. But that bit of cloth with its blue flowers and the smear of dirt on the corner seemed to exist in a vacuum. If any other memories survived Lyndon's death, he wasn't sharing them. Not yet, anyway. Not until Adrian could find a way to open up the deepest parts of himself enough to let Lyndon in.

If only he could figure out how in the hell to do that.

Discouraged, Adrian trudged down the steps from the tower room, through the main hall and across the foyer. He would've liked to stay and try for a little longer, but he was out of time. Greg expected him at the dining hall in twenty minutes.

Maybe he could come back tomorrow. Both of his Wednesday classes were back to back first thing in the morning, Dr. Perez didn't need him at the lab until Friday and Greg was in class from eight until three. If he came by here just after lunch, Adrian would have a good two and a half hours to attempt communicating with Lyndon again. Hopefully the extra time would allow him to relax more. Send himself into a deeper trance. Something, *anything,* to tap into those locked-off portions of his mind he needed to access in order to learn the rest of Lyndon's secrets.

Adrian opened the front door, slipped out into the waning light and used his psychokinesis to lock the door behind him.

He hunched his shoulders against a gust of cold wind. He glanced upward. At least the predicted clouds hadn't materialized. The nearly full moon shone through the bare tree branches, providing him with plenty of light to navigate the gravel drive from the castle to the paved road. He stuffed his hands into his jacket pockets and started walking.

He hadn't gone more than a few yards when he noticed a figure approaching on the otherwise deserted lane. Frowning, he slowed his pace. Who else would be coming to the castle? There were no events going on right now, and even the most desperate students didn't come here for private moments when it was this cold. Especially since people without psychokinetic powers couldn't unlock the doors to get inside.

As the figure drew closer, it passed through a space clear of trees. The combination of the vanishing daylight and a particularly bright moonbeam picked out a familiar head of golden brown curls.

Adrian's heartbeat slowed to a hard, painful *thud-thud-thud*. He stood rooted to the ground, sick with apprehension, and waited. What else could he do?

Gravel crunched as Greg approached. "Adrian."

"Greg. What...?" Adrian swallowed. "What are you doing here?"

"I could ask you the same thing." Greg stared at him, gray eyes brimming with anger and hurt. "We need to talk."

# Chapter Fourteen

*Shit.* Adrian licked his dry lips. "You're right. Let's go to my place. We can talk there."

With a curt nod, Greg turned on his heel and stalked off down the road. Adrian followed, shaking all over with a combination of shock and gut-churning dread. He'd been caught red-handed, with no recourse but to tell Greg what he really should have told him weeks ago.

He just hoped Greg would still be around after he heard what Adrian had to say.

The walk from Groome Castle to Adrian's apartment took eons. Greg marched along at a determined pace without one word or a single glance over his shoulder. Adrian trailed meekly behind him, staring at the stiff line of his spine and wishing they could both go back in time. Just transport backward half a day to that morning, when they had lain tangled together in the warm nest of Adrian's sheets and blankets, Greg's naked body curled against Adrian's side and his head pillowed on Adrian's chest. If he could turn the clock back, Adrian mused, he would tell Greg then. He'd confess the whole thing, before Greg could find out...however it was he'd found out.

"How did you know I was at Groome Castle?" Adrian asked as they walked up the stairs to his apartment. He concentrated harder than was strictly necessary on punching in the entry code, so he wouldn't have to see Greg's face.

"Well, that's a very interesting story." Greg swept past Adrian and into the apartment as soon as he swung the door open. Instead of sitting, Greg took off his jacket, threw it on Adrian's tiny dining table and started pacing. "I got out of class early today. You'd said you were going to be studying at the library, so I decided to head over there. On the way, I ran into your friend Ryan. I mentioned where I was going, and he said to me, 'Oh, Adrian's not at the library anymore. I just saw him heading toward Groome Castle.'"

All the air rushed out of Adrian's lungs. He shut the door, shuffled to his only armchair and fell into it. "Oh."

Greg snorted. "Yeah, 'oh'. So I said, 'Groome Castle? Why would Adrian be going over there?' And Ryan says, 'Oh, he goes there all the time. Didn't you know?'" Crossing the room in a few strides, Greg grabbed the arms of Adrian's chair and leaned close, eyes blazing. "Didn't I *know*? Why, no, I did *not* know. Why is that, Adrian? Why did I not know that my boyfriend makes regular trips out to Groome Castle? Why the fuck does everyone but me know this? And what in the goddamn hell are you doing out there, anyway?" He straightened up and wrapped his arms around himself, making him look uncertain and heartbreakingly fragile. "Why did you keep this a secret from me, Adrian? Are you...are you seeing someone else?"

In his wildest nightmares, Adrian never imagined Greg would have believed he'd cheat on him. Without a second thought, Adrian jumped up and wrapped his arms around Greg's tense body. "No! God, no. There's nobody but you."

Relief shone in Greg's eyes. Nevertheless, he shook loose of Adrian's embrace, walked across the room and sat on the edge of Adrian's bed, still clutching himself as if he'd fall apart if he didn't. "What's going on, then? What's such a big deal that you couldn't tell me about it?"

An angry scowl twisted Greg's features, but the hurt came through loud and clear in his voice. Adrian's chest tightened. "I'm sorry, Greg. I should've told you earlier. It...it's nothing terrible, I don't know why I didn't tell you before. I guess it's just because you don't believe in ghosts and I figured you'd be upset, and..." Adrian made a helpless gesture with one hand. "It seems so stupid now."

Sighing, Greg rubbed a hand over his eyes. "Adrian. Just fucking *tell* me."

Adrian shut his eyes and drew a couple of slow, deep breaths. When he felt sufficiently calm, he opened his eyes again and walked over to sit beside Greg. "Okay. Just promise me you'll listen with an open mind?"

Greg studied him with narrowed eyes for a moment before giving him a brief nod. "I can't wait to hear this." Kicking off his sneakers, Greg curled his legs beneath him and pinned Adrian with an expectant stare.

"All right. Well." Adrian studied his clasped hands, trying to think of the best way to begin. "You know I saw Lyndon Groome's ghost the day you and I first met, right?"

"I know you *said* you did." Greg let out a soft laugh. "I remember thinking you were either lying or completely nuts."

"I'm not crazy." Adrian twisted his fingers together. His heart beat so fast it made him dizzy. "And I told you, I don't lie."

Silence fell. A door slammed across the hall. Footsteps pounded down the stairs outside, fading as they reached the first floor. Adrian waited, staring at his hands and forcing himself to remain still. Part of him desperately wanted to look at Greg. A larger part of him dreaded seeing the expression on Greg's face.

"Let me see if I understand what you're telling me," Greg

said at last, his voice far calmer than Adrian had expected. "You're telling me that you really did see a ghost that day. No lie."

"Lyndon Groome's ghost, yes." Adrian glanced at Greg. His face was unnervingly blank.

Greg nodded. "How do you know that?"

Surprised, Adrian turned sideways and tucked one leg underneath him on the bed. "What?"

"How do you know it was Lyndon Groome's ghost?"

"Well, um..." Adrian scratched his neck, feeling self-conscious. "He told me."

One pale eyebrow lifted. "He told you."

"Uh. Yeah."

"The ghost."

"Yes." Adrian crossed his arms and fought down a rising tide of indignation. "You knew I could communicate with spirits. I haven't mentioned it or demonstrated it again around you, because I know it makes you uncomfortable and because I know you don't believe in it, but I haven't made any secret of my abilities either." *Not those abilities, at least.* Adrian squashed the niggling guilt before it could get a foothold. He wanted to tell Greg about his psychokinesis, but now wasn't the time. There may never be a time for that. "There's no need for you to sound so...*snide* about it."

Greg's cheeks flushed and his eyes darkened, and Adrian steeled himself for a bitter argument. He hated it, but he didn't know what else to do. He no longer allowed anyone to talk down to him. Even if he should have told Greg about Lyndon earlier, he couldn't allow Greg to become an exception to one of his most important rules just because he cared for him.

When Greg slumped forward with a long sigh and rested

his head on Adrian's shoulder, Adrian had to bite back a whoop of relief. He shifted into a more comfortable position, wound his arms around Greg's back and rested his cheek against Greg's hair. Greg smelled like the winter cold. Adrian breathed it deep into his lungs with a smile.

"I'm sorry," Greg mumbled against Adrian's neck. "You realize we haven't discussed this whole ghost thing at all since that night at Groome Castle, right? How you believe it and I don't, I mean."

Adrian's stomach flip-flopped. "I know."

"Mm." Greg unfolded his legs, stretched one across the bed and planted the other foot on the floor. "We probably should."

"Probably." *God, that's not going to be pretty.* Just because the last fight they'd had about ghosts had ended in mind-blowing sex didn't mean the next one would. They'd both been tense as an overfilled balloon at that point. They could've read their grocery lists aloud and it would've ended in sex.

Greg's hands wandered up Adrian's back and clutched his sweater hard. "I don't want to talk about it right now, Adrian. I think this is the wrong time."

Relieved, Adrian nuzzled the silky skin just behind Greg's ear. "I think you're right. We should wait a while. Put tonight behind us. Then we'll sit down and talk it all out once and for all. Okay?"

"Sure." Lifting his face, Greg captured Adrian's mouth in a slow, sweet kiss that made his chest ache. When they drew apart, Greg sat back with a calm but determined expression. "All right. So, you were saying that you talked to the ghost. Is that why you keep going out to the castle? Are you still talking to it?"

"Yeah. But the thing is, it's more than just a simple conversation. I've gotten..." Adrian frowned at the wall, searching for the right way to explain it. "Well, I guess you could say that a few times when I've talked to Lyndon, he's shown me some of his memories. But it's nothing coherent. Just bits and pieces. If I can figure out what I'm seeing, I might be able to find out what happened to him. How he died. I may even be able to find his body, and if I can do that, maybe the school can give him a proper burial and put his spirit to rest. So that's what I've been doing all this time. Trying to communicate with Lyndon. Trying to see what else I can learn about his death, so that I can help him move on."

Greg hid his disbelief well. Adrian would give him that. But Adrian knew Greg well enough to see it anyway. Not that it mattered. He hadn't expected Greg to actually believe everything he said was the literal truth. What he *did* expect was for Greg to know *he* believed it, and to respect *that* truth. He waited, gazing into Greg's eyes with as much calm as he could muster.

After what felt like forever but probably wasn't more than a minute or two, Greg blew out a breath. "Okay. So, you've been trying to solve the mystery of the Groome Castle ghost." He gave Adrian a weak smile. "I guess that's better than you sneaking off to fuck some other guy behind my back."

Torn between relief and worry, Adrian scooted closer and touched Greg's cheek. "Greg, you didn't really think I'd cheat on you, did you?"

Greg shrugged, the very picture of nonchalance, but Adrian saw his answer in the way Greg's gaze slid away to study the bedside table. He'd believed, however briefly, that Adrian was seeing someone else, and he'd been visibly relieved to learn that it wasn't true. Something about that fact gave Adrian's insides a peculiar deep-down quiver.

He traced Greg's jaw with his fingers. The pale stubble tickled his fingertips. "I'd never do that. Never. I don't want anyone but you. Okay?"

"Sure." The answer sounded casual, but Greg's head remained bowed and his fingers toyed nervously with a hole in the knee of his jeans.

Cupping Greg's chin in his palm, Adrian lifted Greg's face. Greg's eyes cut sideways to avoid Adrian's gaze. Adrian shook his head. "Greg. Look at me."

Greg obeyed with obvious reluctance. His face wore the expressionless mask he used when he wanted to hide how he felt, but a storm of relief, confusion and lingering hurt swirled in his eyes. For a moment, Adrian felt as if he were staring into a mirror image of his own tortured eleven-year-old psyche, trying to make sense of all the half-truths and outright lies being flung at him from all sides.

In that moment, Adrian realized in a blinding flash of insight exactly what he'd done, and the shame of it nearly gutted him.

Framing Greg's face in his hands, Adrian leaned their foreheads together. "I never cheated on you," he whispered, his voice hoarse. "But I did lie to you. I deliberately hid from you what I was doing, and tried to tell myself that it wasn't lying, it was just not telling you everything. But it *was* lying, because the whole point was to keep my secret from you. For you not to find out. And that was wrong, it was against everything I believe in. Worse than that, I broke my promise to you, and I am so, so sorry." He stroked a thumb over Greg's cheekbone. "Can you forgive me? Can you give me another chance?"

Greg let out a soft sound. His hands came up to clasp the back of Adrian's neck. Tilting his head, he kissed Adrian in a way that signaled the end of any conversation for the night.

It wasn't exactly the answer Adrian was looking for, but it *was* an answer, and he accepted it as such. He'd learned long ago that Greg communicated physically rather than verbally more often than not. If he was still angry, he wouldn't have his tongue in Adrian's mouth, his fingers wouldn't be creeping into Adrian's hair and he definitely wouldn't be making that hungry noise in the back of his throat. Adrian opened wide for Greg and let his rising arousal wash through him.

By the time Greg broke the kiss and shoved Adrian onto his back, he was so hard it hurt. He opened his legs and moaned when Greg's weight pressed their erections together. Greg shoved Adrian's sweater up to his armpits. "Off."

Adrian grasped the hem of the sweater and pulled it over his head. In the midst of wrestling it over his elbows, Greg bent and sucked Adrian's left nipple. Adrian moaned, his back arching off the mattress. "God."

"Mmm." Wriggling downward, Greg mouthed the crotch of Adrian's jeans. "These need to come off too."

In his haste to get his shoes off, Adrian almost kicked Greg in the head. Greg laughed. Adrian yanked off his sneakers, then nudged Greg's forehead with one sock-clad toe. "I don't see what's so funny."

"You are. So anxious for me to suck your cock that you almost knock me out before I can do it." Grinning, Greg flipped open the button on Adrian's jeans and tugged down the zipper. "Is this what you want, Adrian?" He eased the worn denim down over Adrian's hips, taking his underwear with it, then leaned forward and kissed the tip of his prick. "You want me to suck your cock?" Holding Adrian's gaze, he traced his tongue under the flared head of Adrian's glans in a slow, lazy circle. "You want me to swallow your dick all the way down? Hm? I bet you want to come in my mouth, don't you?"

Adrian bit his lip and nodded, unable to speak. God, but it undid him when Greg talked dirty like that. He was pretty sure

Greg wouldn't consider what he'd just said particularly dirty, but Christian had *never* talked that way to Adrian during sex, and it excited him beyond belief.

Sitting back on his heels, Greg slid Adrian's jeans down his thighs. Adrian lifted his legs into the air so Greg could maneuver the garment down his calves, over his ankles and off. Greg tossed the whole thing over his shoulder, then went to work on his own clothes.

Adrian sat up to help him. Between them, they got Greg's sweatshirt off and his jeans unbuttoned. Distracted by the scent of Greg's skin, Adrian paused to suck up a mark on his neck just below his jaw, one hand fisted in his hair and the other bumping into Greg's as they both fumbled with his zipper.

Greg chuckled, the sound rumbling against Adrian's lips. "Stop helping, you're getting in the way."

"But I want your cock." Adrian bit Greg's neck and grinned when he yelped.

"Move and I'll give it to you." Greg shoved Adrian's hand out of the way. "Greedy bastard."

Adrian fell back onto his elbows, legs splayed obscenely wide just for the pleasure of watching the desire ignite in Greg's eyes. "Hurry. I...I want to suck you while you suck me."

Greg's eyebrows shot up. Heat flooded Adrian's face, but he held Greg's gaze without flinching. For all his blunt honesty in other areas, Adrian rarely talked during sex. He'd certainly never said anything as direct as what he had just now. It made him feel horribly vulnerable. But he loved the way it made Greg look at him—as if he wanted to eat him alive.

Rising onto his knees, Greg shimmied his jeans and underwear down as far as he could, then plopped onto his butt, yanked the clothes off and threw them on the floor. Naked at last, he stretched himself out over Adrian's body. A lazy flex of his hips slid his bare cock against Adrian's. He swallowed Adrian's groan with a kiss.

Adrian planted one hand on Greg's ass, buried the other in his hair and thrust upward. Electricity skated over Adrian's skin. He whimpered into Greg's mouth. God, at this rate he was going to come inside of two minutes.

Greg tore his mouth from Adrian's and pushed up on his hands. "Sorry, but if we don't stop now and rearrange ourselves the fun's gonna be over before it starts."

"I was just thinking the same thing." Smiling, Adrian ran his palms down Greg's sides and grasped his hipbones. "This is fun, though."

"Definitely." Greg leaned down and nipped Adrian's lower lip. "But you mentioned a sixty-nine." He licked away the faint sting where his teeth had dug in, then kissed the end of Adrian's nose. "Once a sixty-nine has been suggested, there's no going back."

"Oh, I see." Adrian slid one hand between Greg's thighs to cup his balls. "Didn't know that was a rule."

"Mm-hm. You learn something new every day." A shudder ran the length of Greg's back when Adrian's fingers curled around his shaft. He moaned, his head lolling downward and his eyelids fluttering. "Jesus, Adrian. Stop, or I'm gonna come."

Adrian stifled a smirk. In the time they'd been together, he'd perfected the art of enhancing his touch with a jolt of psychokinesis. As long as he never completely let himself go during sex, his abilities remained fully under his control and he could use them to ramp up the pleasure for Greg without putting him in danger. Of course it meant holding back a part of himself during an act which ought to be about sharing oneself completely, but he could live with that if it meant keeping Greg safe.

He swiped the pad of his thumb across the head of Greg's cock as his hand dropped away. Greg's body jerked. A droplet of precome clung to Adrian's thumb. He stuck it in his mouth and sucked off the still-warm fluid, staring into Greg's eyes.

Groaning, Greg pushed up until he sat astride Adrian's hips. "If you want to suck something, suck my cock." He turned around to face Adrian's feet and scooted backward until his genitals swung above Adrian's face. "Thumb-sucking tease."

"I never tease." Adrian snaked an arm around Greg's hips. "Come here."

Greg's knees slid apart. Adrian took Greg's cock in his hand and guided it into his mouth. Just as he relaxed his throat to take Greg as deep as he could, he felt Greg's warm, wet mouth engulf the head of his prick and glide down the shaft. With a strangled grunt, Adrian spread his legs as wide as they would go and wriggled his butt, hoping Greg would get the hint. He loved it when Greg fingered his ass while sucking him off.

As usual, Greg got the message. The wet heat drew away from Adrian's cock. He heard a slurping sound. A second later, two slick fingers penetrated him and made a beeline for his prostate. He dug his hands into Greg's thighs and managed an appreciative sound in spite of his mouthful.

Greg laughed, the sound rough and breathless. "I'm getting you a dildo for your birthday."

Adrian had half a second to wonder if Greg was serious. Then that mind-scrambling suction was back on Adrian's cock and he forgot about everything but the wet heat of Greg's mouth and the sweet torture of Greg's fingers battering his gland.

It felt incredible, just as it always did when Greg sucked him. Better, in fact. He'd never engaged in simultaneous oral sex before, but if it was always like this, they were going to have to do it more often. Being sucked off while his mouth was full of cock had to be one of the most intense things he'd ever experienced.

So intense, in fact, that he felt the need to come building low in his belly after mere minutes, and that just wouldn't do. He wanted this to *last*. Closing his eyes, Adrian concentrated on the faint salty flavor of Greg's skin, his musky scent, the hard length of his cock sliding in and out of Adrian's throat. He ran both palms up and down Greg's thighs, paying close attention to the way the hairs tickled his palms. Tiny tremors shook the hard muscles when Greg rocked back into his touch.

Once he felt more in control of himself, Adrian slid one hand up over the swell of Greg's ass and rubbed his thumb over Greg's hole with the light, gentle touch he knew Greg loved. The tiny opening pulsed in response. Greg moaned around Adrian's cock. The vibrations sent shockwaves up Adrian's shaft directly into his brain. His psychokinesis reacted with a blast of energy that raised gooseflesh all over his body and wrenched his orgasm from him with such violence that his hips snapped upward and smacked Greg in the chin.

Through the pulse-pounding haze of his release, he was vaguely aware of Greg's fingers pulling out of his ass, Greg's hands holding his hips firmly to the bed, Greg's skilled and determined mouth sucking him dry. Only when Adrian's prick started to go soft did Greg finally let it slip from his lips. He rested his cheek against Adrian's belly.

Adrian would've laughed if he hadn't had his mouth full. So much for making it last.

"Adrian," Greg panted. His breath felt cool against Adrian's wet, still-sensitive cock. "So close."

The raw need in Greg's voice made Adrian feel better. At least he wasn't the only one who couldn't keep it together for more than a few minutes tonight.

Without the distraction of Greg's mouth on him, Adrian was free to concentrate on nothing but getting Greg off. Circling the base of Greg's shaft with a thumb and forefinger and keeping the other hand on Greg's butt, Adrian guided Greg's cock deep into his throat. He swallowed around the head a couple of times—a difficult trick to learn, but worth it for the way it made Greg cry out in agonized bliss—then drew back, sucking as hard as he could.

That was all it took. Greg's hips whip-cracked forward and he came with a low, pitiful whine, shaking all over. Adrian gagged, grasped Greg by the hipbones and pushed him up until just the head of his cock remained in Adrian's mouth. Eyes watering, Adrian swallowed as best he could. The overflow leaked out the corners of his mouth to trickle down his neck.

He couldn't bring himself to care. Sixty-nine, he decided, was absolutely the most brilliant invention in the known universe. He'd damn well learn how to be on the bottom and not gag, just as long as they got to do this on a regular basis.

Turning his head, he let Greg's cock slip from his mouth and grinned. "Was it good for you?"

Greg let out a satisfied sigh. "Oh, my God. You're such a smart-ass."

"And you apparently wouldn't know a direct answer if it hit you upside the head, so I'm taking that as a yes." Adrian gave Greg's ass a smack. "Come up here."

"Can't move," came the muttered answer from the vicinity of Adrian's groin.

"Yes, you can." Tilting his head just so, he snagged the head of Greg's cock very, very gently between his teeth. Greg squeaked and tried to squirm away. Adrian let go before Greg could hurt himself. "Come on, Greg."

"Fine." Grumbling under his breath, Greg pushed up on his hands, turned himself around and snuggled against Adrian's chest. He grinned, gray eyes sparkling. "You look like a porn star."

Adrian took in Greg's flushed face, swollen lips and wildly tangled hair with amusement. "You're one to talk." He arched an eyebrow. "You have a little something at the corner of your mouth, just there." Grabbing Greg's face in both hands, Adrian pulled him close and licked off the bit of semen drying at the edge of his lip.

Greg laughed. "Man, I am not even pointing out the obvious here." He ducked his head and lapped the stream of fluid from one side of Adrian's neck, then the other. That task accomplished, he leaned in and shared it with Adrian in a long, lazy kiss. When they drew apart, Greg licked his lips. "Mmm. I do love make-up sex."

*Make-up sex.* Adrian's heart lurched. For a while there, he'd almost forgotten why Greg was here in the first place, and the seriousness of the fight they'd had. Now, it all came rushing back. He'd fucked up, badly, and he had to make sure it never happened again. What he had with Greg was too important to lose. Not for Lyndon, not for *anyone.*

Framing Greg's face between his hands, Adrian gazed into his eyes. "It was great sex. But I don't want to have any more reasons for make-up sex. I swear to you, right now, that I won't hide anything else from you, ever. I screwed up, and I don't intend to ever let that happen again."

Something flickered in Greg's eyes and vanished before Adrian could pin a name on it. Greg smiled, his expression warm and open. "We all fuck up sometimes, Adrian. It's okay." He brushed a stray lock of hair from Adrian's eyes. "Can I stay with you tonight?"

Adrian's throat tightened. "Of course you can. You can always stay here, you know that."

"Yeah, I know. I just like to hear you say it." Greg pressed a light kiss to Adrian's lips, then pushed to a sitting position. "I'm hungry. Let's get cleaned up and go eat, huh?"

Right on cue, Adrian's stomach growled. "Spinach lasagna in the dining hall tonight. Let's go."

Greg jumped up and pulled Adrian to his feet. They headed to the bathroom hand in hand. As they climbed into the shower together and Greg melted into his arms, Adrian felt a swell of hope. Maybe everything would be all right after all.

# Chapter Fifteen

The next day, Adrian joined some of his classmates at Alpine Bagel for lunch since Greg was busy, then headed to Groome Castle to try connecting with Lyndon once more. He hummed to himself as he strolled up the gravel road. It felt good to have the whole thing out in the open. He wondered if that honesty would make a difference in his attempts to communicate with Lyndon. Maybe the stress of keeping secrets—*lying*, he reminded himself—had been holding him back all this time. Now that he'd come clean with Greg, maybe he'd be able to break through the last barrier and find the final pieces to the puzzle of Lyndon's death.

Inside the tower room, he settled cross-legged on the cold stone floor and closed his eyes. He drew a couple of slow, deep breaths and relaxed his control over his psychokinesis. All the hairs on his arms stood up as his power crackled through the air. "Lyndon? Are you here?"

When he felt the telltale warmth pulse through him a heartbeat later, he didn't even try to hold back his laughter. He opened his eyes and smiled at Lyndon, who hovered a few feet away. "Hello, Lyndon. I hope you feel like talking today, because I'm ready to listen. More ready than I've ever been."

Lyndon's pale eyes fixed him with the same melancholy stare as always. The phantom lips moved, shaping the only word Lyndon ever spoke—*Cassius...*

The name echoed in Adrian's head, along with a sense of loneliness and loss so huge it made his throat ache with the threat of tears. He blinked away the sting behind his eyelids. "I'm trying, Lyndon. I'm looking for Cassius, so I can hopefully find out what happened to you. But the quickest way for me to do that would be for you to *show* me. I know you remember. We're both going to have to try harder, that's all."

Lyndon didn't answer, but Adrian thought his gaze sharpened a little.

Adrian's pulse quickened in response. He forced it to slow down again. If he was to accomplish his goal today, he couldn't afford anything less than complete relaxation.

"I'm going to go into a trance state now. I'm going to try to go deeper than I have before, and give you more access to my mind. I want you to show me everything you remember. Okay?" Adrian studied Lyndon's translucent features, trying to determine whether or not he understood. His expression didn't change, but then again it rarely did. All Adrian could do was try and hope for the best. He smiled. "All right. Here we go."

Adrian closed his eyes and began the breathing exercises designed to open his subconscious mind. To his delight, the semi-trance state he sought came easier to him than it had in months. It only took a few moments for his body to relax and his mind to focus inward. His awareness of the world around him drifted away until he no longer noticed the room's damp chill, and the susurration of the wind through the branches outside became nothing more than a whisper at the edge of consciousness.

As reality faded, Lyndon's presence grew more solid, until Adrian swore he could almost hear the faint patter of blood on stone and the soft sound of Lyndon's breathing. Adrian concentrated on the thread of Lyndon's energy intertwined with his own and forced all other thoughts from his mind. There was no hurry. He had time. Impatience would only destroy the fragile connection between himself and Lyndon. Stillness strengthened that bond. He pictured his mind as an empty crystal bowl, waiting to be filled with Lyndon's memories, and prepared himself to wait as long as necessary.

Before long, the familiar visions began to flow from Lyndon to him. Adrian watched them as they flickered past, allowed the associated emotions to wash through him and let them go. He'd studied those images in his memory until he knew them as well as he knew the family photos hanging on the walls of his apartment. They held no surprises, nothing new for him to learn.

Adrian breathed in through his nose for a slow count of four, then blew the air out of his lungs through pursed lips for a slower count of five. He did it again, and kept going. By the sixth repetition, his head began to buzz. By the time he lost count, he'd managed a deeper trance state than he'd ever been able to achieve in the past.

Floating in the depths of his own subconscious, he became aware of the urgent push of Lyndon's mind against his. The last of his mental barriers dropped, and he let out an inarticulate cry as a barrage of new images assaulted him...

*...Passing Cassius on the street. A nod, a cool hello, trying to hide the instant flare of love and desire, but God it's so hard when that same desire burns in his eyes too...*

*..."Dirty queer!" A punch to the jaw, another to the gut. Left bruised and bloodied in the alley behind the bar. Cassius curses the two strangers to hell when he finds out, and heals the wounds with gentle kisses...*

*...Lightning, bright white and jagged. Tower stabbing the*

199

*night sky. Bare trees thrashing the castle walls...*

*..."I'm Cassius. Pleased to meet you, Lyndon."...*

*...Leaving, together. Tomorrow. Surely there's a place in this world where men like them can go and not be afraid all the time. Cassius thinks perhaps California...*

*...Rain. Wind. Wet earth. Branches overhead...*

*...White collar. Blue flowers. Smear of dirt on the corner. A stubbled cheek, tendons straining in a sweat-beaded neck, thin lips pulled back in a rictus of fury. Agony drowns the anger and fear, then everything blurs and goes black...*

Adrian came back to himself with tears running down his face. He drew a shaking breath. The final image still lingered, burned onto his retinas. He wondered if he'd ever stop seeing it or feeling the horrible sense of finality that went along with it.

Opening his eyes, he met Lyndon's inscrutable gaze. "I was right, wasn't I? That's when you died. That collar is the last thing you saw."

Lyndon didn't answer—didn't react at all, in fact—but he didn't need to. Adrian knew the truth. He'd felt the sickening crunch of Lyndon's skull cracking, the impotent wrath and panic in the seconds before Lyndon lost consciousness, when he'd realized he was about to die.

"I could almost see his face. Almost." Adrian scrubbed the moisture from his cheeks. "Okay. Wow. I think that's as much as I can handle today, Lyndon. I'm sorry."

Unsurprisingly, Lyndon rendered no opinion one way or the other regarding Adrian's announcement. However, when Adrian rose to leave, Lyndon hovered before him with one bloodied palm out and his colorless eyes staring straight into Adrian's. The ghostly lips moved, but made no sound.

Adrian shook his head. "I'm sorry. I don't understand. If I

was still in a trance state—"

His words dissolved into a strangled gasp when Lyndon's diaphanous form rushed forward and plunged straight into Adrian's chest.

Unlike Lyndon's psychic energy, his physical manifestation felt icy cold. Adrian's body went instantly numb. His breath froze. Yet inside him, deep in his heart and brain and belly, Lyndon's warmth burned like a supernova.

*"Help me,"* a low voice whispered in Adrian's head. *"Find me. Release me."*

As quickly as it had happened, it was over. The sensation of cold and heat and another mind inside his own vanished, and Adrian could breathe again. He bent over and rested his hands on his knees until his head stopped spinning.

When he straightened up again, Lyndon was nowhere to be seen. Adrian didn't bother calling for him. He knew from experience that it wouldn't do any good.

"Goodbye, Lyndon." He raked a hand through his hair. "I don't know when I'll get to come back, but I hope it'll be soon. Maybe this weekend."

Adrian studied the empty room. Sunshine poured through the tall, narrow windows, making the room glow with the same pale golden light it had in Lyndon's memories. The connection between Lyndon's past and his own present made Adrian smile.

With one last look around, Adrian strode to the door and started down the stairs. He had so much to tell Greg.


Greg was still in one of his theater classes when Adrian returned to campus from Groome Castle. It was too cold to wait in the deep shade of the old cemetery's gazebo like he usually did. Instead, he stretched out in a sunny spot on the grass just inside the wall surrounding the graveyard. He had at least forty-five minutes to wait before Greg got out of class, but he didn't mind. A little quiet time in the sunshine to assimilate what he'd just experienced would be a good thing.

The time passed quickly. Adrian was drifting in a pleasant doze, trying to remember why the bit of square jaw in Lyndon's memory seemed familiar to him, when something nudged his ribs. He cracked his eyelids open and squinted up at the person-shaped shadow looming over him. "Hi, Greg."

"Hey." Dropping onto the grass, Greg tucked both legs beneath him. He grinned. "So. What's up? You taking a nap?"

"Nope. Just thinking."

"I see. The college intellectual ponders the mysteries of life while lounging in a graveyard." Greg nodded, his expression dead serious.

Adrian laughed. "Something like that." He sat up, leaned forward and kissed Greg's lips. "I went back to Groome Castle today to talk to Lyndon. I think I made a real breakthrough this time. I'm pretty sure I experienced the moment of his death. I even saw a part of his killer's face. A few more visits, and I think I could actually see enough to be able to identify the person who killed him."

The smile froze to Greg's face. "Oh, really? That's great."

Greg's expression spoke the exact opposite of his words. Adrian's excitement shriveled. He forced himself to speak calmly instead of letting his disappointment turn him waspish.

"Greg, I appreciate what you're trying to do, honestly. But I don't want you to lie to *me* either." Taking Greg's hand, Adrian wove their fingers together. "You obviously don't think what I just said is great. Something about it bothers you. Please tell me what it is."

Greg's shoulders slumped. He fixed Adrian with a guilty

look. "I'm sorry, I really am. It's just that all this stuff about talking to ghosts and experiencing somebody else's death..." He shook his head. "It sounds crazy, Adrian. You have to know it does."

That hurt, even though Adrian knew Greg didn't mean it like it sounded. "That's why I don't usually tell people. They tend to think I'm crazy."

"I don't think that." Greg's eyes searched Adrian's face. "I know you're not crazy. In fact, you might be the sanest person I've ever met. Which just makes it harder to understand when you start telling me about how you've been talking to a ghost and experiencing his death. It's just...disturbing."

Adrian stared at his and Greg's entwined hands, his mind racing. When they'd first started seeing each other, revealing the secret of his psychokinesis to Greg hadn't really been something he'd considered. After all, no one but his family and the BCPI team knew. The few friends he'd made in school had never known. He'd never even told Christian. As far as Adrian was concerned, no one would ever need to know except a long-term partner, and since he'd never expected to have one, he'd been content to leave his secret where it was.

No, he'd had no firm plans to tell Greg, in spite of the vague guilt that prodded him now and then. Yet here he was, at the point where he knew he had to do what he'd never done in his life—tell another human being his entire, unvarnished history, including the truth about his psychokinetic abilities.

The idea terrified him. He swallowed, his throat dry as dust.

Gathering all his courage, he lifted his gaze to meet Greg's. "I think it's time I told you a few things about myself, and my past. So that you'll understand why I can talk to spirits and maybe understand *me* a little better too."

Apprehension crept into Greg's eyes. "What're you talking about? What kinds of things?"

"That's kind of hard to explain without really getting into it." Adrian took a good look around. The sidewalk beside South Road, on the far side of the cemetery, was as crowded as ever with people passing back and forth. The one running not fifteen feet from where he and Greg sat wasn't nearly as busy. A girl in green and black striped leggings loped down the pathway through the graveyard. Other than her, Greg and Adrian, the cemetery was empty. "We can talk here if you want, or go back to my place."

Greg shrugged. "Here's fine with me, if it's okay with you. You're the one who's going to be talking about private stuff."

"All right, we'll talk here." Adrian drew a shaky breath. "I'm really nervous about this. I've never told anyone else what I'm about to tell you."

Greg shifted his position. He looked distinctly uncomfortable. "Adrian, you don't have to tell me if you don't want to. There's no rule that says people have to know every single thing about each other just because they're in a relationship."

"No, it's okay. I've thought about it, and I really think I should tell you this." He smiled, trying to look as though his heart wasn't trying to hammer its way through his sternum. "I *want* to tell you."

For a second, the indefinable *something* Adrian had been glimpsing since Christmas glinted in Greg's eyes, then vanished before Adrian could pin it down. Greg rubbed his thumb over the back of Adrian's hand. "Okay. I'm listening."

"When I was ten," Adrian began, "Sam came to work for my dad's paranormal investigations company. Not long after that, my parents separated and Dad moved out. A few months later, when I was eleven, Mom and Dad divorced, and I found out my father was gay and in love with Sam. The two of them moved in together around the same time my parents got divorced."

"Wow." Scooting closer, Greg rested his free hand on Adrian's knee. "That must've been tough for you and your brother to deal with when you were so young."

"Sean rolled with it like he does with everything." One corner of Adrian's mouth curled upward. "You know me, though. You won't be surprised to hear that I didn't handle it so well."

Greg didn't laugh, or even smile. "You were only eleven. Just a kid." He lifted Adrian's hand and kissed his knuckles. "What happened?"

*This is it.* Adrian took a moment to center himself and calm his racing pulse while he thought of the quickest, easiest way to say what he needed to say.

The straight truth won. "Strange things started happening to me. If I got angry, objects around me would move by themselves, or even break. In my room at my mom's house, I would sometimes see...things. Very weird, frightening things. Things that didn't belong there."

Greg's brows drew together. "Adrian—"

"No, wait. I know it sounds weird, just...let me finish. Let me tell you the whole thing before I lose my nerve."

Something uncomfortably close to pity softened Greg's expression. "All right. Go on."

Adrian squeezed Greg's hand to convey his thanks. "My mom didn't believe me when I told her what I was seeing. She blamed my dad and Sam because of all the stress of the divorce and Dad being gay and all. At first, I thought she was right, that I was imagining all of it. I thought I was going crazy."

"God, Adrian." Greg's hand tightened on Adrian's knee.

Afraid that if he stopped he'd never again have the nerve to finish his story, Adrian plowed on. "Then something happened when my dad and Sam were there. I had gotten in trouble at school, and my dad was trying to talk to me about it. I was *furious,* and a bulb in the overhead light just broke. That's when Dad and Sam figured out that I had developed psychokinesis, which is the ability to make things move with your mind. Sam has the same ability. I wasn't able to control it, and to make a really long story short enough to tell in an afternoon, I ended up accidentally opening a portal into another dimension in my mother's house the night before Thanksgiving, two thousand and five, when I was eleven. Something came through. It almost killed my whole family before Sam helped me send the thing back where it came from and close the portal." Adrian let out a short bark of a laugh. "Wow. It feels so strange to say that out loud. It sounds so surreal."

Through this speech, Greg had remained still and silent. He twisted his hand free from Adrian's grip and stood. "Okay. Well, that was some story. Why don't you call me when you're ready to stop jerking me around, huh?" Spinning on his heel, he strode off toward the path leading through the cemetery toward South Road.

Shocked, Adrian scrambled to his feet, lunged after Greg and caught his arm. "Greg, I'm telling the truth. I know it all sounds strange, but I swear it's all true." He grasped Greg's shoulders when he broke away and spun him around to stare hard into his eyes. "You have to believe me. Please."

Greg shook off Adrian's grip and backed up. His eyes glittered with a painful war between the desire to believe Adrian and the obvious fear of being the butt of a joke. "I thought you were going to tell me you'd had some kind of psychotic break, or...or something. Something *real.* And...and then you tell me *this* shit?" He shook his head. "Fuck you."

Adrian hadn't known mere words could hurt so much. He'd laid himself bare for Greg, told him things no one else knew, and Greg had done the verbal equivalent of cutting out Adrian's heart with a dull razor.

Mortification and anger twisted into a burning knot in Adrian's belly. He felt his heart rate increase, his breath coming faster. Electricity sizzled over his skin, and he knew his control was slipping.

For once, he didn't care. If Greg refused to believe the truth in words, maybe he'd believe his own eyes.

"I don't lie," Adrian growled, eyes narrowed. "Hold still."

"What the f—" Greg's words cut off with a sharp hiss of intaken breath as the zipper on his jacket undid itself.

Gathering every ounce of his concentration, Adrian used his psychokinesis to yank Greg's jacket down to his elbows and hold it there. He tugged on the jacket arms, forcing Greg's hands to crisscross over the front of his body and plant themselves on the opposite hip. A thought tightened the leather until it dug into Greg's flesh.

Greg let out a tiny, distressed sound. "Adrian. Stop."

Adrian couldn't help the surge of triumph he felt. "Do you believe me now?"

"Yes." Greg licked his lips. "S-stop. Please. It hurts."

Fear threaded through Greg's voice. Adrian took one look at Greg's dead white face, and the enormity of what he'd just done hit him like a concrete block to the head.

Adrian dropped his psychokinetic control of the jacket. Greg's arms flopped to his sides. The jacket slithered downward. The arms turned inside out, the cuffs catching on Greg's wrists. Greg stood still, staring at a spot somewhere over

Adrian's left shoulder.

"Greg? Are you okay?" Closing the distance between them, Adrian reached out to touch Greg's cheek. Greg flinched away, and Adrian's stomach rolled over. "I'm sorry. I didn't mean to hurt you."

Greg's gaze focused on Adrian's face, and the sheen of fear in those gray eyes tore at Adrian's heart. "Harrison never did either."

*Oh, God.* Adrian rubbed both hands over his face. He supposed it had been selfish of him to hope Greg wouldn't make that connection. "I'm so sorry," Adrian repeated, his voice cracking. "I just...just wanted you to believe me. That's all. I have excellent control over my...my abilities. It'll never happen again, I promise."

"You're right, it won't." Greg shrugged his jacket back on. His hands shook. "Goodbye. Don't call me."

Adrian stared, stunned into silence, as Greg turned on his heel and started walking. It wasn't until Greg stepped onto the path toward South Road that Adrian realized Greg was leaving him. *Leaving him.* Maybe for good.

Panic spurred Adrian into action. He ran after Greg. "Wait!"

Greg didn't even slow his pace. "Go away, Adrian."

"But if you'd just listen for a minute." Adrian stretched out his arm and brushed his fingers over Greg's shoulder.

Greg shook off Adrian's hand, whirled around and pinned Adrian with a furious glare. "Don't you fucking *touch* me. Don't talk to me, just..." Tears welled up and spilled down his cheeks. He dashed them away with a couple of sharp, angry movements, then turned his back to Adrian. "Just leave me alone."

Watching Greg walk away and not stopping him was the

hardest thing Adrian had ever done, but he clenched his hands at his sides and forced himself to do it. With every step Greg took, Adrian's heart squeezed harder, faster. His breath came in short, shallow gasps. The rush of blood in his skull drowned out the noise of the traffic on South Road and the sigh of the wind through the branches overhead.

When Greg turned the corner onto the South Road sidewalk without a single glance in Adrian's direction and strode out of sight, the shields keeping Adrian's psychokinesis reined in shivered under a wave of despair like he hadn't felt in more than a decade.

Adrian spun and started running. He didn't think about his destination, just let instinct drive him forward. His vision blurred, his feet faltered, but it didn't matter. Nothing mattered but reaching the one place he knew he would be safe.

The "walk" signal went off before he got to the crosswalk on the far side of the theater. He darted through the intersection anyway. A powerful blast of mental energy slowed the traffic barreling from either direction enough to keep him from being crushed. He reached the opposite sidewalk with the blare of horns cutting through the static in his ears. His shoulder collided with a broad, suit-clad chest. He swerved sideways and stumbled down the tree-lined street, chased by the faint buzz of the man's curses.

As Adrian approached, Groome Castle's front door unlocked itself and swung open so hard it hit the wall with a bang. Adrian bolted through the foyer and toward the tower room stairs without slowing down. The door slammed shut behind him.

He hit the steps at a dead run, took them two at a time, flung open the door at the top with a twist of his mind and skidded to a halt in the middle of the room, panting. "Lyndon?

God, please be here. I need you."

A swirl of dust turned in the sunbeam pouring through the southernmost window. The silence felt barren.

Squeezing his eyes shut, Adrian dropped his mental shields, leaving his psyche naked to whatever forces the castle contained. A vague sense of sorrow lapped at his mind like cold, dark water. It seemed to emanate from the stone all around, as if the castle itself had absorbed the emotions experienced here.

Twenty-four hours earlier, Adrian would've found the phenomenon fascinating. Now, he didn't care. He needed the only being in the entire universe who knew what he was capable of and not only wouldn't judge him for it, but couldn't be injured by whatever his uncontrolled psychokinesis might do.

Adrian let his senses expand the way Sam had taught him all those years ago. Electricity crackled through the air. His hair swirled around his head. At the edges of consciousness, a dim, scattered spark pulsed. Lyndon, Adrian realized after a moment's hard concentration. Communicating with Adrian earlier must have rendered him unable to manifest physically, this soon at least. Adrian had no idea how long it would be, but at the moment it didn't matter. He needed Lyndon *now*, not later.

All this time, he'd been helping Lyndon. Doing his best to find out what had happened to him, so that he could locate Lyndon's body and lay him to rest, allowing his spirit to move on. In fact, Adrian's work with Lyndon had been a major factor in Greg leaving him.

The resentment simmering in Adrian's gut exploded into blind fury. Opening his eyes, he threw his head back and screamed at the ceiling. "You fucker! You should *be* here for me!" The light bulb in the old-fashioned fixture overhead shattered. Instead of falling to the floor, the glass shards surrounded Adrian in a glittering whirlwind. "He left me, Lyndon! Greg fucking left me. Because of *you*. Because of *this*."

*Because of you, Adrian. Because you couldn't control your anger. It's always been about that, hasn't it? Your family almost died ten years ago because you couldn't control your anger. And now you drove away the first man you ever loved because you couldn't control it. You have no one to blame but yourself, and you know it.*

Adrian stood stock-still, staring wide-eyed out the window at a crooked branch as the realization of what he truly felt sank in.

He wondered if it would've made any difference if he'd figured it out earlier.

The urge to bare his throat to the blur of glass tempted him so strongly he took a step forward, neck arched, before forcing himself to stop. He sent the tiny fragments raining to the floor before he could act on his impulse.

For reasons he couldn't fathom, the tinkle of glass on stone broke something inside him. He sank to the floor, curled his body forward and buried both hands in his hair. How the hell had it come to this? He'd been doing so well in school, with his investigation here at Groome Castle and with Greg. He'd been *happy*. And now that happiness was gone, all gone, because he'd forgotten the principles he'd sworn years ago to live by.

Truth. Control. Always. No exceptions.

Adrian drew a deep, shuddering breath. Drawing his knees up, he rested his forehead against them. He'd never felt more alone in his life. The worst of it was, he didn't know if it would've helped anything if he'd realized before now that he was in love with Greg, or if telling him would've just driven him away earlier.

Ally Blue

Tears stung Adrian's eyes. This time, he didn't try to stop them. He covered his face with his hands and cried.

# Chapter Sixteen

Adrian woke in the dark with his cheek pressed to cold stone. The left side of his body was numb where he'd curled up on the floor of the tower room.

He pushed to his feet, wincing as a thousand aches and pains born of sleeping on the rocky floor flared to life. A look at the fluorescent hands of his watch told him it was just after one in the morning. He felt weak and wrung out, and his head throbbed, but his mind was clear and uncluttered. An emotional breakdown followed by eight plus hours of sleep— even if it *was* on the floor of a cold castle room—would do that.

He laughed, the sound harsh and humorless in the empty room. Anyone else would have some major explaining to do in the morning. Friends, lovers, roommates or study groups to whom they'd have to explain their unexpected absence. He had no one. His family didn't expect him to call at any particular time, and now the only person in his life who would've noticed his disappearance no longer wanted to see him.

The giant hook that seemed to have buried itself in the center of his chest dug in a little bit deeper. He scowled, impatient. *Stop feeling sorry for yourself. You can't change the past. All you can do now is try to talk to him, tell him how much you regret what happened, and wait for him to be ready to take you back.*

He refused to consider the possibility that Greg truly might not want him back. He knew that might be the case, but his emotions were far too fragile to dwell on it. Besides, the two of them couldn't have lasted this long if Greg didn't care about him enough to at least *try* to get past this.

Right?

Shoving the dark thoughts to the back of his mind, Adrian crossed the room to the door. The moon had already set, and the night was pitch dark. He picked his way down the narrow spiral staircase and across the main hall downstairs by feel in the inky blackness. He left the castle and locked the door behind him, making a mental note to bring a light bulb and a broom with him next time he returned.

The temperature had dropped several degrees in the time Adrian had been in the castle. He zipped his jacket, stuffed his hands in his pockets and hunched his shoulders against the icy breeze. He started toward his apartment at as brisk a walk as he could manage in the darkness. Then he remembered his bed would be cold and empty, and he slowed down. No point in hurrying when all places were equally lonely now without Greg.

"You're being ridiculous," Adrian admonished himself through chattering teeth. "Stop it."

Since he knew he wouldn't be able to stop thinking about Greg, Adrian decided to analyze Greg's behavior from the previous afternoon and try to figure out what had been going on in his head. He'd been far too upset at the time to pick up on the small clues which would no doubt shed some light on what had happened. Maybe looking at it now—with a clearer head—would give him some idea as to what had made Greg angry in the first place, and how to approach him.

Adrian did not, however, speed up his pace. He'd rather freeze on the street than be alone in his apartment any sooner than absolutely necessary.

As he strolled along, he reviewed the previous day's conversation word by word. In spite of the pain it caused, he also conjured the memory of Greg's face and studied it with as much scientific detachment as he could muster. He noted the discomfort in Greg's expression when he first said to Greg that he wanted to tell him something he'd never told anyone else, then the swift flash of whatever-it-was that Adrian *still* couldn't label but which made his heart beat faster anyway.

When his memory-self assured Greg that he wanted to tell him this and he saw Greg's expression soften with an unmistakable tenderness, Adrian knew he'd found the crux of the problem. The way Greg's eyes shone with betrayal for a heartbeat before his face froze at the mention of psychokinesis and portals told Adrian all he needed to know.

He groaned. This explained everything. Greg had thought Adrian was trusting him with an event of major importance from his past, knowledge with which he'd never trusted anyone else. The fact that it was true didn't matter, in the end. What mattered was what Greg believed. And if Adrian was right, Greg believed Adrian had built him up to a huge revelation, only to feed him a deliberate lie, probably to make him the butt of a particularly bad joke.

Adrian thought he detected Harrison's fingerprints on Greg's fears. He wondered how often the bastard had abused Greg's trust in such a cruel way, and if he'd done it as often as he'd abused Greg physically.

*That's something you have in common with Harrison now. You've both hurt Greg physically. Just because you didn't use your fists doesn't make what you did okay. Never forget that.*

The memory tasted bitter, but Adrian wouldn't allow himself to shy away from it, no matter how sick it made him.

Until the day he died, he needed to remember the flat gleam of terror in Greg's eyes and the tremor in his voice, as a reminder of what could happen when he lost control.

When he reached Country Club Road, Adrian stopped at the crosswalk, torn. His apartment wasn't far now, only a couple of blocks away. He looked forward to getting out of the cold, but the idea of facing his lonely apartment didn't appeal to him any more now than it had fifteen minutes ago.

Another picture floated to the front of his mind—the vision of a stubbled jaw, a tense mouth and a straining neck, a drop of sweat rolling into a soiled white collar embroidered with blue flowers. Maybe he could stop by his place long enough to grab his laptop, then head over to Davis Library and try to figure out why the partial face from Lyndon's memory struck such a familiar chord. He had no idea where to begin, but that hardly mattered. In fact, he considered it a plus at this point. The mental exercise would fill the long hours until morning brought the campus to life and his day began.

His plan in place, Adrian jogged down the sidewalk toward his apartment. With any luck, by the time classes ended today Greg would be willing to listen to what Adrian had to say.

~ \* ~

Unfortunately, Adrian never laid eyes on Greg that day, or the next. He saw Greg at the dining hall Saturday night, looking pale and red-eyed. His phalanx of friends closed ranks around him the instant they spotted Adrian. Sandy shot him a glare that told him beyond a doubt that she, at least, had heard some version of what had happened Wednesday afternoon.

Sighing, Adrian took a tray and loaded a plate without paying any attention to what he was getting. It didn't matter, since he'd lost his appetite. He sat within sight of Greg, picked at his food and wondered what Greg had told his friends to make them look at him like he was evil incarnate.

While Greg shoved his pasta around his plate, his friends gradually finished eating and drifted away until only Sandy and a boy whose name Adrian couldn't remember remained at the table. When Greg rose to leave, Adrian jumped up and followed. "Greg. Wait."

Greg stopped, his back stiff. "I told you to leave me alone."

Adrian swallowed against the tightness in his throat. "Just...just give me one minute, okay? Just to tell you something. Then I won't bother you anymore. I promise." Saying those words hurt, but Adrian had sworn to himself that he'd tell Greg what he needed to then back off. The next step had to be up to Greg, or it meant nothing.

Stepping in front of Greg, the boy—Steve, maybe?—glowered down at him. "He doesn't want to talk to you. Now fuck off, before I smash your face in."

"Steven, no." Greg grabbed Steven's muscular arm and pulled him away. "I don't want anyone getting hurt." Greg turned his troubled gaze to Adrian. "Okay. Let's talk."

Adrian licked his lips. "Can...can we talk alone?"

"No." Sandy crossed her arms. "We're not leaving him alone with you, asshole."

"Sandy, don't." Greg darted an annoyed look at his friend, then gave Adrian a short nod. "All right."

He turned back to the table he and his friends had just left, slid into the booth and sat staring at his clasped hands. Adrian sat across from him, heart aching. He hated that he'd done this to Greg, however inadvertently.

"You're not talking." Greg twisted his fingers together so

hard his knuckles turned white. "Talk."

"Oh. Right." Adrian stuck his hands beneath his thighs to keep himself from reaching across the table to touch Greg. "Well, I just wanted to say that... Well, first of all, you can't possibly know how horribly sorry I am that I let my temper get away with me like I did the other day. Ever since my abilities first manifested, staying in control of myself has been one of the guiding principles of my life. I lost sight of that on Wednesday, and I regret that more than I can tell you. I wanted to tell you that I'm sorry, that I'll never, ever let myself forget what I did, and I'll never let it happen again as long as I live."

One corner of Greg's mouth quirked upward. "Never is a long time, Adrian."

"Maybe. But I can try." Hope surged in Adrian's heart when Greg's expression didn't change. "I also wanted to say that I think I know why you were so angry with me after I told you...what I told you. But I swear to you—I *swear*—that everything I said was the complete truth. I wasn't lying, and I wasn't making fun of you. For me, it was a huge step to be able to tell you those things. I've never trusted anyone enough to tell them about what I can do, or about what happened to me when I was eleven. You're the first person outside my family who's ever been that important to me."

*I love you.* Adrian longed to say it, but the fear that Greg would think it simply a ploy to win him back stilled his tongue.

Greg closed his eyes. The dark circles underneath them stood out like bruises against the unhealthy pallor of his skin. "I don't know what you want me to say."

*Yes, you do!* Ignoring the part of him that wanted to scream until he got what he wanted, Adrian forced his voice to remain soft and calm. "You don't have to say anything. I know I hurt you, and I know I scared you. I'll regret it forever, but I can't change it now. What I *can* do is give you the time you need to decide what you want to do. I hope you'll still want to be with me. And I'll be waiting for you when you're ready, if that's what you want. If you don't..." Adrian's voice broke. He cleared his throat and made himself go on. "If you don't want me anymore, I'll respect that."

Silence fell. Adrian waited, his stomach churning. After a long moment, Greg opened his eyes and stared into Adrian's. "I do want to be with you, Adrian. Nothing in the world could make me not want to be with you."

After nearly three days of sickening uncertainty, this rare moment of blunt truth from Greg felt like a benediction. Adrian planted his elbows on the table and rested his head in his hands as relief left him dizzy. "Thank God. I was so afraid."

"Adrian. Wait."

Something in Greg's voice made the bile rise in Adrian's throat. He met Greg's gaze with trepidation. "What?"

Greg gave him a sad smile. "I want to be with you. But I don't know if I can."

Adrian's heartbeat stumbled. "What do you mean?"

"I mean, I don't know if I can do it. Mentally, I mean. Emotionally." Leaning back in his seat, Greg rubbed the side of his face with one hand. "My arms are bruised where my jacket dug into them, Adrian. I know it sounds stupid since it's just a couple of bruises, and it was just that one time with you and you've always been so good to me, but I can't help it. I think to myself, what would happen if it wasn't the *only* time, but the *first* time?" He turned his head to stare out the window at the clouds slowly covering the blue sky. "The first time Harrison hit me, I told myself I should overlook it because it was just that once and he'd always treated me great up 'til then. But of course that wasn't the only time. It was just the first time. After

I left him, I promised myself I'd never let there be a second time again."

Adrian nodded, even though what he wanted was to prostrate himself at Greg's feet and beg until Greg relented and gave him another chance. "I understand. I won't bother you anymore." Sliding to the edge of the booth, Adrian stood. He stuck his hands in his pockets so Greg wouldn't see how badly they shook. "I'm so sorry, Greg. I'd give anything to take it back. I'd turn back time if I could. And I'll never, ever forgive myself for ruining the best thing that's ever happened to me, or for hurting you like I did."

The tremor in Adrian's voice reached the breaking point. He snapped his mouth shut, spun and hurried toward the door without looking back.

He made it halfway across the quad before his knees decided he was done walking. Dropping to the ground, he stretched out on his back and contemplated the increasingly gray sky beyond the bare branches above his head. He felt numb. Greg had just broken up with him. He hadn't run away in anger or misguided fear. No, this was a calm, rational decision. Something to which Greg had clearly given a great deal of thought.

Who could blame him? *You hurt him in a fit of anger. Maybe his fear isn't misguided. Maybe he's right to be afraid of you. Maybe you're a potential abuser, just like Harrison, only with powers that let you cause damage without ever laying a finger on a person.*

The idea horrified him. He'd never thought of himself as that sort of person. Then again, he'd never before loved anyone outside his family. It seemed counterintuitive to him that his feelings for Greg brought out the worst in him sometimes, but there it was. Maybe being in love simply turned him into a monster. Maybe he was destined to be alone forever.

"I don't believe that," he declared aloud, as if trying to convince himself. "I will not believe that."

Regardless of what he believed, Greg's decision left Adrian alone now.

An invisible truck parked itself on Adrian's chest. Squeezing his eyes shut, he pressed his palms to his forehead and drew slow, deep breaths until the urge to scream and sob and rail against the universe passed.

Once he got himself under control, Adrian pushed to his feet and started toward the physics lab. Life didn't stop, no matter how much he might want it to right now, and he had work to do.

~ ✳ ~

The librarian looked up with a smile when Adrian walked in. "Hello, Adrian. Back again so soon?"

He smiled back automatically, even though he didn't feel it. "Hi, Mrs. Wickham. Yes, I still have quite a few papers to get through. I have the rest of the afternoon free, so I'm going to stay until closing and get as far as I can, if that's all right."

"Of course, dear." Taking her keycard from the drawer, she walked out from the enclosed desk area. "The machine is free. I doubt anyone will need it. We rarely have any requests to view any of our microfilm collection these days."

"Well, I'm glad you have it. Otherwise I'd be out of luck. Davis Library has a lot of the town's newspapers scanned from microfilm into digital, but they haven't gone back as far as I need yet."

In the past fifteen days, twenty-one hours and forty-five

minutes since Greg had broken up with him—not that he'd been keeping track—Adrian had spent most of his free time researching the sparse clues to Lyndon Groome's death. With very little idea of what to do, he'd decided to go through all of the Chapel Hill newspapers from the last three months of nineteen-oh-five to see if he could find anything helpful. For the past two days he'd been a fixture here at the Chapel Hill Public Library, skimming through the old newspapers on microfilm in whatever spare time he could scrape together. He hadn't seen anything interesting yet, but he wasn't prepared to give up. Lyndon Groome vanished on Halloween. Adrian's gut told him that if there was anything to be found in the newspapers, it would be in the editions published soon after Lyndon's disappearance. He'd wanted to read the October papers mostly to see if anything had happened in the days leading up to Lyndon's disappearance.

He trailed the librarian's neat salt-and-pepper braid into the rear of the building and waited while she retrieved the film he needed and set it up for him. When she'd finished, she patted him on the shoulder. "There you are, dear. You know how to use the machine, and you know where to find me if you need me."

"Yes, ma'am." He gave her a more genuine smile than he had when he'd first walked in. "Thank you. You've been a huge help to me with this project, and I really appreciate it."

A faint blush tinged her dark cheeks. "You're most welcome, Adrian. It's good to see young people taking an interest in this town's history."

Adrian just nodded. Mrs. Wickham was a sweet lady, but she didn't need to know about his abilities or his precise reasons for wanting to read Chapel Hill's old newspapers.

She glanced behind her at the open door of the microfilm

viewing room. "Well. I suppose I should get back to my desk. Let me know if you need anything, dear."

"I will. Thanks again, Mrs. Wickham."

She nodded, turned and left, closing the door behind her. Once she was gone, Adrian settled himself in the chair in front of the viewing machine. He set his iPhone on the desk provided in case he needed to take notes, then started scrolling through the November nineteen-oh-five papers.

The moment he saw the few short paragraphs near the back of the November second morning edition, he knew he'd found the missing piece to his puzzle.

*November 2, 1905*

*CHAPEL HILL—According to a police report filed on the afternoon of November 1st, Sir Lionel Groome of Groome Castle was accused of murdering his nephew Lyndon during the Halloween festivities held at the Castle on Halloween night. Lyndon has been a guest at the castle since late spring and is currently attending the University of North Carolina at Chapel Hill as an exchange student from Oxford University in England. The Groome family has social and financial connections with both universities and with the town of Chapel Hill going back to the late seventeen hundreds.*

*Anonymous sources inform this reporter that police have spoken to Sir Lionel but have found no evidence with which to charge him. Lyndon himself has not been seen since Halloween. Sir Lionel has filed a missing person's report on his nephew and according to my sources appears most distraught. As for the man who accused Sir Lionel of murder, his name is listed on the police report as John Davis. However, many people around town say his name is actually Cassius Wellington. Furthermore, many whisper that Cassius Wellington and Lyndon Groome have been spotted about town in frequent and intimate company. This reporter has to wonder if perhaps friendship turned sour and Cassius Wellington, not Sir Lionel, is the one who knows Lyndon Groome's fate.*

Adrian leaned back in the chair, his heart racing. It was hardly definitive proof, but along with Lyndon's memories it at least gave him a solid lead to follow.

*God, his own uncle. How awful would that be?*

Maybe it wasn't true. Adrian hoped it wasn't. Just because Cassius thought that's what had happened didn't mean he was right.

*Unless he saw it. Maybe he was hiding somewhere nearby and witnessed Lionel Groome killing Lyndon. My God, what a horrible thing.*

Adrian shuddered. There was no point in creating nightmare scenarios in his head, especially when he could attempt to extract the information directly from Lyndon's memories the next time he went to the castle. With any luck, having this information would make connecting easier.

In the meantime, he needed to finish reading through the papers. There might be more clues, and he didn't want his excitement over this one clue—huge though it may be—to make him miss anything else.

Picking up his iPhone, he thumbed it on and called up the notes function. He keyed in the pertinent information from the article, as well as its location on the microfilm spool, then went back to reading.

As he'd suspected, Adrian found nothing else of interest in the nineteen-oh-five papers. The library closed before he was quite finished with the December editions, but by that time he'd already decided there wouldn't be anything else mentioned. He found it puzzling, actually, that there could be an accusation of murder against one of the town's prominent citizens with only one mention in a back page column bordering on gossip.

Maybe the "financial connections to the town" bit had something to do with the lack of further coverage. Walking out into the cold, damp night air, Adrian resolved to ask around and find out what the chances were that an influential man like Lionel Groome might have paid off someone at the paper to keep his name out of the headlines.

With his brain busy laying plans for visiting Lyndon and reading further in the Chapel Hill newspapers—maybe finding out what had become of Cassius—the walk to his apartment passed quickly. He punched in the entry code, swung open the front door and climbed the stairs to the second floor. When he reached the top of the steps he stopped and stared, shocked.

Greg sat on the floor outside Adrian's apartment. He stood as Adrian approached. "Hi, Adrian." His voice sounded rough and hoarse, and Adrian wondered if he was sick.

"Greg." Adrian clutched the stair rail, his heart thudding so hard it left him breathless. "How'd you get in?"

"Lori let me in when she came home." Greg gestured at the door across the hall, where Adrian's neighbor Lori Young lived. "I'm sorry, I know I didn't have any right to bust in like this, especially after I broke things off with you, but..." His gaze fixed on Adrian's face, Greg moved closer. "Something happened today, and I just had to see you. I had to talk to you."

Adrian studied Greg's face. His skin was deathly white, gray eyes wide and glazed. Worse, Adrian thought he saw...

Forgetting all about his own wounded heart and the two weeks of hell he'd endured after the breakup, Adrian gently pulled aside the collar of Greg's jacket. What he saw made his chest constrict.

"Oh, my God." Adrian stroked his fingertips over the purple

bruises marring the skin of Greg's throat. "What happened?"

"Harrison was waiting for me outside my dorm this morning." Greg dropped his gaze to the floor at his feet. "He tried to kill me."

# Chapter Seventeen

Anger stained Adrian's vision red. He breathed it away. Greg needed him calm and gentle, not enraged, regardless of the target of his fury.

Resisting the urge to take Greg's hand, Adrian walked to his apartment door on trembling legs. "Let's get inside. I still have some of that mint tea you like. I'll make you a cup and you can tell me what happened."

Greg followed him inside without a word. He sat in the armchair while Adrian filled a large mug with water, stuck a mint teabag in it and popped the whole thing into the microwave. They waited in silence while the tea brewed. When the microwave beeped, Adrian took the mug out and stirred in a dollop of honey. He handed it to Greg, then dragged a chair over from the dining table.

"All right." Adrian settled into the chair, all his attention on Greg. "First of all, please tell me that bastard Harrison is behind bars right now."

The corners of Greg's mouth curved upward. "Yeah, he is. Steven sat on him until campus security got there, and the cops showed up not long after that. They carted him off to jail."

"Good." Adrian clasped his hands together. The temptation to pull Greg into his arms and hold him was hard to resist. "What happened? You said he was waiting for you when you left your dorm, right?"

"Yeah." Kicking his shoes off, Greg curled his legs beneath him. He took a sip of tea. When he lowered the cup, his shaking hands caused the liquid to slosh almost to the rim. "I don't know where he was, exactly. Maybe behind that big oak tree. Steven and Sandy were with me when I left the dorm, but none of us saw him until he attacked me. He ran at me and tackled me from behind, got me on the ground and started strangling me. He was yelling something at me, but I couldn't understand him." One of Greg's hands went to his throat. His eyes took on a haunted look. "Steven and Sandy were both trying to get him off me, but they couldn't. I could hear Sandy screaming for help. Finally, Steven kicked him in the face just when I thought I was going to pass out. That made him let go. Steven pinned him to the ground and *literally* sat on him while Sandy called nine-one-one. By that time other students had noticed and someone had called campus security too. I don't know the time frame, but I know it wasn't long before security got there, then the paramedics and cops showed up. It's all kind of a blur after that."

"I bet." Adrian eyed the bruises on Greg's neck with concern. "Are you all right? I assume if the paramedics were there they at least checked you over."

"Oh yeah." Greg let out a hoarse laugh. "They took me to the ER, and I got scanned and X-rayed and prodded within an inch of my life. The doctor said I have a little bit of swelling in my windpipe and vocal cords but it's mild. She said the bruises make it look a lot worse than it is."

Relief brought a genuine smile to Adrian's face. "Still, I'm surprised she didn't want you to stay overnight, just to watch you and make sure it didn't get worse."

Greg's pale cheeks colored. "Um. Actually, she kind of did."

He lifted his mug and took a long swallow of tea.

"But you refused." Adrian shook his head. "Why? I thought you had better sense than that."

One of Greg's shoulders hitched up in a falsely casual shrug that didn't fool Adrian for a second. "I don't like hospitals, that's all. Waking you up to give you a sleeping pill and that sort of crap. And have you seen those stupid beds? It's like they're designed to keep people from getting a good night's sleep." He stirred his tea with one finger, watching the swirling liquid as if it was the most fascinating thing in the world.

Warmth suffused Adrian's insides. The fact that Greg had come here—not his dorm room, not any of his friends' room, not even his parents' house—spoke volumes. The truth was, he'd simply wanted to be with Adrian, not alone in a hospital bed. After enduring the past sixteen days alone, Adrian was content to know that without having to hear it spoken out loud.

"You have a point there." Adrian watched Greg drain half his mug in one draught. "I'll tell you the truth, Steven and Sandy haven't exactly been my favorite people lately, and you know why, but I'm very glad they were with you this morning. They saved your life."

"I know. Believe me, I know." Greg snorted. "I've thought all day about how ironic that was, that they've been hanging all over me to protect me from you, when all along it wasn't you I needed protection from at all. It was *him*."

A suspicion wormed itself into Adrian's brain. He aimed a narrow look at Greg. "What are you saying? I thought he'd left you alone lately. You didn't mention anything to me about him bothering you."

Greg stared at the blue and white UNC mug in his hand for a moment, as if it held the answers to all life's most pressing questions, then leaned over the arm of the chair and set it on the floor. Unfolding his legs, he scooted to the edge of the chair, reached out and took Adrian's hands in his. "Adrian, I owe you a massive apology. And I owe you the truth. The whole truth, for a change. You've given me that. I realize that now. And you deserve the same from me."

Cold dread settled like a block of ice in Adrian's stomach, but he didn't let it show. He curled his fingers around Greg's and nodded. "I'm listening."

For a second, the fear and worry melted from Greg's features and his eyes shone with the elusive light Adrian had noticed on and off ever since that last night in Mobile. Only this time, it didn't fade away. It remained, bright and beautiful, even when Greg's brief smile vanished and the furrow dug into his brow once again.

Adrian stared, fascinated, his pulse galloping and his mouth dry. Finally, *finally*, he thought he could put a name to what he saw in Greg's eyes. But he refused to voice it, even to himself, because being wrong would destroy him. Instead, he forced the revelation to the back of his mind and focused on what Greg was about to say.

"Harrison never left me alone." Greg's fingers kneaded the backs of Adrian's hands, a sure sign of his nervousness. "In fact, the stalking's gotten worse since that day we saw him on the street."

Adrian nodded. He'd expected something like that. "And to think I thought I'd scared him away. Stupid of me, really."

Greg frowned. "What do you mean?"

"I gave him a little taste of my psychokinesis. Just enough to scare him off, or so I thought." Adrian shrugged, feeling his cheeks heat as Greg's eyebrows shot up. "I know it was dumb. It just made me so angry, the way he treated you."

"I know. And I'm not starting *that* fight again." One corner of Greg's mouth turned up in a wry half-smile. "I guess that explains why he kept telling me you were a demon."

"Probably." Adrian ran a thumb over Greg's knuckles. "I'm sorry. I hope I didn't make things worse for you."

"With Harrison, it's pretty hard to tell, but I'd say you didn't." Greg sighed. "Anyway, up until this morning he's mostly been either calling me or showing up out of the blue to tell me that you're a demon who'll steal my soul away to hell, or that I belong to him and we're destined to be together. A few times he's told me that he's coming back to take me away to paradise, whatever the fuck that means."

Adrian blew out a breath. "Good grief. He sounds certifiable, Greg. Why didn't you try to get any kind of protection from him?"

Greg's eyes flashed. His jaw took on a familiar stubborn set. "I didn't take out a restraining order because I know Harrison, and it would've just set him off and made him violent. And before you say it, yes, I know what happened this morning. That was completely out of the blue. I didn't expect it." The defensiveness disappeared from Greg's face. His shoulders slumped. "I actually talked to the cops earlier about having him committed, and I found out it would be impossible for me to do since I'm not next of kin. The police said I could do a restraining order, but that was my only option until Harrison actually attacked me or something."

"Jesus." Unable to help himself, Adrian lifted Greg's hands and kissed them both. "I'm so sorry you've had to go through all that. I'm glad he's in jail. I hope they put him away for a long, long time."

"Me too." Twisting his hands in Adrian's, Greg wove their fingers together. "Now for the apology I owe you. I'm sorry I accused you of lying when you told me about your...your abilities, and what happened to you when you were a kid, with the portal and all. It must have been really hard for you to tell me that, and I threw it in your face, just because I was scared of being hurt."

Adrian swallowed against the tightness in his throat. "Well, to be fair, I *had* lied to you about Groome Castle, and Lyndon."

Greg shook his head, his intense gaze never wavering from Adrian's face. "Yeah, but it's not exactly the same thing. In all the time I've known you, you've never, *ever,* told a deliberate lie to someone's face. You've never said something that's completely untrue. And you're certainly not the type of person to make fun of somebody the way I accused you of doing. I should never have said those things to you, and I'm sorry." His hands tightened around Adrian's. "Can you forgive me?"

Adrian didn't even have to think about his answer. "I forgave you ages ago."

Relief lit up Greg's face. He slid closer, his knees bumping Adrian's. "Can we try again?"

Happiness made Adrian lightheaded. Still, he had a responsibility to make sure Greg wasn't just reacting to the trauma he'd suffered.

*You have the potential to hurt him worse than Harrison ever dreamed of doing. Never forget that.*

Dislodging Greg's grip on his right hand, Adrian touched Greg's cheek. "I want that so much it hurts. But you have to be sure of this. After what I did—"

Greg cut him off with a hand against his lips. "I know what you did. And I know what I said about it. Believe me, I've thought about this a *lot* over the last couple of weeks. And I realized that in spite of what you did in the cemetery, you don't have it in you to be an abuser."

Adrian blinked. "But... But I..."

"You got angry. You lost your temper, like all of us do sometimes." Greg ran his fingertips across Adrian's cheek and over the corner of his jaw. "I'm not excusing what you did. If I'd gotten pissed off at you and punched you, there'd be no excusing that either. But the thing is, if I did that, I know—I *know*—it would only happen once. I'd be so horrified by what I'd done that I'd make damn sure it never happened again. And see, I know that's how you feel. I know you'll never hurt me again." A smile tugged at Greg's mouth. "In fact, I have extra confidence in you because you have more self-control than anyone I've ever known. You're almost super-human that way."

That surprised a laugh from Adrian. "I'm definitely no Superman. But I *do* want to be with you again. God, yes, I want that."

"Good." Greg rose from his chair to straddle Adrian's lap. "You promised you wouldn't lie to me, and I'm promising right now that I won't lie to you either. I'm still a little scared. But I trust you." He let go of Adrian's hand, cradled Adrian's face in both hands and pinned him with a stare that pierced him to the core. "Don't make me regret that."

Adrian shook his head, his throat tight. "Never."

"I know." Beaming, Greg leaned in and pressed a soft kiss to Adrian's lips.

It felt so good Adrian wanted to cry and whoop with joy at the same time. He settled for wrapping an arm around Greg's waist, burying the opposite hand in his hair and taking the kiss deep. Greg's resulting moan sounded sweeter than any music to Adrian's ears.

When they drew apart, Greg rested his forehead against Adrian's. "Can I stay with you tonight?"

*Tonight, and every night. I want you with me forever.* Adrian ran his fingers through Greg's curls. "Of course. You don't even have to ask, you know. You have an open invitation to stay here with me."

Greg's breath hitched. His fingers dug into Adrian's shoulders. "Thank you."

Tilting his head, Adrian brushed a chaste kiss across Greg's mouth. "Come on. I think you should lie down and get some sleep. You've got to be exhausted."

"It's not even ten yet," Greg protested, but he stood anyway and let Adrian lead him to the bathroom to brush his teeth and change into a borrowed pair of sleep pants and a T-shirt.

Adrian had planned to work on his math paper before going to bed. The sight of Greg in his bed changed his mind. He set his alarm for an hour early the next morning, brushed his teeth and changed, and crawled under the covers with Greg instead. Greg curled into Adrian's embrace, his back molded to Adrian's chest and their legs tangled together. Adrian hooked an arm around Greg's waist and breathed in the familiar scent he'd missed so terribly.

*I love you*, he mouthed into the bend of Greg's neck. Maybe one day soon he could speak the words out loud. Maybe he'd even hear them in return.

Warmed by the thought, Adrian closed his eyes and let the rhythm of Greg's breathing lull him to sleep.

# Chapter Eighteen

Adrian waited until Saturday to broach the subject of visiting Groome Castle. Partly because he wanted a time when he could communicate with Lyndon without worrying about classes, but mostly because waiting put five days of distance between Greg's assault and the need to have the Lyndon conversation with him.

Of all the things they needed to talk about, Adrian dreaded that one the most.

He made cheese omelettes for breakfast, then took the plunge while they were still sitting at his table sipping their coffee. "Greg, I have something I'd like to discuss with you."

"Uh-oh. That sounds serious." Greg set his mug on the table, his expression wary. "What is it?"

Adrian rubbed both thumbs nervously over the Bellingrath Gardens logo on his mug. "Well, I hope it isn't. The thing is, on Monday night when you came over here, I had just found a major clue to Lyndon Groome's death, and I was thinking that maybe I'd go over to the castle today and...you know, talk to Lyndon. See if I could find out if what I learned could possibly be true."

Greg gazed at him in thoughtful silence. Adrian drew a deep swallow of coffee, then another, and tried not to fidget. Finally, Greg leaned forward, a determined look in his eyes. "I want to come with you."

Of all the responses Adrian had imagined, that hadn't been one of them. He gaped at Greg in astonishment. "You... What? Really?"

"Yeah."

"I thought you had play practice today." Greg had landed the role of Fiyero in the school's upcoming production of *Wicked*, and he'd spent at least a portion of most days lately at practice.

"Not today. We only have the theater for half the day and the director wants the chorus to spend that time working on a couple of numbers I'm not in." Greg bit his lip. "If I'd be in your way, I'll stay here. It's just, I feel like there's things I never knew existed before now, you know? Like, I had no idea there was any such thing as psychokinesis, but you can do that, you can really *do* it. I've *seen* it and *felt* it. I know it's real. So if that's real, maybe I've been wrong about ghosts and stuff all this time too. And if that's the case, then I want to be there when you talk to a real ghost and find out how he died."

Shock gave way to a warmth like nothing Adrian had ever felt. A wide smile spread across his face. "Of course you can come with me. And no, you will *not* be in the way." Grabbing Greg's face in both hands, Adrian surged forward and kissed him hard. "You're amazing."

Greg laughed. "I'm not. I just have enough sense to admit when I'm wrong. At least sometimes." He returned Adrian's kiss with extra tongue. "Let's get dressed and go now. Can I do anything to help, or should I just hang back and be quiet?"

"Honestly? I have no idea. I've only ever done this alone. But I promise to tell you if there's anything I think you can do." Adrian stood and began gathering the breakfast dishes. "Come on. It'll only take us a minute to get this cleaned up."

Greg hopped to his feet. Within fifteen minutes, the two of them had the kitchen clean and themselves showered and changed. They left the apartment and headed hand in hand for Groome Castle.

"So what's this clue you're chasing?" Greg asked as they strolled down the sidewalk.

"There was a short piece I found in the November second edition of the Chapel Hill paper. It said a man named Cassius Wellington accused Lyndon's uncle, Lionel, of murdering Lyndon during a Halloween party at the castle." Adrian squinted up at the bright blue sky. The weather had turned unseasonably warm, and he was glad. It was still chilly, but not the bone-numbing cold it had been lately, and the sunshine felt nice. "In the memories Lyndon's sent me before, Cassius was the name of the man Lyndon loved. If this is the same Cassius, it's possible that he witnessed the murder or had some other insight that made it likely he was right and that Lionel Groome really did kill Lyndon."

"Wow." Greg shot a wide-eyed glance at Adrian. "You said you got a glimpse of Lyndon's death through his memories, right?"

"Yeah. Just bits and pieces, really." *Stubbled jaw. Straining neck. Soiled white collar, blue flowers.* So familiar. Where in the hell had he seen that curve of jaw before? And did it really belong to Lionel Groome?

"There's a picture of him in the castle's main hall."

Adrian stopped so suddenly Greg stumbled. "Who?"

"Lionel Groome. We had to take it down for the haunted house. I remember it was a big pain in the ass because it was original to the castle so we had to get permission to move it." Greg frowned. "Adrian, are you okay?"

"Yeah. Fine." Adrian chewed his lip, thinking hard. Now

237

that Greg mentioned it, he remembered having seen the picture hanging on the wall behind the head of the long oak dining table. He'd been one of the ten students it had taken to move the massive piece of furniture for the haunted house. "I need to look at that picture."

"Yeah, I figured you'd want to. I mean, if the old guy really was the murderer, and you saw part of his face—well, kind of— then you'd be able to identify him if you saw his picture, right?" Shifting closer, Greg cupped Adrian's cheek in his free hand. "Adrian, what's wrong?"

"Nothing, really, it's just that I kept thinking the part of a face I saw in Lyndon's memory looked really familiar for some reason." Adrian laid his hand over Greg's. "It's been bugging me."

Understanding dawned in Greg's eyes. "Oooh, okay. I hate that. When you *know* you know something and you can't pin it down."

"Me too. My memory's usually much better than that."

Greg lifted a skeptical brow. "Adrian, you might have a nearly photographic memory, but you're always misplacing the picture albums."

Startled into laughter, Adrian rewarded Greg's insight with a long, lazy kiss. For once, it didn't matter that they stood on a public sidewalk on a particularly fine mid-February Saturday morning, for the whole world to see. All that mattered to Adrian at that moment was the taste of Greg's mouth, Greg's hands in his hair, the warmth of Greg's body molded to his. God, he'd missed this during those terrible two weeks like a drowning man misses air. He never wanted to be without it again.

The only things missing now were three little words. Adrian was willing to wait for that.

They drew apart before things could get too heated and

started walking again. When they reached the castle's front door, Greg frowned. "How are we supposed to get in? It's locked."

Adrian grinned. "I can move things with my mind, remember?" He gave a mental twist. The lock clicked. He opened the door and swept his arm forward. "After you."

Greg's eyes saucered. His fingers clamped down on Adrian's. "Holy shit."

"Yeah, that was pretty much my reaction when I was eleven and did it on purpose for the first time." Adrian moved forward, tugging on Greg's hand. "Come on. We don't want to stand here too long. People do walk past here sometimes, and I don't want anyone to see us going in here."

"Oh." Greg shot a hunted look over his shoulder. "We're not gonna get in trouble, are we?"

Guilt needled Adrian's gut. "I don't think so. I always try to leave everything the way I found it. Except that time I accidentally broke the light bulb in the tower room. And I *did* replace that."

Greg shrugged. "Well, I guess it's a little late to worry about it now anyway, since you've already been in here more than once."

Adrian shut and locked the door behind them with a thought. Greg cast a skittish look at it, but said nothing. Hands still linked, they crossed the foyer into the main hall. Sunshine poured through the arched windows. The brilliant light brought out veins of red and rich gold in the dark wood of the dining table.

As they approached the opposite end of the room, Adrian's gaze zeroed in on the eight-by-ten photo hanging on the wall behind the head of the table. His pulse sped up as they drew nearer and the sepia tones of the old picture revealed a man in high-waisted pants, suspenders and shirt sleeves rolled up to his elbows. Pale hair spilled in a riot of curls over a wide brow, and a huge smile split his handsome face. One foot was planted on the front bumper of a gleaming—and expensive-looking—car, and his arms were crossed over his chest.

Now that Adrian saw it, he remembered his one quick glimpse of it before it was removed for the haunted house. Hardly a typical portrait to hang in the hall of one's castle, but the gleam in Sir Lionel Groome's eyes instantly labeled him a maverick, so Adrian supposed he'd be one to hang a scandalous portrait if he damn well pleased.

Walking closer, Adrian studied the photo in detail—the line of the neck, the curve of the jaw, the tilt of the smile. He grimaced. "It's him, all right."

Greg pressed against Adrian's shoulder, staring at the picture in fascination. "So you think he really murdered Lyndon?"

Adrian nodded. "His face is the one I saw in Lyndon's memory. I'm sure of it."

"And you're positive that what you saw is the memory of Lyndon dying?"

He was, he knew it in his bones, but... "Well, I didn't see the whole thing, so I can't really say for sure, I guess. I need to see more of the memory to be certain."

"Okay. Then you'll just have to get Lyndon to show you all of it." Greg marched toward the back hallway with the fire of resolution in his eyes.

Adrian followed, grinning. Greg's enthusiasm was contagious. Especially since it was so unexpected.

They had to let go of each other's hands to climb the stairs to the tower room. Adrian led the way, since he'd occasionally opened the door in the past to find Lyndon already hovering in the musty air. If Lyndon decided this was a day to manifest without being called first, Adrian wanted that extra second to prepare Greg for what he would see.

*If he sees Lyndon at all*, Adrian reminded himself, remembering the day he'd met Greg.

At the top of the steps, Adrian turned the knob and swung open the door. Sunbeams cut through the dust set swirling by the door's motion. Lyndon wasn't there.

Adrian reached out with his senses and felt the familiar energy sparking close enough to touch.

Excitement raised the hairs on his arms. Today, he would finally have all the answers he craved. He knew it, as surely as he knew his own name.

"Adrian? What the hell's that?"

Greg's voice was sharp with a mix of curiosity and fear. Turning toward him, Adrian took his hands and squeezed. "Tell me what you're feeling."

"It's like..." Greg trailed off, brow scrunching in concentration. "I don't know. Like electricity, only not really. The weirdest thing is, I could swear I've felt something like this before. It seems familiar. Which is just *wrong.*"

"No, it isn't." Pulling Greg closer, Adrian wound an arm around his waist and kissed him. "What you're feeling is my psychokinesis. It acts up every time I get turned on, so you've felt it plenty of times before. And that ability is linked to other psychic abilities, such as the ability to sense spirits. I was using that just now to see if I could sense Lyndon's energy. You picked up on that and recognized it."

Greg's eyebrows went up. "Wow. There's a mind fuck if I ever heard one."

Laughing, Adrian let Greg go. "Don't let it bother you. I can put that connection to some very interesting uses."

"Cool. I'm totally holding you to that when we get home." Greg shot him a filthy leer, then wandered over to lean against the nearest windowsill. "All right. So, what happens now? I mean, I know you're going to try and contact the ghost, but how do you do it? Is there some kind of ritual?"

"Not really. I usually just sit on the floor, close my eyes and do a few breathing exercises to clear my mind and relax my body. Nothing terribly exciting."

Greg nodded. "I think I'll just sit over here, if that's okay." He sat on the floor, leaned his back against the wall and looped his arms around his drawn-up knees.

"That's fine." Seeing the nervousness in Greg's eyes, Adrian gave him a reassuring smile. "Don't worry. I'll be fine, and I seriously doubt anything'll happen other than Lyndon hovering in the air. That's all he ever does."

"Okay." Greg gnawed on one thumbnail. "What's he look like? I heard he's all bloody and stuff."

*Shit. That's right.* Adrian gave himself a mental smack for not having thought to warn Greg earlier about Lyndon's appearance. He himself was so used to it he didn't even notice anymore.

"There's blood all in his hair and running down his neck onto his shirt." Adrian lowered himself to the floor and crossed his legs beneath him. "It's really hard to tell, since he's usually pretty transparent, but I think maybe the back of his head was smashed in when he died. He's got, well, brains coming out of his head."

Greg paled. "Oh." He swallowed, Adam's apple bobbing. "Okay. Ready when you are."

Adrian held Greg's gaze for a long moment. When Greg gave him a nod and a faint smile, Adrian shut his eyes and turned his focus inward. He drew a deep, slow breath in through his nose and blew it out through his mouth, imagining all his tension exiting his body along with the air.

A few breaths was all it took to send Adrian into the lightest of semi-trance states. Lyndon's energy caught and held his in a grip stronger than he remembered. He felt the warm rush through his blood, felt the very air around him swirl and condense, heard Greg's surprised shout, and knew he'd been right before. Today was the day.

He opened his eyes. Lyndon bobbed a few feet away, between two wedges of sunlight, more solid than he'd ever been before. Transparent crimson dripped from his battered skull onto the floor, vanishing even as it hit. His pale eyes burned with purpose. The bloodless lips opened, moved. *Ssssshowwww...yyyooouuu...*

"Oh, shit." Greg pulled his legs closer to his chest. His face had gone dead white. "He talked. He fucking *talked*, Adrian, oh shit. Oh shit."

Adrian blinked, startled. He was positive Lyndon hadn't spoken out loud before. Then again, he'd never said "show you" before either.

Everything about today seemed stronger, more vivid. A jolt of excitement shot up Adrian's spine.

Keeping his gaze on Lyndon, Adrian held out a palm toward Greg. "It's okay," he whispered. "Stay there. Don't move, no matter what. Stay calm. Promise me."

Greg drew a hissing breath, but nodded. "Promise."

Reassured, Adrian let his eyelids fall shut. "Show me." He dropped all his shields and left his mind open to Lyndon.

*...Halloween party. Five hundred invited guests. Cassius wasn't one, but snuck in anyway. He makes a dashing Musketeer...*

*…Sneaking up the stairs to the tower room together. "Hush, now. No one must know."…*

*…His naked skin glows in the flashes of lightning from the storm outside. So lovely…*

*…God, yes, right there, oh…*

*…Dress swiftly after. It's been nearly an hour. Someone might notice…*

*…Door bangs open. Jump apart, quickly now. Did he see the kiss? An introduction, a smile, a handshake and a clap to Cassius's shoulder. Perhaps he didn't see after all…*

*…Confusion and fear in Cassius's eyes. So blue. Shaking hands as Cassius leaves, because there's no other choice now. Goodbye, love…*

*…Rage, such rage. He saw, dear God, he saw. He locks the door…*

*…Hands squeezing, choking, cutting off breath. Uncle Lionel's straining neck, his tight jaw and furious snarl, eyes bulging beneath the fall of sweat-damp curls. "Fucking…little…sodomite…whore!" Each word punctuated by a burst of agony like a bullet to the back of the head…*

*…I am going to die…*

*…Lightning flashes. The soiled white collar of Uncle Lionel's pirate shirt shines in the light, its embroidered blue flowers a pure Carolina blue. Anger, futile anger that such beauty could coexist with such evil. Then the pain flares again, and shadows swallow the world…*

Adrian emerged from the memories with a start. His eyes flew open. Lyndon hadn't moved, though he seemed a bit less solid than before. His gaze seemed to bore straight through Adrian's skull. Adrian's throat constricted. *I'm so sorry, Lyndon. So sorry.*

"Adrian? What happened?"

Taking a deep breath, Adrian turned to meet Greg's worried gaze. "I saw it. The whole thing, this time."

"And?"

"And Lionel Groome really did murder Lyndon." Adrian rubbed both hands over his face. "He caught Lyndon and Cassius kissing, and after Cassius left he killed Lyndon by smashing the back of his head against the stone floor here in the tower room until he died."

"Oh, Jesus." Greg rubbed his arms, eyeing Lyndon with sympathy. "That's horrible."

"It is. It was awful, watching it. The bastard just..." Adrian couldn't say it, not with Lyndon floating there, staring at him with a century of sorrow and loss in his eyes. "Okay, so. I know what happened. Now I just have to figure out how to find his body and lay him to rest." He sighed. "I was kind of hoping his memories would give me a clue to that too, but they didn't."

Greg shoved his hair out of his eyes. "Can't you just ask? I mean, maybe he can lead you there. Ghosts know where their bodies are, right?"

"I think it depends on the circumstances of their death." Adrian looked over at Greg. "In any case, Lionel Groome was bound to have taken Lyndon's body outside the castle, and I'm not sure Lyndon is able to leave the castle. He's only ever been seen outside this room once, and that was downstairs, during our haunted house."

He glanced at Lyndon, seeking confirmation. Lyndon didn't move, but Adrian thought he caught a wisp of regret from the spirit's mind.

"Hm." Tilting his head, Greg studied Lyndon with a thoughtful expression. "Well, do you think he..." Greg waved his hand toward the door, "...you know, saw where his uncle took

245

his body? Do you think maybe he could show you any memories of that?"

A vision flashed into Adrian's mind—Lyndon hovering at the tower's southeast window, gazing out at the stretch of winter grass leading to the woods behind the castle. The puzzle pieces clicked into place in Adrian's mind.

He stared at Greg in stunned surprise. "Oh, my God. Greg, you're a genius."

Greg beamed. "I am?"

"You are. I should have thought of this before. Of course I'm not sure I could've established a strong enough connection with him before now. Things just seem to be different today." Adrian gazed up at Lyndon. "I'm pretty sure his body's in the woods behind the castle."

"Okay, I feel like I missed something."

"Lyndon tried to tell me before. He stared out that window there, right at the woods." Adrian pointed at the pertinent aperture in the wall. "I just didn't get the hint until now. But I still need to figure out exactly where he is."

Greg nodded. "You think he can tell you?"

"Hopefully. I doubt he'll be able to show me memories of precisely what his uncle did with his body. Not clear ones, anyway. But there are certain theories that say a spirit can be at least partly tied to the physical body for a while after death. No one's sure how long, but the author of the original article I read hypothesized up to twelve hours."

"And whatever Lionel did with the body, it would've had to have been fairly soon after the murder, so there's a good chance you'd see *something* through his eyes, even if it doesn't make a lot of sense." Pushing to his feet, Greg took two steps toward Lyndon and stopped, eyes wide. "Wow. Poor Lyndon."

"Yeah. I guess I'll need to try to hook up with him again. I've never tried to do it twice in one day, but—" Adrian broke off as a realization hit him. "No, wait. I think I know."

"You do?" Greg sidestepped toward Adrian and crouched beside him, a hand on his shoulder. "How?"

"Some of the stuff from Lyndon's memory. I remember a few things I couldn't make sense of at the time, but now..." Closing his eyes, Adrian focused his mind inward and rifled through the blurry watercolor images permanently imprinted on his brain.

A brief vision of the castle from outside, jagged white lightning illuminating the bare trees and the tower reaching toward the black sky.

Rain. Wind. Wet earth.

Adrian's heart gave a sickening lurch. Fingers scraping at the stone of the tower floor, he hunched his shoulders and dug deeper, looked harder, found details of the memory he'd never noticed before...

...*Jostling movement. Tower tilting. A thud, and the movement stops, the castle halting at an odd angle. Edge of a tree trunk, smooth grass, then the castle's back porch...*

...*Solid thunks. Wet, tearing sounds. Cursing...*

...*Trees, grass, castle, sky, all wheeling in crazy circles...*

...*Rain. Wind. Wet earth pressing in all around, tunneling up toward bare branches. Roots sticking out. Soupy smack of mud blots out the lightning...*

Adrian opened his eyes. Beside him, Greg sat, darting worried looks back and forth between him and Lyndon. "Adrian? Everything all right?"

"Yeah." Adrian laid a soothing hand on Greg's knee. "I think I know where to find Lyndon's body."

Greg's gaze snapped into focus on Adrian's face. "Really?"

"Yes."

"Where?"

Adrian smiled at Greg's eager expression. "Just inside the edge of the woods, not too far from the back porch. We were right. I saw the exact spot through Lyndon's eyes."

Greg's mouth formed a silent "oh". "Do you think you could find it?"

"It might take a while, but there might still be traces of Lyndon's psychic energy lingering around his body. I can use that to zero in if I need to. We have plenty of time, anyway." Excitement surged through Adrian's blood. He scrambled to his feet. "Are there any shovels or anything around here?"

"There's a gardener's shed out back. It's padlocked, but I'm sure that's not a problem for you." Greg stood and linked hands with Adrian. "Come on."

As they headed for the door, Adrian stopped and gazed at Lyndon, who still hovered in the middle of the room. For the first time, his melancholy gaze seemed to hold a certain measure of peace.

*We'll find you, Lyndon. I promise.*

~ ✳ ~

The woods had grown closer to the castle since Lyndon's time. It took Adrian almost two hours to locate the area with the angle best corresponding to the one from his vision. After that he spent another twenty minutes pacing back and forth with his eyes shut, his arm linked through Greg's and his psychic senses wide open to follow the faint trace of Lyndon's energy to its source.

Finally, he stopped in a small, sunny space between two young dogwoods and opened his eyes. "Here. He's right here."

Greg glanced down at the unimpressive patch of dirt and weeds. "Here? You're sure?"

"Positive." Dropping to the ground, Adrian laid his cheek against the earth, his face toward the castle. "Yes. The angle's perfect. This is definitely it." He pushed to his feet again. "Okay. Let's get the shovels."

Greg stuck his hands in his pockets. "Should we mark this spot?"

"Probably. Or you could just stay here while I go get the shovels."

"That works." Greg pointed toward a green wooden building nearly hidden in the bushes on the other side of the back lawn. "That's the shed over there."

"Okay." Laying his hands on Greg's cheeks, Adrian leaned close and kissed him. "Be right back."

Greg's lips curved against Adrian's. "I'll be here."

Adrian jogged over to the shed. A simple padlock secured the door. He unlatched it with a mental nudge, slipped it free of its metal loop and swung the door open. Inside, garden tools hung in neat rows from hooks on the walls. Skirting the mower with its attached leaf collector which took up half the floor, Adrian lifted two shovels from their hooks and left the shed, leaving the padlock hanging on the loop.

Forty-five minutes of hard digging later, he and Greg had carved out a roughly circular space in the ground about three feet across and four feet deep. There wasn't room for both of them to dig in the shallow pit at the same time, so they'd started taking turns. Right now Adrian was scooping earth from the trench onto the growing pile at the edge while Greg sprawled on the thin grass a yard or so away.

So far, they hadn't found anything more exciting than a couple of quarters, and Adrian had begun to doubt himself.

Sighing, Adrian thunked the blade of his shovel into the red clay at his feet and used his forearm to wipe the sweat from his brow. "Maybe this is the wrong spot after all. We haven't found a thing."

"Doesn't mean it's the wrong place. We don't know how deep he's buried. Plus I bet bones are hard to find by digging." Greg rolled onto his side. "You want me to take over again? It's probably about time."

"It isn't, and you know it. I can't possibly have been digging for more than five minutes this turn." He managed a tired smile. "But thanks anyway."

Adrian curled his fingers around the shovel handle and yanked. The blade came free with such surprising ease that Adrian lost his balance and fell onto his butt in the dirt. The shovel slid from his grip and came to rest against the side of the pit.

"Oh, shit. Adrian?" Leaves rustled, and a moment later Greg peered over the edge. "You okay?"

"Yeah, fine. I just pulled on the shovel too hard, I guess." Adrian planted a palm on the cool clay to push himself to his feet, and stopped. Something brownish stood up from the ground where the shovel blade had dug in, something with a different texture from the earth around it. "Hang on a second, there's something here."

"What, that brown thing there?" Greg bent dangerously far forward. "What do you think it is?"

"I'm not sure, but it looks like leather." Leaning closer, Adrian rubbed a thumb over the material. A tingle shot up his arm, and for a moment the world around him blurred behind a vision of a lightning-split night sky, wind-tossed trees and the castle wall looming in the rain.

He knew what it meant, even though he couldn't see the bones yet.

He turned wide eyes up to meet Greg's. "Oh my God, Greg. We did it. We found Lyndon."

# Chapter Nineteen

At first, Greg didn't want to call the police. He was afraid he and Adrian would get in trouble for excavating on college property. Adrian argued that while they might face some sort of punishment, they had an obligation to notify the authorities.

Greg hedged up until Adrian offered to remain at the castle alone while Greg returned to his dorm. At that point, he relented and let Adrian dial nine-one-one from his iPhone. No way, he said, was he letting Adrian go through any of this alone.

After three hours of standing around broken up by brief bouts of questioning by the police, Adrian was incredibly grateful for Greg's presence. Especially since the officers weren't predisposed to believe Adrian's tale of how he'd found the body in the first place.

"Oh, my God," Adrian groaned as he and Greg shuffled into his apartment that afternoon. "I'm exhausted. Who knew just *finding* a hundred-year-old body would take up so much of a person's time?"

"No kidding. But at least we didn't get busted for digging up college property. I had no idea the property ended at the tree line, but damn, I'm glad it does. Thank God for cops who know their property lines." Toeing off his sneakers, Greg stripped out of his filthy jeans and sweatshirt and headed toward the bathroom in his underwear, his dirty clothes hung over his arm. "I'm taking a shower. Care to join me?"

Adrian's cock twitched at the thought of naked, wet Greg. "Oh, yes." He followed Greg's black-brief-clad rear, pulling off his sweater as he went.

Greg laughed. "No shower sex. I'm too tired to stand up and fuck at the same time."

"And here I thought you'd be in great shape with all that dancing you do for theater." Grinning, Adrian dodged the swat Greg aimed at his head. "Kidding, kidding. I agree with you, actually. We'll get clean, *then* have fun."

"That's what I like about you. You're so smart." In the bathroom, Greg dropped his jeans and sweatshirt into the laundry basket in the corner, turned and started working on Adrian's button fly. "So. Now that the mystery of Lyndon Groome's murder is solved, is his ghost going to be gone forever?"

A pang of loss tugged at Adrian's heart. "I expect so, yes." He put a hand on the sink to steady himself while he took off his mud-caked sneakers. "I know it's what I set out to do, and what's best for Lyndon. But I have to admit I'm going to miss him. There were a couple of times over the past few weeks when I felt like he was my only friend."

Greg's shoulders tensed. He said nothing, however, even though the meaning behind Adrian's words couldn't possibly have escaped him. Keeping his gaze downcast, he hooked his thumbs into the waistband of Adrian's jeans, snagging his underwear as well, and worked the garments down over Adrian's thighs. Adrian took over from there, and they each finished undressing in silence.

Neither said anything else until they'd finished bathing and Adrian shut off the water. Greg stepped out of the shower first.

Adrian stood just inside the half-drawn blue plastic curtain, wiping water from his eyes and wishing he'd kept his mouth shut. He could've shared his fondness for Lyndon without adding that bit about him being Adrian's only friend. The days of his and Greg's breakup were in the past. Bringing up that time now—especially in a way serving only as a reminder of how much Adrian had been hurt—was unnecessary and petty.

Adrian drew the shower curtain aside and stepped onto the bathmat. "Greg, I'm sorry, I—"

Greg cut him off with a hard kiss. Both arms wound around his waist to pull him close. Adrian opened to him, a tiny involuntary whimper escaping as their tongues slid together. Almost four months to the day after their first kiss, electricity still sparked along Adrian's skin every single time Greg's mouth found his.

When the kiss broke, Greg stepped back enough to meet Adrian's gaze with his. "I'm sorry too. But that's all over. We hurt each other, we've moved on, and it's all in the past now." Taking Adrian's hand, he walked backward toward the bathroom door. "Come on. Let's go to bed and fuck 'til we drop, then we can order pizza."

Happiness bubbled up in Adrian's chest. He laughed. "Sounds like a perfect plan to me."

"I know. I'm a genius that way." Greg reached behind him with his free hand, felt for the door and opened it. In the cooler air of the main room, he shivered. "Wow. It's cold. You need to turn up the heat in here."

"I'm about to." Pulling his hand from Greg's grip, Adrian dove forward and swooped Greg into his arms.

Greg yelped in surprise. "Hey, be careful!"

"What, afraid I'm gonna hurt you?"

"No, dumbass, I'm afraid you're gonna hurt yourself. I'm

not exactly a delicate flower here." Greg let out an *oof,* then snickered when Adrian dropped him on the bed. "Caveman."

"You bring it out in me."

"Yeah? What else do I bring out in you?"

The wicked smile on Greg's face brought Adrian's cock from half-mast to diamond hard in two heartbeats. Climbing onto the bed, Adrian nestled between Greg's open thighs and rocked his hips. Greg moaned, and a shiver of excitement ran up Adrian's spine. "You make me want to try things I've never tried before." He kissed Greg's lips. Did it again, because it tasted so damn good. "I guess that means you bring out the adventurer in me."

The warm light which always made Adrian's heart beat faster rose in Greg's eyes. Without a word, he buried both hands in Adrian's hair and angled his head to kiss him deep.

As usual, the feel of Greg's bare skin against his, the strong legs winding around his waist and the long fingers cradling his skull, kicked Adrian's psychokinesis into overdrive. He tamped it down with an effort. After four months, he had gotten much better at keeping his gift under control, but it was never easy.

Several glorious minutes later, Greg tore his mouth from Adrian's. "Shit. Are you using your mojo on me?"

Adrian frowned, trying to think past the waves of lust thumping through him. "My mojo?"

"Yeah. You know, your moving stuff with your mind thing." Letting his legs fall away from Adrian's waist, Greg slipped both hands down to squeeze his ass. "I could come just from kissing and humping. That can't be normal for a suave and worldly guy like me."

"Actually, I think that sort of thing is perfectly normal for guys our age, no matter how suave and worldly they might be." Adrian arched an eyebrow at the flushed and grinning naked man underneath him. "But yeah, my 'mojo', as you call it, was acting up. It always does when we're together. I can control it, but it doesn't really go away. It does make for an enhanced experience, though."

The fire that flared to life in Greg's eyes created an answering heat in Adrian's belly. Greg extended one arm toward the bedside table, rummaged through the drawer and emerged with a tube of lube, which he handed to Adrian. He didn't say anything. There was no need.

Sitting back on his knees, Adrian opened the lube. He squeezed some onto his fingers, then reached down behind Greg's balls, slick fingertips sliding into the crease of his ass. Greg lifted his legs and spread himself open with both hands, staring straight into Adrian's eyes the whole time.

*God, the way he looks at me. Like he wants to eat me alive.* It was almost enough to make Adrian feel like he could come without ever being touched. He clamped his free hand around the base of his cock and started counting backward from one hundred by sevens in his head until his belly stopped tightening and the pressure in his balls eased.

Biting his lip, he pressed two lubed fingers deep into Greg's ass. He pumped and twisted to spread the slick stuff around both inside and out. Greg moaned. One hand went to his cock, curling around the shaft. His thumb caressed the flare of the glans, but otherwise his hand didn't move. Almost as if he wanted to wait for Adrian to be inside him before he started getting himself off. Adrian found it oddly sweet.

When his fingers penetrated deep enough to nail Greg's gland, Greg let out a sharp, desperate cry. "Ah! Jesus, just...I know you like to finger my ass, but right now I want your cock in me so bad I could *die*." Greg unfolded one leg, rested his foot on Adrian's shoulder and used muscles made strong by hours on the stage to urge Adrian closer. "C'mon, Adrian. Fuck me."

The need in his voice intensified the hot ache in Adrian's groin. Pulling his fingers from Greg's hole, Adrian managed to coat his cock with lube in spite of Greg adding the other leg to the fight to get him horizontal. He tossed the half-empty tube over the side of the bed just in time to keep it from being trapped as he finally gave in and let Greg yank their bodies flush against one another.

"You're awfully impatient today," Adrian observed, attempting to wriggle into position without rubbing all the lube off his prick. "Anyone would think I didn't take care of your needs."

In response, Greg bit his neck. "Too much talking. Fuck me."

Adrian snickered. "Trying."

Propping himself on one elbow, he bent his right hip just enough to get his hand in the space. He grabbed hold of his cock, fumbled with it a moment, finally got it aimed in the right direction and slid home.

They let out identical groans. For what felt like the hundredth time in the last few weeks, Adrian thanked whatever deities existed for long-term monogamy and reliable disease testing, because fucking Greg bare felt incredible. If he had his way, they would never use a condom again.

Greg's thighs tightened around Adrian. One heel dug hard into Adrian's lower back. Bare toes wove into his still-wet hair and pulled so hard his eyes watered. Wincing, he dislodged Greg's leg from his shoulder. The overly enthusiastic toes wrenched free of his hair. Probably took a few strands with them, he figured. For some reason, the thought made him smile.

The smile dissolved into a heartfelt moan when Greg's pelvis tilted upward, creating a mind-melting friction against his cock. Greg's ankle hooked over his other one across Adrian's back. "Adrian. God, please. Move."

Greg's hips rocked, back and forth, and Adrian's vision blurred with the force of the energy pulse that hit him. Curling his forearms beneath Greg's shoulders, he dug his knees into the mattress and set up a firm, steady rhythm. Forceful enough to satisfy Greg—who liked to be fucked hard and deep—but slow enough for Adrian to keep control of his powers. He felt himself trembling on the edge already. Not close to orgasm, but to losing his grip on his psychokinesis. The strength of it still took him by surprise sometimes, when he and Greg were together like this.

A tender caress on his cheeks brought his attention into sharp focus on Greg's face. Greg's smile was dazed, but his eyes glinted with the determination Adrian had come to both adore and dread. "Don't."

Adrian shook his head. "Don't what?"

"Don't hold back."

"I'm not." Adrian gave a hard thrust to prove his point, and grinned when Greg's back arched and his eyelids fluttered. "I know how you like it. I never hold back with you."

"Not...what I meant." Visibly gathering himself, Greg lifted his body up enough to kiss Adrian's lips. "Your mojo. I can feel it. I want to know what it's like to feel *all* of it." He stroked Adrian's hair, his jaw, ran a thumb over his lower lip. "Don't hold back. Let it go."

Whatever Adrian had expected, that wasn't it. If it weren't for the undulating grip of Greg's insides on his prick, he would've gone soft. He shook his head. "No. I can't. It's too dangerous. If I don't control it, you might get hurt."

*Like I hurt you before. Only so much worse, because I won't be in control anymore.*

As good as it would feel to give himself up completely to the experience of making love with Greg, he couldn't do it. Couldn't risk it. If he did and anything happened to Greg, he'd never forgive himself.

Greg framed Adrian's face between his hands and stared into his eyes. "Don't be afraid, Adrian. You won't hurt me."

Adrian swallowed. "If I'm not in control, I might."

"You won't. Your subconscious mind won't let you." That *look*, the one Adrian knew but feared to name, shone in Greg's eyes. "I trust you."

*I trust you.* They weren't the three words Adrian most wanted to hear, but they reverberated in his soul anyway. Bending forward, he hid the tightness in his throat behind a slow, searching kiss.

He didn't stop until his flagging arousal recovered and the familiar psychokinetic energy began to spark along his spine. By the time he pulled back, he was fully hard again and Greg had gone back to moaning and seesawing his hips.

"All right," Adrian whispered, watching Greg's face. "I won't hold back. Promise you'll tell me if you want me to get control again."

Greg blinked a few times, then nodded. "Promise."

Bracing himself on his elbows, Adrian shut his eyes and concentrated. He'd never deliberately dropped all the careful controls he'd built over the years. It was harder than he'd thought it would be.

Finally, he pictured his restraint of his power as a giant hand. He imagined the fingers unfolding, the palm opening and his psychokinesis bursting out like a flock of birds.

The effect was instantaneous. The familiar sensation prickled over Adrian's skin, magnified to a near-painful intensity. He let out a cry. Greg echoed it, his back arching off the bed. His hole clamped down on Adrian's cock, and it was all Adrian could do to keep himself from coming right then.

"Oh fuck," Greg gasped, his thighs shaking. "Fuck, 's good."

"Y...you like it? Oh, God." Adrian ducked his head and started pounding into Greg as hard as he could when another wave of energy hit him. He couldn't help it. He felt dizzy and breathless with the urge to *move*, to fuck with everything in him. And *God* it felt good to just let go and do it. "Okay?"

Greg nodded. "'M okay. Close."

Something blunt scraped across Adrian's lower belly. After a moment, he realized it was Greg's hand, trapped between their bodies, moving hard and fast on his cock.

Knowing that Greg not only wasn't hurt, but *got off* on the jolt, killed the last of Adrian's qualms. Burying his face in the curve of Greg's neck, he drove his cock into Greg's ass in a punishing rhythm.

His power swirled over and around and through him like a drug, and *God,* it felt incredible. Through the rush of blood in his ears, Adrian heard books tumble from the shelf near his bed. An electric current buzzed and sparked all over his skin. Invisible fingers pinched, scratched, yanked his hair, toyed with his balls. The smell of male sex rode the air like a powerful perfume, much stronger than it should have been. In the lust-ridden haze of his brain, Adrian wondered if Greg felt it too, and what he thought of it if he did.

As if in answer to Adrian's half-thought question, Greg moaned, his free hand clutching at Adrian's back. "Oh. God. Coming, oh, oh *fuck*!"

His body shook, his ass rippling around Adrian's cock. Warm, slippery fluid spread between his belly and Greg's, and the feel of it was one sensation too many. Adrian came with a keening cry, his cock buried deep in Greg's body and Greg's scent all around him. He sought Greg's mouth and claimed a messy but passionate kiss while his release thumped through him.

After a blissful eternity, the floaty feeling began to fade from Adrian's head as he came down from his orgasmic high. Allowing his softened cock to slip from Greg's hole, he broke the kiss and rolled sideways, pulling Greg into his arms. He cast a glance around his apartment. Books littered the floor near the bookshelf, all his cabinets stood open and his comforter had somehow ended up on the other side of the room, but there didn't seem to be any major damage.

Turning back to Greg, Adrian studied him with a critical eye. He looked to be completely unharmed, and Adrian knew that he himself wasn't hurt. "You okay?"

"Mmmmm." Greg propped his chin on Adrian's chest and gazed at him with half-closed eyes and a sated smile. "I am beyond okay. I am fucking *drunk* with goddamn well-fucked."

Adrian laughed. "That doesn't even make sense."

"Sure it does. It means you and your awesome mojo fucked me upside down and sideways and I love it." The smile widened to a goofy grin. "We are *so* doing that again."

Looking into Greg's contented face, Adrian felt the burden he'd carried for the last ten years fall from his shoulders. *I let go. I let my psychokinesis have free rein, during* sex *of all times, and nothing terrible happened. Greg's okay.*

Relief made Adrian bold. Laying a hand on Greg's cheek, he finally found the courage to say the words he'd held inside for far too long. "I love you, Greg."

Greg looked startled for a moment, then his face lit up brighter than the winter sunshine pouring through the window. "That's good, because I'd hate to be in love all by myself."

*He loves me. I was right.*

Pure happiness ballooned in Adrian's chest until he thought he'd burst. Smiling, he tucked a tangled curl behind Greg's ear. "So. You hungry?" He yawned.

"Not really. But I'm as wiped out as you look." Stretching forward, Greg pressed a kiss to Adrian's lips. "Let's have a nap. We can call for pizza later."

"Okay." Adrian's eyelids drooped. He hauled them back up. "You want me to grab a washcloth so we can clean up a little?"

Greg rolled off of Adrian, grabbed the corner of the sheet and swabbed the semen off both of their bellies. "There. All clean." He gave Adrian another kiss—longer this time, and with more tongue—then snuggled against his chest with a contented sigh. "Now go to sleep."

Chuckling, Adrian put his arms around Greg and rested his cheek on Greg's head.

Drifting in the twilight just below wakefulness, in love for the first time and lying in bed with Greg naked in his arms, Adrian felt a perfect peace wash through him. After all he'd been through in his life, he thought he deserved a little happiness. He sure as hell intended to enjoy it.

Adrian nuzzled Greg's hair and let sleep carry him away.

# Epilogue

The spring semester had been over for a week, but the UNC campus was more crowded than it had been since basketball season ended. School officials had even elected to leave one of the dorms open for any students who wanted to stay for today's event. A couple hundred—mostly history and anthropology majors—had chosen to remain.

Adrian couldn't blame them. After all, it wasn't every day the school held a memorial service for a man who'd been murdered over one hundred years ago. If he hadn't already been staying in town for the summer to work with Dr. Perez, he would've hung around for the service anyway.

He was just glad Greg had agreed to share Adrian's apartment and had been able to find work in town. As much as he looked forward to the cutting-edge research in which he'd be involved, a summer without Greg would've been unbearable.

On this particular May morning, however, Adrian thought his life looked pretty damn spectacular. He drew a deep breath scented with flowers and smiled as he and Greg made their way to the Old Chapel Hill Cemetery.

Lyndon Groome's memorial service was scheduled to begin shortly. After an exhaustive process to positively identify the skeleton whose name Adrian already knew, the school had decided that since Lyndon had no surviving family, he should be given a place in the old cemetery. The body had been buried in private the previous day, tucked into a green corner of the graveyard and marked with a modest stone. A memorial obelisk was being placed near the center of the cemetery today, to tell what was known of Lyndon's story and honor his memory.

Adrian kept the truth about Lyndon and Cassius mostly to himself. He couldn't bear the thought of exposing their doomed romance to the scrutiny of thousands of strangers.

He only wished he could have found out what happened to Cassius. After almost a month of filing near-daily police reports under his John Davis pseudonym, the man had vanished from the face of the earth. Adrian had spent two solid weeks of digging, but had failed to turn up any further information about him. Unless the unidentified body the police found in a Chapel Hill alley in early February of nineteen-oh-six was him. Adrian fervently hoped it wasn't.

"Wow, look at all the people," Greg said when he and Adrian rounded the side of the theater and the cemetery came into view. "Good thing we have VIP passes."

Laughing, Adrian squeezed Greg's hand. "I keep telling you, there *are* no VIP passes. We just get to stand up front because we found the body, that's all."

"*You* found the body. I just helped you dig." Greg glanced up and down the road, then trotted across, pulling Adrian with him. "I'm glad they decided to put Lyndon's memorial next to the gazebo, where it's shady. I don't think I could take standing out in the blazing sun in a damn suit." He shot Adrian a reproachful look. "Speaking of which, I can't believe you talked me into wearing a suit for this thing. How'd that happen?"

Adrian grinned. "You'll agree to anything for up to seven minutes after sex."

One pale eyebrow arched up. "Not anymore."

"Uh-huh." Hooking his arm around Greg's waist, Adrian pulled him close and kissed him. "You look absolutely gorgeous in a suit. Just so you know."

The stern look melted from Greg's face. "Thanks. So do you. But then again, you look gorgeous in everything. Or nothing." He bit Adrian's chin, eyes sparkling. "Come on, we're gonna be late."

They weren't, but Adrian let Greg hustle him along anyway. It was probably a good idea. Every time they got too involved in kissing, or touching, or sometimes even just staring at each other, Adrian's psychokinesis reacted in ways that couldn't be ignored. *Mr. Mojo rising*, as Greg would say, usually right before he tackled Adrian and tore his clothes off.

As much as Adrian loved those episodes, he didn't think anyone else at the memorial service would appreciate watching.

He and Greg threaded their way through the press of people standing in groups on the pathway and in between the graves. A few minutes later, they reached the steps of the gazebo, where the chancellor and selected others stood.

Chancellor Wild gave them a wide smile. "Mr. Broussard. Mr. Woodhall. I'm so happy you could both make it." She held out a ring-covered hand to Adrian. "Thank you for coming."

"Thank you for letting us stand up here with you, ma'am." Adrian fought not to hunch his shoulders as he shook her hand. He felt horribly self-conscious with everyone watching him like he'd done something special. "Please, ma'am, just call me Adrian."

"And I'm Greg. Mr. Woodhall's my dad." Flashing the smile that never failed to charm everyone around him, Greg took the chancellor's hand and shook. "Adrian and I are just happy Lyndon Groome is being honored."

"So am I, Greg." She retrieved her hand and surveyed the

crowd. "Well. I think it's about time to begin." With a nod and a smile for Greg and Adrian, she walked up the steps into the gazebo, where a man with a long ponytail and battered Bible stood waiting. She faced the crowd, and the conversation drifted into silence. "Ladies and gentlemen, we are here today to honor the memory of a young man who died far too soon..."

Later, after the ceremony ended and the crowd dispersed, Adrian and Greg wandered off to the corner where Lyndon was buried and sat with their backs against the spreading oak that shaded the grave. Greg stripped off his shoes and socks so he could dig his bare toes into the cool grass. Adrian wound his arm around Greg, and Greg rested his head on Adrian's shoulder. Overhead, a bird warbled somewhere among the rustling greenery.

Adrian let out a happy sigh. This was such a lovely, peaceful spot. He thought Lyndon would've liked it.

"It was a nice ceremony," Greg murmured, snuggling closer. He slipped an arm around Adrian's waist. "I liked that poem the chaplain read."

"'Black Marigolds'."

"Hm?"

"That's the poem. 'Black Marigolds', by E. Powys Mathers. He only read the last verse, though. The whole thing's a lot longer."

"Oh." Greg stirred in Adrian's embrace. "Well, it was nice. I thought it fit."

Adrian's throat constricted. He'd gone to the chaplain in confidence before the ceremony, hoping to give him a sense of Lyndon as a person so he'd have more than dry historical narratives to work with when writing his memorial. It had worked better than Adrian had dared hope.

Closing his eyes, he repeated the words of the poem in his head.

*Even now,*

*I know that I have savored the hot taste of life,*

*Lifting green cups and gold at the great feast.*

*And just for a small and a forgotten time*

*I have had full in my eyes from off my girl*

*The whitest pouring of eternal light.*

It *did* fit, in spite of the female reference. Even though Lyndon and Cassius had been forced to hide what they felt for one another, they hadn't let disapproval or even very real danger keep them apart. And in the end, Lyndon had paid the ultimate price.

*We're lucky, Greg and I.* Adrian raked his fingers through Greg's hair, kissed his forehead, cupped his cheek in one hand. *I hope we never lose sight of how lucky we are.*

A warmth Adrian had felt many times before caressed his mind. Startled, he glanced around. Only a few feet away, in the dappled shade over the new grave, hovered two translucent figures. One was tall and wide-shouldered, with dark hair and sparkling blue eyes. The other had short, sleek blond hair and gray eyes so familiar it made Adrian's chest ache. The only thing unfamiliar about that face was the lack of blood and the wide, joyful smile.

Lyndon. And Cassius.

Adrian stared, his heart racing. Part of him had longed to see Lyndon again, just once. Just to know for certain that he was happy.

*I guess I got my wish.*

The push against Adrian's mind intensified. Instinctively, he allowed his shields to drop. Lyndon's energy flowed into him, and he let out a tiny gasp.

Greg sat up. "Adrian? You okay?"

Adrian couldn't answer. He nodded.

Lyndon's lips moved. *Thank you.* The words echoed in Adrian's head. He smiled, his heart full.

Realization dawned in Greg's eyes. Weaving his fingers through Adrian's, he glanced toward the spot where Lyndon and Cassius stood. "Adrian? What do you see?"

Adrian pressed a soft kiss to Greg's lips as Lyndon and Cassius faded into the sunshine. "Just a couple of old friends."

# Author Note

Hello, readers. Ally here, with some quick notes to give credit to a couple of poets whose works I've referenced in *Love, Like Ghosts*. In the scene where Adrian and Greg are walking down Franklin Street, headed for Pita Pit (a real place, by the way, with great pitas) and Adrian is thinking to himself how uncomfortable he is with PDA, the line "I have known the eyes already, known them all" goes through his head. That line is from the poem "The Love Song of J. Alfred Prufrock" by T.S. Eliot, © copyright 1995 The Oxford Companion to American Literature. Many of you might already be familiar with that one thanks to English Lit classes in college. If not, Google it and read it, it is *awesome*!

In the epilogue, the last stanza of a poem is read at Lyndon's memorial service. That poem is "Black Marigolds", by E. Powys Mathers, © copyright renewed 2004 Margaret Gibson and Lucy L. Painter for the estate of E. Powys Mathers. I guess this one's not quite as famous as old Prufrock, but it's a beautiful, amazing work. Definitely look it up and read it in its entirety.

One other thing I'd like to mention, because I always get questions about it. If you ever read a scene in this book—or any of my books, actually—and think to yourself, "Hm, would the moon really be out that early?" or other such moon-related questions, the answer is "yes". I refer you to my favorite website on the whole entire internet, the U.S. Naval Oceanography portal's site for complete sun and moon data for any one day anywhere in the world:

http://aa.usno.navy.mil/data/docs/RS_OneDay.php

Yes, I'm a dork.

# About the Author

Ally Blue is acknowledged by the world at large (or at least by her heroes, who tend to suffer a lot) as the Popess of Gay Angst. She has a great big penis hat and rides in a bullet-proof Plexiglas bubble in Christmas parades. Her harem of manwhores does double duty as bodyguards and as sinspirational entertainment. Her favorite band is Radiohead, her favorite color is lime green and her favorite way to waste a perfectly good Saturday is to watch all three extended version LOTR movies in a row. Her ultimate dream is to one day ditch the evil day job and support the family on manlove alone. She is not a hippie or a brain surgeon, no matter what her kids' friends say.

To learn more about Ally Blue, please visit www.allyblue.com. Send an email to Ally at ally@allyblue.com or join her Yahoo! group to join in the fun with other readers as well as Ally! http://groups.yahoo.com/group/loveisblue/.

LaVergne, TN USA
05 August 2010
192250LV00003B/1/P